D1431189

Taming
MR. FLIRT

USA TODAY BESTSELLING AUTHOR
A.M. MADDEN
JOANNE SCHWEHM

TAMING MR. FLIRT

Table of Contents

CHAPTER 1

Kyle

THE CROWING OF AN IRATE cock in the distance caused a spontaneous snort laugh to escape my mouth. My best friend Jude had a hate/hate relationship with that cock, and the fact that rooster chose to keep crowing every five minutes couldn't be more hilarious. I warned my friend when he told us they planned to get married on his future in-laws' farm that it would be a bad idea. Did he listen? No.

Another squawk, another snort, and when Jude shook his head I couldn't be sure if the rooster caused it, or me. The way the minister cleared his throat, and the bride-to-be, Brae, glared at me over Jude's shoulder, supplied all the confirmation I needed.

I didn't dare look behind me at my other best friend, Luca. If he were on the verge of losing it as well, Jude would kick our asses. A flip of the coin won me the coveted best man responsibility. Jude couldn't decide between Luca and I. When I won the toss, the asshole groom said, "*Best two out of three?*"

Jude Soren had no faith I could play the part of best

man, and proving him right I had to force every muscle in my body into lockdown mode to keep from laughing again. When I met Vanessa's eyes, the sight of her lips curling over her teeth to keep from losing her shit had my body convulsing. Clearly, the maid of honor had the same sense of humor as I did.

I felt like a kid again when I'd get a fit of hysteria in church. But instead of my mom pinching my arm, a solid punch to the middle of my back by Luca made matters worse.

The squeak that escaped my lips caused the bride and groom to stare at me, as did the minister and Brae's bridal party. "Sorry," I mumbled while looking down. I could also feel the eyes of every guest attending this wedding on me, including Jude's family who flew in from Sweden.

The warm Indian summer day made for a perfect wedding day, but it also caused me to break out into a sweat. It felt like we'd been standing in that tent for days, and not minutes. Because of the unprecedented warm temperatures for October, the inside of the tent felt like a sauna. The combination of flowers and about a hundred different scents of perfume and cologne were giving me a headache... an unfortunate occupational hazard.

It felt like an eternity passed after the happy couple said their vows. The minister recited a good portion of prayers. As he went on and on, absolving us all from our sins, I ran a finger between my shirt collar and my damp skin.

Dammit, when will this end?

I wanted out of that tent, and I'd love a feisty brunette to be the one to settle me down. My eyes caught Vanessa's eyeroll as the minister droned on and on. Christ, he could talk. Her audible sigh almost initiated another snort laugh. She made an even worse maid of honor than me a best man. Since Brae also couldn't pick one out of her three best friends, Vanessa won her role today by drawing the longest straw.

For the record, Vanessa should have been a supermodel. Her long brown tresses fell like silk over her shoulders. The way her green eyes sparked to life when she spoke could have any man forgetting his own fucking name. But her tall, lean body could make a man beg. The thought of her long legs wrapped around my waist had me acting like a male dog chasing a female dog in heat.

Personality wise, the chick couldn't be more opposite of Brae and her friends. She loved partying, dancing, and having a good time… my kind of woman. She also had a thing for nicknames. She dubbed Jude, *Mr. Wrong,* the day we met at the game show where I pranked him into participating, and until now the name stuck.

We'd been out a few times with the lovebirds. Vanessa nicknamed me *Mr. Flirt,* which suited me fine since that was all I'd done from the moment I laid eyes on her.

A few passionate moments passed between us on the dance floor when we all hung out at a bar called Dispatch. Another time we made out in the engine room on the yacht where Jude and Brae had their engagement party. Every one of our encounters, four to be exact, had been steamy foreplay… that was until last night.

During the rehearsal dinner, Miss Vanessa Monroe blew my cock, and my mind, in the coatroom. I couldn't wait to see her today and hoped to take the flirting to the next level. The next level in my mind meant being horizontal, if and when the damn ceremony would fucking end already.

I should've been happy and elated for Jude. After all, those two pledging eternal devotion today wouldn't be happening if not for me. Long story short, I pranked him and then he wanted to kill me. My little stunt sent him to a deserted tropical beach for six weeks with a complete stranger. Within a year, Jude went from plotting my death to planning his wedding to Brae.

I couldn't relate to the way Jude stood beside me while staring at his bride, like his very existence depended on her. I'd known Jude Soren my entire adult life, and this man making goo-goo eyes was an imposter.

Sure, Brae was a stunning brunette and just his type. But I couldn't help but wonder if she drugged him while living on that secluded beach. He left a cocky prick and came back a sap in love.

Of course, I was happy for my best friend who *claimed* he found the love of his life. Did I believe he did? Fuck, no. With almost eight billion people on earth, how could one person be destined as a soul mate?

The scientist in me argued that mathematically finding love with one person didn't make sense. I believed in love, but to love just one? Again, fuck no. Things like curiosity, creativity, statistical thinking, and *logic* meant something better was at the next discovery.

Discovering new things was the reason for my existence.

In my job, that next discovery translated to a beaker filled with an exotic combination of liquids ready to be made into an intoxicating scent. In my personal life, that next discovery could slam into me at every turn. I met beautiful women all the damn time, and I was supposed to choose one forever?

Yeah, no.

There were too many decisions in this world, whether it be in the cosmetics creation process or in choosing my next lay.

Applause brought me back to the Hallmark movie we were forced to endure. Party time. As the only groomsman, Luca offered his arm to Brae's two bridesmaids, Cassie and Desiree. I followed behind with Vanessa.

The short black dresses they each wore complemented their bodies. Where Cassie was blonde, small, and petite with some impressive curves, Desiree was brunette, taller, and slimmer, similar to Vanessa.

I admired the two women walking ahead of me, with Luca sandwiched between them, before looking down at the hottie on my arm. "Damn, Brae has some beautiful friends."

"Why, thank you," Vanessa chirped beside me. I couldn't help but smile at her. Most other females would have taken offense to my declaration.

Leaning toward the gorgeous woman whose hand rested in the crook of my arm, I took an exaggerated whiff. "Miss Dior?"

Her head snapped toward mine. "Why did you just sniff me?"

Before I could explain, the happy newlyweds were getting ready to greet family and friends. Vanessa released me and stretched her arms out to Brae. When she leaned over, I appreciated her long toned legs. The short black dress hugged her assets, and by assets I meant her perfect tits and great ass.

With the women in some sort of female huddle giggling, I held my hand out to the groom. "Well, you did it, Soren. Again, you're welcome."

"I already thanked you a million times," Jude said as he shook my hand. "You're fired by the way."

"No, I'm not. Any best man would have snorted."

"I wouldn't have," Luca quipped.

"Fuck you." I turned back to Jude and asked, "This is the thanks I get? I should have been best man without a coin toss. You met her because of me."

"Yeah, yeah, you're responsible for getting us together. I take all the credit for making her mine." He looked at Brae who looked right back at him with a smile. "Today, that gorgeous woman is my wife. So, I thank you for being the jackass who forged my name on a contract. Try not to be a jackass during the toast."

"Ingrate."

Luca clapped my back. "Let's get a drink. Looks like there are some single women at the bar."

Speaking of women, I needed to get Miss Dior alone. As if she heard my thoughts, Vanessa looked at me with a mischievous glint in her eyes. From my calculations, we had about an hour before we were due to deliver our toasts. That was more than enough time.

The women all looked at me as I sauntered up to them. I kissed Brae on the cheek. "Congratulations, Mrs. Soren. I wish you all the luck in the world with that crazy Swede." After a roll of the eyes, Brae smiled. There was nothing anyone could say to her that would make her smile falter. "Vanessa, can I see you for a minute?"

Our friends looked at us. "We're rehearsing our toasts. We wouldn't want to disappoint anyone."

Before anyone of them could comment, I took her hand and led her out of the ceremonial tent. When everyone turned right toward the one for the reception, I pulled Vanessa left.

"What toast?" she asked as we reached the barn. "I didn't prepare a toast. I was just going to say, 'Congrats and you have my permission to ditch the rest of your wedding to start consummating as husband and wife.' Not appropriate?"

"That sounds like the perfect toast to me, although Brae may not think so. But speaking of consummating, we have an hour to get nasty ourselves."

"Good plan," she drawled with a salacious grin. I slid open the barn door and our eyes scanned the surroundings. Just as I tugged her inside, Vanessa's nose crinkled. "It stinks in here."

"Trust me, in a few minutes the last thing you'll be thinking about is the scent." I squeezed her hand and pulled her toward the bales of hay.

"Speaking of scents, how did you know what perfume I was wearing?"

"It's what I do."

"What does that mean? Do you hang out in department stores and memorize fragrances? Wait, are you one of those perfume-spritzing guys at Macy's? Please tell me you are." She laughed, but I didn't.

"No, smartass, I'm a chemist. I create fragrances and I can tell you, Miss Dior, although popular, isn't what you should be wearing." Her eyebrows shot up. "Not that you don't smell great, because you do. Believe me, I've wanted to devour you since you devoured me last night."

We both stood staring at the hay strewn all around the barn. "That looks very scratchy," Vanessa said with a frown.

"Allow me." I removed my monkey-suit jacket and spread it over a mound of hay that was closest to us. A quick glance toward the door ensured we were out of sight if someone were to walk in. "Better?" With an enthusiastic nod, Vanessa lowered herself on my jacket, rested on her bent elbows, and stared up at me. I looked down at her and considered all the things I could do to her with my tongue. "That dress looks amazing on you, but I bet having it pushed up around your waist would make it look even better. I can't wait to see if there's a thong under it or lace panties. I'm a thong guy."

"You talk a lot. Are you just going to flirt with me or are we going to put this hay to good use? You owe me an orgasm."

"Oh, you'll get one. Trust me." My dick was in agreement as it came to life in my pants. Poor thing had struggled throughout the entire ceremony. With each look and smile Vanessa gave me, my cock responded. There were a few times I had to glance at Brae's great aunt Myrtle just to calm him down. But now, there was no calming down in his future.

There wasn't anything romantic about this encounter, then again she didn't seem to be into that bullshit. Neither was I, and that was what made our connection perfect. Hovering over Vanessa, supported only by my left arm, I skimmed my right hand up her leg.

Warmth filled my palm with each stroke of her soft skin. Once my fingers reached the hem of her dress, I pushed it up right where I wanted it. She raised her ass a bit to allow the fabric to gather up around her waist. Fuck me, she was naked under her dress. "Okay, this is my new favorite," I said, cupping her bare skin. "Do you always go without panties?"

"Depends on my mood."

"Thank fuck I didn't know that during the ceremony or I never would have made it through." She giggled at my admission, but I was dead serious.

Shifting my body, I settled my head in between her

legs. "Spread." Vanessa dropped her bent knees to either side. Her bare pussy glistened with anticipation. Jesus Christ, she was going to make this quicker than it already needed to be.

Taking a moment to appreciate the beauty in front of me, I stared at her. "You're fucking gorgeous." My thumbs spread her open. Vanessa moaned and lifted her hips. "Just a minute, beautiful, I'll get you there. I want to play for a bit." And that's just what I did when I teased her with my tongue.

Her chest still covered by her dress rose and fell with each deep breath she took. When I slid one finger in, she moaned—when I added another, her hips bucked as I finger fucked her. "You like that?" She nodded and before I continued, I removed my fingers from her tight channel and put them in my mouth. "Delicious."

"Oh, God. Kyle… I need… you… inside… me. Now." Vanessa's words came in halted, short commands. Before I knew it, she yanked on the end of my bow tie and pulled until it slid off my neck.

I stood to remove my pants, first retrieving a condom out of my wallet. Her green eyes resembled lasers as they zoned in on the motion of me rolling it over my cock. With a devious smirk on my face, I again positioned myself between her legs, but this time with the tip of my dick pressed against her entrance. "For the record, this is going to be a quick hard fuck."

"I'm good with that," she purred. "But first…" She wrapped the bow tie around the base of my cock with a devilish grin.

"What are you doing?"

"Impromptu cock ring." Damn this woman was perfect. Tying the end in a bow, she added, "Okay, I'm ready now." On her consent, I leaned down and kissed her at the same moment I thrust into her.

Fuck me.

Her heat encased my cock tighter than the condom and bow tie I had on. Our tongues mimicked the movements of our hips. Everything about this woman was perfection. Rocking our way to chase an orgasm, I slowed down.

"Don't stop, I'm almost there, please." Cupping her face with my hands, I lowered my lips back to hers. Stiff hay scratched my knees, and if it weren't for my jacket beneath her I imagined it would also be marking her ass—something I'd like to do myself one day. "I'll get you there, don't you worry." We sped up our movements. She crossed her ankles on my lower back, causing the heels of her shoes to dig into my ass. Her pussy pulsed around me, milking every ounce of my climax. Our mouths devoured each other's as we swallowed one another's groans.

"Fuck me, that was fantastic," I said through labored breaths.

"Isn't that what I just did?" She looked up at me with her gorgeous green eyes and grinned.

"Yes, and we will be doing that again before the cake is served." As soon as I pulled out of her we heard voices. "Shit. Pull your dress down." I slid off the condom, tied it off, and put it in my suit coat pocket. My fingers tried and failed at working the knot on my bow tie. "Where the fuck did you learn how to tie a knot like this? Girl Scouts?"

"No, the Boy Scouts." Vanessa laughed.

"Why are you laughing? This isn't funny." The voices grew louder and panic set in. "I need to put the bow tie back around my neck where it belongs."

"Your dick is out and you're worried about the bow tie?" She shimmied her dress down and with steady dexterity removed the bow tie from around my cock. Her fingers brushing against him almost set things in motion again. With one deft movement, the noose was removed, and my dick was freed.

Fuck. I dusted off strands of hay stuck to my legs before rushing to put myself back together. When I inspected Vanessa to be sure she looked as she did when we walked in, it was my turn to laugh. "You might want to get the straw out of your hair."

She raked her fingers through the long dark strands only to make matters worse. "Holy shit. How much is in here? It's like a goddamn nest!"

Just as I was assisting her in the straw removal, Jude cleared his throat behind us. "Cleary."

Uh oh. He used my last name. Vanessa and I turned to find Jude and Brae. "Soren."

Brae stood with her mouth in the shape of an "O" and Jude glared at me with eyes narrowed into slits. "What are you doing in here?"

"Well, nothing now." The sound of me raising my zipper echoed in the barn. Vanessa snickered when I added, "A minute ago we were fucking. Why are you in here?"

"Same reason, but we're entitled… it's our wedding day." His irritated voice made us laugh.

"And we're entitled to celebrate our best friends' wedding day."

"And as maid of honor and best man, you should conduct yourselves with a touch more class." Brae added her two cents.

"My wife is right. Shouldn't you two be out there ensuring our guests are having a good time instead of Kyle's cock?"

Vanessa clucked her tongue against the roof of her mouth. "Oh, calm your jets Jude-alicious." Jude furrowed his brow and all I could do was stare at her.

"What did you just call him?"

"It's my nickname for Jude," Brae chided. "She stole it."

Vanessa turned to me. "Since I can't call him Mr. Wrong any longer, then Jude-alicious it is."

"I can't wait to see what I graduate to if this clown is whatever you just called him."

Vanessa shook her head. "You are and will always be Mr. Flirt. Now let's get out of here and let these two consummate their marriage."

I clapped Jude on the back. "Have fun and watch out for that hay. It's brutal on the knees."

At that, Vanessa plucked a few more pieces out of her hair and quipped, "And your bare ass if you don't use his jacket as a buffer."

Brae looked up at Jude who tossed his arm around his wife. "Bedroom?"

She nodded with a firm, "Yes."

"Don't take too long, or you'll miss our speeches," I reminded them.

With my hand on the small of Vanessa's back, I walked her out of the barn and into the tent where the reception was held.

She smiled at me. "That was fun."

"Getting caught or screwing?"

Her tongue wet her lips. "Both. Although, getting

caught in public is a complete turn-on, I was referring to the sex."

Who was this woman? The thought of fucking her in public made my dick go hard once again. Grabbing her hand, I grumbled, "I need a drink."

What I needed was to calm the fuck down before I threw her over my shoulder and cut out of the wedding way too soon. Jude would definitely kick my ass, but once the reception was over, all bets were off.

Chapter 2

Vanessa

GUESTS GATHERED AROUND THE TABLES enjoying the cocktail hour. We spotted our friends at the bar, because where else would they be? When we approached them, Luca's face lit up while Desiree and Cassie's jaws dropped.

"What are we drinking?" I asked casually.

Desiree leaned forward and plucked something from my hair. She held it up and examined it. "What were you doing?"

"Mucking out stalls. What do you think we were doing?"

Two gasps from my friends preceded Luca's snide remark. "You're lucky your balls are still intact. If Mr. Daniels would have caught you messing around, they'd be picking more than hay out of you in the emergency room."

Kyle and I stood there both smug and content not bothered by the way they continued to bust our chops. Before we could order another drink, the bandleader announced dinner would be served.

"Hmm… I wonder where the guests of honor are?" His voice boomed, and several people including the bride's parents stared at him. Cassie's head dropped in her hands. Kyle looked around in an over-exaggerated manner. He turned to the crowd, "Folks, have a seat and enjoy your meal. I'm sure the bride and groom will join us when they're done consummating their union."

Gasps filtered throughout the tent, yet one person laughed—me. All of a sudden a firm slap to the back of Kyle's head forced him to snap his gaze to where the assailant stood.

"Jackass."

Kyle rubbed his head. "Shit, what the hell?"

Jude pulled Brae to his side. "Maybe Luca should give the speech."

"Calm your nuts, Soren. My speech is perfect." On demand the band summoned the best man and maid of honor to the microphone. Brae's face paled and Jude glared at Kyle. "Don't worry, buddy, we've got this." Kyle clapped him on the back, a bit harder than normal, and guided me toward the makeshift stage.

The waiters filled flutes with champagne and Kyle and I were each handed one. As soon as the guests' glasses were in hand, we began. He leaned toward the mic and a high-pitched whistle rang through the tent. "Oops, sorry." When I looked at the guests, Luca was giving Kyle two thumbs up with a mocking smile.

Kyle whispered in my ear, "Ladies first." He grinned, reached over, and pulled a piece of straw out of my hair. "Looks like you were rolling in the hay. You should learn to control yourself."

I laughed and took a turn at the mic. "Hi, I'm Vanessa, the maid of honor, and Brae's voice of reason. When I first met Jude, I told her she needed to climb that man like a tree." Gasps once again rang out. Kyle on the other hand laughed. Brae and Jude just stared at me, although Jude looked proud.

"They didn't meet the conventional way. But, I knew from the start that he was Mr. Right, even though Brae was convinced he was Mr. Wrong." Jude looked at his bride who smiled with a shrug. "All kidding aside, if there were two people meant to be together it would be Jude-alicious and Sparky." I tossed an exaggerated wink their way announcing the nicknames they had for each other. "I wish you both a life filled with mind-blowing sex, love, and happiness." I raised my glass. "To Jude and Brae."

Kyle waited until the tinkling sound of glasses hitting each other subsided. I handed him the mic and smiled. I couldn't wait to hear what he had to say. He lowered the mic away from his mouth. "That was very tame."

"Make it fast. I have hay in places it shouldn't be."

"Picturing those places doesn't do much for my concentration." He raised the mic. "Hi, I'm Kyle, the reason these two lovebirds are together." The crowd laughed and so did I, but Kyle leaned over to me and said, "I was being serious." I couldn't help but laugh harder.

When the chuckling wouldn't subside, Kyle spoke over them. "Funny, but true. Anyway, I never thought the day would come that Jude Soren would settle down. When we first met at Yale, Luca, Jude, and myself took dating to a new level. We made it an art form." Kyle laughed, although no one else did. "Tough crowd." He cleared his throat. "Brae…" When he said her name, she looked up with narrowed eyes. "There isn't anyone else I could see bringing this man to his knees like you have. In case he hasn't told you, he admitted to Luca and I that you were the best thing that has ever happened to him." The suspicion fell off her face as her eyes shimmered with emotion.

"He also said you were the best sex he's ever had." My solitary applause echoed in the quiet tent. Our eyes met and we both laughed, until Brae's father cleared his throat. "Sorry, Mr. Daniels."

I leaned into him. "Just wrap this up, will you? I'm starting to itch."

Kyle smirked and brought his attention back to the task at hand. "In closing, Jude Soren would give his left nut to help someone out. He's my best friend and although he reverts back to his native tongue to curse at me in Swedish, I know deep down he loves me. Raise your glass and join me in congratulating the perfect match. Jude and Brae, may your spark continue to ignite into a roaring flame. Thanks and enjoy the rest of your evening."

When Kyle and I stepped off the stage, the band started playing dinner music as white-gloved waiters began to deliver cloche-covered plates to the guests. It was evident Jude did his best to bring The Plaza to the farm.

After dinner and a few dances, it was time for the obligatory wedding stuff. Kyle and I tried to sneak back to the barn before the cake was served, but the bride and groom were on to us. They each kept delegating maid of honor and best man duties we were convinced they were making up as they went along. Of course, Jude wanted to leave the moment after they gingerly fed each other a piece of cake, but there were still more traditions to be had.

Brae grinned as she waved the small bouquet in her hand. "Ready, girls?" she asked, turning her back to all the single ladies. After a short countdown, she tossed it behind her. I wanted to lace my fingers behind my back, but when the flowers came careening into my chest, there was nothing I could do but catch them. I could feel all the blood drain from my face. Brae turned and winked at me–the bitch did it on purpose. I should have realized it when I saw Cassie and Des step away from either side of me. They'd pay for this.

Jude removed the garter with such reverence and ceremony. Once it was off Brae's leg and in his hand, he kissed the bare skin where it was positioned and then the thin scrap of lace. I was sure that if he didn't have an audience, he would have tossed her over his shoulder caveman style and left the reception. Instead, he turned his back to the available men.

Luca and Kyle stood like mannequins. Clearly, neither one wanted to be the bearer of the ideology that came with catching the garter. And with the flowers in my hand, I didn't want Kyle to catch it or it would put Brae in full matchmaker mode.

In slow motion, the garter flew right toward Kyle. Out of nowhere, Luca's hand snatched the garter from mid-air, causing him and Jude to burst out laughing. Meanwhile, I thought it was weird when Kyle glared at Luca.

Before I made my way to the chair in the middle of the dance floor, I heard Kyle say to Luca, "Don't go too high, I know for a fact she isn't wearing anything under that dress."

Luca smirked. "Was that meant to deter me?"

Before Kyle could respond, they turned and caught me listening. Ignoring their surprised expressions, I took my obligatory position on the chair. On bent knee, Luca glanced up at me with soft eyes and a warm smile.

The feel of his long fingers sliding the garter up my leg at a snail's pace should have turned me on. Although handsome, I felt no attraction toward Luca. Maybe because in my mind he was the romantic of the three, much like Romeo… and I wasn't a fan of romance. Proving me right, Luca stood and kissed me on my cheek.

As the night wore on and guests left, Jude and Brae made their escape back to the island of St. John where their romance began.

It was time for us to head back to our motel in the middle of nowhere. Brae secured us each a room, but when we arrived there were only two available.

So, as I lay there in bed next to Cassie, with Desiree in the bed next to us, the inquisition began.

"You had sex in the barn?" Cassie prodded.

"You say that as if there was something wrong with it. I'll have you know that Jude and Brae showed up to do the same."

Desiree tsk'd. "They did just get married."

I waved my hand back and forth. "Don't guilt me. The sex was great aside from the straw." An uncharacteristic giggle-snort escaped me. "You should have seen his face when I tied his bow tie around the base of his…"

Desiree thrusted her hand in the air. "TMI! We don't need the details."

Cassie smiled. "Speak for yourself!"

🍁 🍁 🍁

Kyle

FUCKING VANESSA ON THAT OLD dryer was a pretty fabulous way to start our day. Once again, an article of my wardrobe served a great purpose by protecting her gorgeous ass from the rusty metal she sat on. The machine rattled in time with our thrusts, and the coins we fed it were almost out.

"Come, already," I demanded through gritted teeth. Her eyes locked with mine just as her ankles tightened around my back. Seconds later, she contracted around me causing an explosive release. "Goddamn," I said as our bodies fed off each other's, causing our orgasms to seem like they went on forever. "Shit, woman. I'm glad I texted you 'good morning.'"

"I'm glad I sexted you back." My text arrived when she was fresh out of the shower, and the visual of the boob shot she sent me set the chain of events in motion—a quick pack, stupid excuses to our friends, and hooking up in the laundry room.

"Me, too," I said, pulling out before removing the condom. Deja' Vu hit when a voice called out from a few feet away. My jeans were buttoned and zipped in an instant. In slow motion, Vanessa hopped off the dryer, slid on her thong and adjusted the skirt of her dress. "Seriously? Hurry the hell up."

"Relax," was her last word when Cassie came barreling into the laundry room.

Her eyes raked over first Vanessa, and then me. "What the hell, V? We've been looking for you. It's time to leave." She then pointed a manicured finger at me and added, "Your buddy is ready to kick your ass or I assume he is, since he's muttering in Italian."

"Calm your titties," Vanessa said with attitude. "We're ready."

With that, Luca plowed through the door and his already livid expression worsened when he saw the condom in my hand. "Are you fucking kidding me, Cleary? Get your ass in the car!"

"Why is everyone in a rush?" I made the mistake of asking. Cassie and Luca both began rambling off a long list of shit that they needed to get done, and three seconds in I was bored. "Shut it, I'm sorry I asked."

Vanessa seemed completely unaffected, not only by what just had occurred between us, but by the pissed off twins glaring at us. "I just need to grab my bag," left her mouth nonchalantly. Meanwhile, every cell in my body was still pulsing as an effect of the orgasm I just had. I couldn't understand if it was the fact we had to go that irked me, or the fact I wanted more and she had moved on.

"I'm leaving in sixty seconds, with or without you," Luca said over his shoulder.

Cassie quipped, "Ditto," following after the asshole who clearly needed his own good fuck.

"I don't know about you, but I'm not walking home." Vanessa leaned up and kissed my cheek. "It's been a blast, Kyle. See you around."

A blast? This woman rocked my world in a coatroom, a barn, and a laundry room and that's what she considered it... a blast? It wasn't that I disagreed with her, because she was every bit of the hot fuck I thought she'd be... and yes, my body *blasted* into her a few times, but it wanted more.

"Yeah, you'll see me." My dick wouldn't forgive me if we didn't indulge in her again.

Out in front of the motel, her friends started their car, and Luca's brake lights lit. That was our cue to run. Luca shifted into drive at the exact moment my ass hit the front seat. A flippant wave through the window was all I saw as the girls' car drove past ours in the parking lot.

"You're an asshole."

He glanced my way with a smirk. "You're funny. I hauled your suitcase down to the car for you, and I was nice enough to wait for your dick to deflate, all without a thank you. But I'm the asshole?" My lack of a response had him adding, "You have nerve, Cleary. It's not always about you getting laid, you know."

"Maybe you need to get laid yourself, eh?" I voiced my thoughts.

"Or you need to keep it in your pants once in your life... *eh?*" He shook his head, and I failed to see why he was so aggravated. "You fucked her what, two times in two days?"

"Technically, three if you count her mouth as one."

"Nice." A heavy sigh came right as he released a sarcastic laugh. "Kyle, do you know anything about this chick, besides her being Brae's best friend? Which in itself should have deterred you."

"Why?"

"Let me fast forward. You fuck her over, Jude kicks your ass for hurting his wife's best friend."

"Pfft, I'll be the one she hurts," came out of my mouth before I could stop it. The quick surprised expression he threw at me forced me to add, "Forget I said that."

"Oh, no way. She will hurt you how?"

"Like I said, forget it. My brain is still trying to recover from the lack of oxygen due to the many orgasms I had." Luca rolled his eyes. "What? It's true."

"Are you going to see her again? Or was this just a weekend fling?"

"Of course, I'm going to see her again, dumbass, since as you said, she's Brae's best friend."

"That's not what I meant and you know it."

"My cock wants to, is that what you meant?" Just picturing her on her knees in the coatroom, on that pile of hay in the barn, and on the rusty dryer at the motel, created a surge of energy in my pants. My cock was as hard as it was when it pounded into her.

"I really don't want to talk about your cock. All I want is to get back to the city where life is normal. I'm exhausted."

"Dude, seriously." I waved my hand over my crotch. "Just thinking about her makes my cock hard."

The car swerved toward the open land on my right just before it stopped. "Get out. I swear to God, you say the word cock once more and you're walking back."

"What if you're about to hit a rooster in the road? I can't yell, 'look out for that cock!' so you don't run it over?"

"Rooster. Just call it a rooster."

"Fine and when did you become such an altar boy?" Luca pulled back onto the road.

"You want to tell me about tits and ass, I'll listen. Cock talk you can keep to yourself."

"Can I talk about her magical pussy? She does this thing where…"

"Do I need to pull over again?"

Chapter 3

Vanessa

"**M**ISS MONROE!" HIS ANNOYING, NASALLY voice screeched from behind his closed door. The sound of it had me wanting to stab him in the heart with my letter opener. Actually, a letter opener to the heart would be too compassionate.

I hated that man more than anything.

Scratch that, I hated my job more. When put together, that was a lot of anger boiling within me. Every day, since day two, I've plotted ways to kill him without getting arrested. It had become somewhat of a game for me.

I tried looking for another job, but the actual job wasn't the problem. I'd only end up replacing this idiot with another out there convinced it was his responsibility to better humankind through his pathetic career choice. My real problem, I wasn't qualified for a job that would make me happy. My other real problem, I wasn't meant to work in an office. Unfortunately, my liberal arts degree hadn't given me the opportunity to travel the world.

Looking back, I was dumb—end of story. When I lost the love of my life, I spent the rest of my college years numbing myself. That involved taking the easiest courses I could while keeping my GPA within a respectable range. I was somewhat of a dreamer, and that was exactly what I did most of the time. Before I knew it, I had my degree in my hand and had no clue where to go next.

Stupid.

I dutifully grabbed my notepad and dragged my ass to his office. "Yes, sir?" I asked after opening the door with no enthusiasm.

"Did you book my flight and hotel?" he barked without looking away from his computer screen.

"Yes, sir." I waited a pause, because he usually ordered me to fetch him some coffee or a donut from the snack room.

"That's all," came with a dismissed wave of his hand... no thank you, no pleasantries, no smile. I closed his door behind me, and in a very mature manner stuck my tongue out at him knowing damn well he couldn't see me. Fuckhead.

The last thing I wanted to do on this Monday morning was book a flight to Paris for Mr. Boyd. I should have been booking a flight to Paris for myself. All I've ever wanted when I was a little girl was to travel around the world and live, truly live life to the fullest. Financially, I wasn't able to do that, not yet. At least I lived my life to the fullest while off the admin-clock. Weekends were my salvation.

Why couldn't there be a contest I could enter, like Brae did, to win money—less the man, of course? The day she told us she had signed up for some dating game of sorts, for a cash prize, I was intrigued. Even more so when the man she had to spend six weeks with on a tropical island could be described as sex on legs. Sure, they had to do without Internet or cell phones, but damn who needed that when you had a fine specimen like Jude Soren to "play" with?

Believe me, I was so very ecstatic for my friend. If anyone deserved happiness it was Brae. Married to that hottie and no longer having financial issues to worry about made my heart smile for her.

But, I wasn't looking for the happily ever after with a man… I wanted a happily ever after with myself. What would it be like to relax without having to worry about making appointments, booking flights, and kissing a suit wearing ass… the latter of which I did every fucking day of my life?

Mr. Boyd flew first class and stayed at the best hotels all on the company's dime. After I booked his suite with a view of the Eiffel Tower, my anger rose to the point where if I didn't talk to my girls, I'd quit my job, and that wasn't an option.

Once I had the confirmation numbers for his trip, I tapped out a text.

> **Me:** Happy Hour? I need drinks.
>
> **Cassie:** It's not even 10.
>
> **Desiree:** Are you okay?

Shit. It's only ten?

> **Me:** I'm fine. Drinks, yes or no?
>
> **Desiree:** I can't, I have a late meeting.
>
> **Cassie:** Dispatch at 5:30?
>
> **Me:** See you there.

At least I had that to look forward to. I needed to endure seven more hours of work before I could breathe.

Nothing had changed from when I first started working for Mr. Boyd, who I promptly nicknamed *Boyd-Who-Annoyed*. His title, Executive VP of Commerce, went straight to his big, fat, bald head. I'd say it looked like a penis, but that wouldn't be fair to my favorite part of the male body.

My thumb clicked the top of my pen at rapid speed while the clock moved at a snail's pace. What in the hell was I doing with my life? The obvious answer was—marriage, kids, yada, yada, yada, and none of which were in the cards for me.

Being a witness at Brae and Jude's wedding did nothing to make my heart crave the same thing. However, in just two days Kyle Cleary did manage to make my body crave something. That man was talented. Between his ability to sniff out the type of perfume I wore, which for some reason turned me on like no tomorrow, to the orgasms that wracked every part of me, I should have been in a better mood. Maybe, I would be, if I were listening to the carnal pleasures of a man rather than orders being barked at me.

"Miss Monroe! Get in here!"

Motherfucker.

My eyes cut to the stapler sitting on my desk. Nah, that wouldn't be enough to kill him.

The streets were flooded with people escaping the confines of their offices. Most were probably headed home. All I wanted was to hang out with my friend and a very large margarita.

While I waited for Cassie, I scoped out the place. Even for a Monday night, happy hour still thrived.

Businessmen and women occupied the small tables and stools in front of the bar. A few handsome faces looked familiar. One of them caught my eye and smiled with a wink. *Hmm,* I thought, and quickly dismissed the idea because I wasn't there to score a man; I was there for a reality check and to unwind.

Cassie slid into the booth, shrugged off her jacket, and smiled. "So, why are we drinking on a Monday night?" Her smile alone brightened up my mood. I loved my friend.

"Does it matter what day it is?" She shook her head. "That's what I thought. My day was horrible and I wanted to chill out before going home."

Her eyes studied me. "Nope, not buying it. You sent a text at ten in the morning. There must be more to it than just *chilling out*. What happened?"

"Life happened. Well, it's not happening and that's the problem."

"You lost me." Cassie's eyes softened. "Is it Kyle?"

I could feel lines on the bridge of my nose form as I crinkled my face. "No, it isn't Kyle. Why would you even think that?"

We flagged the waitress down so Cassie could order a dry martini. "Well, I just thought because of your sexcapades this weekend, maybe you…" She shrugged one shoulder. "I don't know what I thought."

"It's not Kyle. It's not any man. Well, that's not entirely true. My boss is a pain in my ass, and I want to murder him."

"This isn't a newsflash. Please don't go to jail. I can't deal with the stress that would come from visiting you in the pen."

I took a healthy sip of my drink. The tart liquid did

nothing to ease my frustration. "I can't make any promises. I just hate my job so damn much. All I want is to live my life the way I want to live it. I need to start playing the lottery."

"Don't you have vacation time?"

"Two weeks is not enough time."

"Then take a leave of absence. Does your company allow that? Call it a mental health break. I'm sure you can get a note from your doctor. You're friends with him, right?"

Her idea wasn't completely far-fetched, but just because I may or may not have gone out on a date with Dr. Nichols, didn't mean he'd do that for me. "Maybe. I suppose I could look into it. Still, that would also be a temporary fix. Eventually, I'd need to return to that god awful place I work at." If I could slam my head on the wood table in front of me without bruising myself, I would have.

"Look, V, you are a smart, beautiful woman. If you want to take a life break, then do it." Just as I opened my mouth, her hand went up to stop me. "Yes, I know you're worried about money, but you don't need to do anything drastic. Start out small, go to Florida or Los Angeles. Hell, you can go to a spa on Long Island and it would feel like a vacation. Any place away from work and the city is an escape."

Cassie was right, I knew what she said made sense, but I wanted more. That wasn't living. It was putting on a Band-Aid. "I want to experience the top of the Eiffel Tower, put on a beret and dance in the streets of France. I want to see Italy and have lunch at a street side cafe in Rome, or maybe have wine in Tuscany. I want to salute the guards in front of a palace in London, swim with sharks in Australia—these are the things I want to do.

Yes, your suggestions sound great, but it's not enough." I wasn't frivolous. I did have a savings account, but it wouldn't last a year with all the places I wanted to see.

"Sharks?"

"Okay, dolphins. The point is I'm wasting my life." If I didn't know my own age, I'd think I was in the middle of a midlife crisis. Sad eyes stared back at me. It was time to change the topic. "Tell me about your day, it had to be better than mine," I said with a bright smile.

My sweet friend smiled back. "My kids are starting to settle into a school day routine after summer break." Cassie went on to tell me about her kindergarten class's antics. The smile on her face grew with each tale, while some of them horrified me. Yet, I knew my friend loved her job, and that part I envied.

"I have a little boy named Mikey, who I have to admit has become my favorite. He's so sweet, V." Tears suddenly shimmered in her eyes.

I reached out and held her hand. "Cass, what's wrong?"

"Ugh," she said, waving her other hand in frustration. "Every time I think about it, I get upset. He lost his dad last year. I had a conference with his mom, Sabrina. She wanted to let me know just in case Mikey had a hard time adjusting to a classroom setting. The thing, V, he's so eager to learn. Even at his age, his little brain is trying to deflect the sadness he feels by making new friends, talking about what he's going to be for Halloween, and everything a child who hasn't experienced a devastating loss does."

My heart ached for this family. Losing people sucked, and moving on without them was worse. "That poor little boy. How's his mother? I can't imagine raising a little human let alone doing it on my own."

"From what I can tell, having just met her, she's doing okay." Cassie frowned. "Her husband was in the military so the possibility of him not returning was always present. Except, he died in a car accident." Tears swelled and an involuntary gasp escaped as Cassie looked at me with confusion. I think I could count on one hand how many times my friends saw me cry.

Predictably, Cassie reached across the table and grabbed my hand. "What is it, V? You look like you're going to be sick."

I had never uttered the words that were clawing their way to the surface. My friend sat patiently waiting for me to explain my A-typical behavior, but I couldn't go down that road today, so instead I said, "Their lives changed on the turn of a dime and it's just so unfair. How does this poor woman cope?"

"Maybe being a military wife for so many years had prepared her for the possibility that something could happen. There's definitely sadness in her eyes, but when she speaks of Mikey she's strong. I'm sure that's because her little boy needs her. She's all he has left."

The tears we held back ran down both our faces. "I'm sorry, I made this night worse. Here you wanted to escape and we're sitting here crying. Some friend I am." Cassie handed me a tissue. "I suck."

We both laughed through our tears. "No, you don't suck. But, you did prove that your job is rewarding while mine sucks hairy balls. Mikey does have someone else. He has you. In my opinion, he's a very lucky kid. Can you imagine if he had me?"

She tsk'd in disagreement. "He'd be just as lucky."

I cradled my head in my hands. My fingers gave a

quick rub to my temples before returning my attention to Cassie. "Your story about Mikey once again proves my point. I could die tomorrow without having seen even one of the Seven Wonders. I'll just wonder what they were like."

"You do know the Eiffel Tower isn't in that classification, right?" she teased. When I gave her a blank stare, she continued. "Here's my opinion, if you don't want to ask for a leave of absence, find another job. And before you say it, I know you've tried before, but maybe you'll find what you're looking for this time. Why stay in a job that makes you miserable? You do realize we spend more time at our place of employment than we do out of it."

"Yes, I do realize that. Hence my mood."

"What about Jude? Maybe he has a position for you at Soren Enterprises."

"The only way I could work for him was if it were in Paris, and even then I'd probably be fired because I'd be calling in sick every other day. I'll come up with something." I lifted my glass toward her and she followed my lead. "To hitting the lottery."

"To hitting the lottery," she repeated before tapping her martini against my margarita. "And if not, to you finding the job of your dreams."

"Always the practical one," I said while wondering if my friends would approve of me becoming a high-class, traveling escort.

Chapter 4

Kyle

TOP NOTE OF BERGAMOT ORANGE followed by middle note of grapefruit with a bottom note of vanilla.

The liquid swirled around the beaker when I mingled the fragrance notes with a glass stirring rod. I brought the mixture to my nose and inhaled. It missed something, but I couldn't figure out what. With swift movements, my fingers tapped over the keyboard of my laptop as I meticulously wrote every metric measurement down.

Frederick, my senior lab assistant, opened my door forcing me to break concentration. "Sorry to barge in, but I knocked three times. Where did you drift off to? The fields of Ireland… the beaches in Tahiti?"

"Bali." The new line of fragrances were each modeled after a romantic destination, designed to transport the customer from their everyday life. "I'm just trying to nail down this fragrance, but all I keep thinking of is that sickly sweet creamsicle ice cream bar I loved as a kid."

"Did you try cutting it with cardamom?" I shook my head, and Frederick knew not to question further. When I was in my lab, my staff let me work my mad scientist skills without influence. Of all the divisions in Cleary Laboratories, fragrance creation was my baby. I delegated well when it came to cosmetics, hair products, and even men's fragrances. But anything to do with a woman's scent was all me. At my silence, he added, "Okay, boss, I'm calling it a night. You should, too."

My first instinct was to say that I had a few more hours, but for some reason today I wasn't able to focus on something that usually came as easy as tying my shoes. Instead, my brain was recounting the events of the past weekend.

"I'm right behind you. See you in the morning."

I closed up my lab, shutting lights along the way, and locking up. The moment I sat my distracted ass in my Model S Tesla, boredom hit. Unless I was at work, entertaining a woman, or hanging out with my friends, most of the time I felt antsy. I was the type of person who needed activity at all times. After such a busy weekend, I should have welcomed the opportunity to chill out and relax. Yet, the week stretched ahead in a looming way.

The drive home from Queens to the Upper East Side with not much traffic only took fifteen minutes. I parked my car, grabbed my tux from my backseat, and walked to the cleaners on the corner.

Metallic bells sounded when I strolled in. Natasha, the woman behind the counter smiled. "Hi, Kyle."

"Hey, Natasha. How's the dirtiest beauty in the cleaning business?" Her Eastern European features gifted her with striking bone structure and a long lithe body. Her flaxen straight-angled bob currently sported a fuchsia streak that framed the right side of her face.

The sweetest smile crinkled the corners of her ice blue

eyes. "That's not fair. I only did that once in my life, and that was with you. Having sex in my family's place of business never occurred to me before you came along. Not that I'm complaining because it was fun."

"It sure was, although I'm lucky to still have my balls after your dad stopped in on his day off. And I'm still thanking the gods I didn't burn off anything important on that long iron thing."

"It's called a pant press," she corrected.

"Whatever. It still could have permanently branded my ass." A few months ago, Natasha and I were having a great time on the back counter when her father, who owned the cleaners, walked in on us. Needless to say, when we heard the linebacker-built man mumbling in Russian at the front of the store, it was that day I found out I'd make a great firefighter. The way I jumped off of her and into my clothes was quite an accomplishment. I smiled at my agility, then frowned at how close I came to death.

Natasha giggled at the look on my face. "When he said…" She puffed up her chest and deepened her voice three octaves to imitate the grizzly bear that was her father. "'What you doing back here?' That was hilarious." Then mimicking her father's actions, she thrusted her blue painted, manicured finger toward the door. "Out!"

"Yeah, haha. So, funny." I dumped the suit on the counter, and Natasha robotically began to check my pockets.

"Aw, you handled it well. *I'm fascinated with garment conveyors, Sir.*" She now altered her voice to sound like a high-pitched Mickey Mouse.

"I don't sound like that."

"You did that day," she quipped with a grin. When

she pulled out a few strands of hay from my tux jacket, her eyebrow arched. "I thought you were going to your friend's wedding, Kyle?"

At the sight of the stiff pale yellow straws, my cock sprung to life in my slacks. "I did. It was in a barn." There was no way I'd think of hay the same way again. Not that I ever thought of it to begin with.

"Uh huh." Natasha gave me an all-knowing smile. She started taking inventory of what I'd brought in. "One pair of pants, one vest, one shirt, one suit coat." Natasha moved the pieces into a bin. "No bow tie?"

The memory of where that bow tie had been turned my semi into a full-blown hard-on. I stepped closer to the counter to camouflage the issue in my pants.

Natasha gave me a smirk. "Did you lose it or was it a casual affair?"

"I guess I must have misplaced it."

"Uh huh," she repeated with a wink that meant she was on to me. She gave me my receipt and said, "It'll be ready by Friday. In case you have another bow tie-less barn hosted wedding to attend."

"No, nothing in the near future. None of my other friends are signing their lives away in marriage."

"You're terrible. You're going to die a dirty, old, lonely man."

"I'll make you a deal. If we're both single when we're eighty, I'll make an honest woman out of you." Thinking in my head that her father would be dead by then.

"Oh, great. That'll give me fifty-five years to find the perfect dress."

"You probably shouldn't wear white," I said as I limped away. The chimes on the door did little to hide her laughter.

A few minutes later, I was back in my apartment in need of food and drink. Not bothering to change out of my work clothes, I opened a beer and began to scarf down a slice of cold pizza. I wondered where that damn bow tie ended up. With half a slice still dangling from my lips, curiosity caused me to dig through my overnight bag that still sat packed in my bedroom. I pulled out boxers, socks, and low and behold poking out the side of the condom box was the black tip of my bow tie.

"Oh, yeah." I remembered how and why I had shoved it into the box… which led to remembering Vanessa spread eagle on a mound of hay… which then led to a fierce need to have a quickie with my hand like a teenage boy.

Luca's text a few hours earlier commanded I meet him at Dispatch. After a boring week, I jumped at the request. Friday nights usually drew in all the Manhattanite female population for Happy Hour, which put all the guys on alert. Luca beat me there. I approached in time to see him drain a beer and smack the empty bottle onto the worn mahogany table with a thud.

"What now, eh?" I asked at the scowl he gave me as a greeting.

"One of Jude's huge clients, Waldon, wants my balls on a fucking platter. Whenever Jude isn't available, a convenient crisis appears. I didn't give a fuck what he said, I had no intention to contact Jude on his honeymoon, and because of it the prick has made my life miserable for the last two weeks."

"I'm actually surprised you haven't heard from the Swede. When we sent him away for six weeks…"

"*We?* What the fuck? *You* sent him away for six

weeks."

"Technically, Brae sent him away for six weeks. She picked the cocky bastard." I raised my hand to get the waiter's attention.

"Well, when he's with Brae he has a one-track mind, and it's not focused on Soren Enterprises or Howard-fucking-Waldon. Like last time, he left me at the helm and having to deal with that pazzo."

"Please don't start with the Italian." The waiter came over and looked at us expectantly. "A Molson for me, please, and another Stella," I said to the dude before turning my attention back to Luca. "Can you blame him? Would you be thinking about an old, bald billionaire if you were tapping Brae?"

"If you repeat that to Jude, he'd…" Luca stopped to reach over the table and slap the side of my head.

"Ow, you fuckhead. You said the same once. You just don't have the balls to say it to him."

"No… I have the brains not to say it to him."

Our heads turned simultaneously when two female forms appeared at the end of our booth. "Fancy meeting you here." The petite blonde said. My eyes instantly looked behind Cassie and Desiree for the brunette I'd been lusting over. When I didn't see her, Cassie picked up on the disappointment written on my face. "She's not here."

"Who's not here?" I played dumb.

Luca's laugh made me want to punch him. "Yeah, okay. Good try, Cleary." He turned toward the girls as his ass shifted sideways on the seat. "Join us."

Without hesitation, Desiree slid next to Luca, leaving Cassie no choice but to sit beside me. At that moment, the waiter appeared with our beers. "What can I get you ladies to drink?" he asked when he saw they didn't have anything as of yet.

"Cosmo," Desiree said before Cassie added, "A lemon-drop martini."

Once we were alone again, Cassie's face brightened with a smile. "So, Des and I were just discussing ways to surprise the newlyweds when they get home tomorrow. We thought we'd get flowers and scented candles…"

"Jude hates surprises," I interrupted. "Plus, those scents will destroy your nasal passages." They both looked at me like I had two heads. "Truth."

Desiree looked toward Luca, her brow quirking up in question. "He's all about the smells."

"I'm afraid to ask what that means," Desiree responded.

"I own my own cosmetics lab, specializing in fragrances."

That caught their attention based on the wide-eyed, enthusiastic expression on their faces. "Ooh, your girlfriends must love that."

"I don't do girlfriends." As if my words were attached to a plug that has been pulled, their smiles fell in an almost comical way. I felt the need to apologize. "Sorry. Didn't mean to disappoint you, are you offering?"

"No, not offering nor am I disappointed, but your comment makes sense now," Desiree said. "You and V are two peas in a pod. The term boyfriend would cause her to break out in hives. After a date or two, her attention span significantly plummets. Tonight is date number two for her, and it's almost time for me to text her and check in."

"Check in for what?" Luca asked.

"We have a texting system. She'll respond with a yes

or no, and if no then we know she'll be joining us soon." Cassie lifted her phone and added, "I'll check in now."

My eyes shifted toward her screen, but she angled the phone away from my view. A few seconds passed and a response came quick. "All good," Cassie said. "Which means we won't be seeing her tonight."

And why the fuck that bit of information annoyed me was unexpected.

"Now we know Vanessa doesn't do boyfriends, but why aren't you two attached?" I took the opportunity to change the subject.

"Desiree is married to her job, and I just haven't found my Prince Charming."

"Uh oh. I'm guessing you're the romantic in the bunch." I took a sip of my beer. "Just like you, Benedetto."

"You say that like it's a bad thing," Cassie said in a defensive tone.

"He's right, I'm a dreamer, and Kyle's a scientist. His world doesn't run on emotion, but instead facts and measures."

A waitress I recognized appeared with their drinks. "Hey, Kye," she said when her eyes noticed me. They roamed from face to face before settling back on mine with a sexy smirk. "How have you been?"

"Good, you?" Luca did his typical throat-clearing-sarcastic-chuckle thing. "Where's the dude who was serving us before?"

"He's on break. I have mine in fifteen, if you want to catch up." Her pink tongue came out and skimmed over her full ruby lips.

"Is that what they call it," Luca mumbled. My glare caused the prick to laugh in my face.

"Maybe another time, Lynn," I said, thanking God she had a name tag on… because there was no way I would've remembered it. "I'm on the early shift tomorrow if you change your mind. Plus, it'll be my last day." She winked and walked away while Cassie groaned in obvious disgust.

"Seriously? I could have been your girlfriend."

"Is that a proposition?" I asked with a teasing smile.

She smacked my arm. "It's rude… and whore-ish."

"Just his type," Luca shot out.

The girls both shook their heads, and I felt the need to defend myself. "That's not true. I have standards."

Desiree lifted her Cosmo and said, "Yeah, I can see that," before taking a sip.

"He does. I was just busting his balls. Kyle loves a strong, independent woman who is smart as a whip. It helps if she's cut from the same cloth… facts and measures above candlelight and flowers."

The girls' eyes met across the table and they both said, "V," at the same time. "Anyway, you two should be there tomorrow night. We'll bring the food and you bring the liquor," Desiree suggested.

"Speaking of, your idea on how to surprise Jude and Brae tomorrow night has a potential to backfire."

"Why?" they both asked together.

"First of all, instead of the flowers and candles maybe you should consider handcuffs and blindfolds. Soren is a kinky fucker, and that may distract from the fact that he can't consummate his marriage the moment he walks through the door with his bride."

"They've had two weeks to consummate," Cassie said with a dismissed wave of her hand.

"I'm just saying.'" I raised my hands defensively. "We all know what a caveman he is around Brae. He may still be a kinky fucker, but now he's a fucker in love." I pretended to shudder, which earned me another smack on the arm.

I threw my arm around Cassie's shoulders and planted a soft kiss on her cheek as an apology. "Fine, we'll be there. Who are we to deny two beautiful women?"

"Now I know why Vanessa calls you Mr. Flirt."

"I could be called worse."

"Like dickhead… prick… jackass… Canadian cocksucker…" Luca paused and then quickly added a few more in Italian for good measure.

"Okay, that's enough, asshole." I leaned across the table and kissed Luca in the same way I kissed Cassie. He shoved me away, but I knew he loved me.

"What's this?" Cassie pulled out a bright orange flyer that was nestled in the menu holder on the table. "Oh! This sounds like fun, listen." She cleared her throat. "Join us next Saturday for our first annual Halloween Bash. Awards will be given for best single, couple, group, scariest, funniest, and most original costume." Luca grumbled. "Oh, hush. It will be fun! Let's do it!"

"I hate to break it to you, Miss Festivus, but Soren will not don a costume. When we were in college, he wouldn't even wear a toga."

Cassie smirked. "If Brae asks him to, he will."

Luca sighed in defeat. "She has a point, but that doesn't mean Cleary and I have to."

"Oh, come on, we'll make it interesting. Girls versus boys. If we win a prize, we drink on your tab for a month. If you win, you drink on us."

"So if we win, we get to do body shots off you for a

month?" I clarified.

"Um, no. You get to drink *free* on us, not literal."

"Whatever. We can iron out the details later." I offered Cassie my hand and added, "Game on."

"Game on," she repeated with a firm shake, but Desiree and Luca didn't look as enthusiastic as we did.

Chapter 5

Vanessa

"**D**EEP BREATH, IN THROUGH YOUR nose and out of your mouth." The yogi's soothing voice along with the instrumental harp music grated on my nerves. The girls and I met every Saturday for yoga, and it had yet to relax me.

"Breathe in… hold… exhale. Move into your Downward Dog position."

Breathe, my ass. I was not cut out for this shit and only tolerated it once a week to spend quality time with my friends. Ironically, it was Brae's idea to take the early Saturday class, and then have breakfast at our favorite uptown bistro ala Sex and the City, one of her favorite shows.

But, the witch had been MIA, more times than not, since the day she set eyes on that Swede. Mr. Wrong-turned-Right barely let her out of his grip, especially on the weekends.

"Speaking of downward dog," Cassie leaned over and whispered, "how was your date last night?"

"Slowly rise… long spine… breathe in… hold…

release." A long exaggerated sigh echoed through the room, and she continued with, "And position, Warrior One."

We followed her command and stood like statues on our rubber mats. "Ugh," I whispered back. "When the dickweed pulled out a condom from his pocket, he sent his wedding band twirling through the air and we watched it land with a clink at my feet."

"No fucking way!" Cassie exclaimed.

"Shh!" Desiree said just as the sound of a gong silenced us, with every head in the room turning to glare. That gong was a rare proverbial slap on the wrist, but somehow we managed to have it hit every week with our antics. It was a miracle we hadn't been kicked out of this stupid-ass class.

Undeterred, the breathy voice once again came over the speakers. "Slowly rise… long spine… breathe in… hold… release… and Warrior Two."

Once her commands resumed, and we were again being ignored, Desiree looked past Cassie and threw me the evil eye. She was a goody two-shoes, but we still loved her. Cassie came to my defense and whispered, "He was married."

"What a dick!" Suddenly, Miss Goody Two-Shoes fell out of Warrior Two pose and landed on her ass, earning us another gong, and all eyes on Desiree's beet red face.

"Ugh, this fucking class," I whispered. "Yogi Wan Kenobi doesn't even use the gong in the right way. It's supposed to transport us to peaceful bliss. It just pisses me off."

"Shh!" the group of college co-eds in front of us quipped.

"Oh, fuck you!" I rolled up my mat, bowed to the

class, and exclaimed, "Namaste," before walking out of the room. The bitch at the front desk watched me condescendingly as I grabbed my jacket off the hook, put on my sneakers, and took the walk of shame out the door.

They left me sitting outside the studio on the sidewalk for twenty fucking minutes. When they finally emerged, each holding a piece of paper, they had the nerve to be pissed at me.

I looked at the papers they held and said, "Did you get A's for being teacher pets, you kiss asses? What the friggin' hell? My grand exit would have been more poignant if my two *supposed best friends* followed me out!"

"Oh, no worries," Cassie said with a tsk. "We're not allowed back in. Good job, V. This is the second one in six months. You're making it so we'll have to travel to Brooklyn for yoga. Brae is going to be pissed."

"Fuck Brae. This is all her fault. And if I come near that Yogi Wan bitch again, I'm shoving her gong right up her tight ass." A few passersby shook their heads at my crass comment. "What is with people today? Are we not in New York?" I asked louder than I needed to. "Not sure if my need to punch Yogi Wan in the face or all that heavy breathing is what made me light-headed. Time for food." I stalked down the street, hearing their rubber sneakers pattering behind me.

The aroma of baked goods and coffee lifted my mood a tad. Just as we sat down at the four-top and picked up the menus, a perky waitress approached us. "Hi, my name is Raine and I'll be your server today. Would you like some green tea or coffee?"

"We'll all have coffee," I said grumpily.

Raine's ponytail bobbed. "We have two specials this

morning, an egg-white, spinach and kale omelet or…" She paused to scrunch her nose. "The chef's special, a three egg, cheddar, bacon, and sausage frittata served with home fries and…"

My hand shot in the air. "I'll have that."

"Texas toast," she finished her spiel.

"Even better," I quipped. "Toss in a blueberry muffin while you're at it. I'll have that as my appetizer." The girls placed their orders, choosing the healthy special, and Raine scurried off into the kitchen like a tiny mouse. "That special will taste like ass. What exactly is kale? Brae's not here to police our meals and you order egg whites with kale?"

"Some of us need to watch what we eat, Miss Perfect Metabolism."

"Sex… it works wonders for your core muscles. Fuck yoga. My plan is better, more fun, and I get to scream as much as I want."

"Oh, Vanessa," Des said in her loving way.

Coffee arrived, and after adding a healthy dose of cream and two packets of sugar, a few sips later and I felt back to my fun-loving self.

"Okay, so finish telling us what happened after you found out he was married," Cassie said before sipping her black coffee, which was vile in my opinion.

"I fucked him."

"You did not!"

"Of course not! Jeez, what do you take me for? I kicked his ass out." I should have been pissed at the relief written on their faces. "What did you guys do last night?" I asked, bringing my mug to my lips.

"We went to Dispatch and hung out with Kyle and

Luca." The sip of coffee sitting in my mouth came shooting out at Cassie in a violent way. A spray of brown dots now decorated her brand new white zip-up hoodie.

"I'm so sorry, Cass."

"What the hell, V! What is wrong with you?"

"That damn class makes me a nervous wreck," I lied. Just hearing they spent time with them caught me off guard. "So, how are the guys?" I went for nonchalant, but failed miserably.

Des smirked with a nod. She was so on to me. "In case you're wondering, your name did come up." My eyebrows arched. "Don't worry, it wasn't anything bad. We came to the conclusion that you and Kyle are one and the same."

Still not satisfied, I continued to look at my friends for clarity. Cassie interjected, "We found out you both aren't into commitments when he told us what he did for a living."

"Oh, that he makes perfume?" Now they were the ones with their eyebrows arched. "What? He told me at the wedding when he sniffed me."

"He sniffed you?" Des asked. "Where?"

"My neck, the first time. Where did you think he sniffed me?"

Des rolled her eyes. "I meant where on the farm."

"Oh, on our way out of the ceremony. Then again later in the barn, while his pelvis was between my legs." The group of older women looked my way. What the fuck was with everyone today? "When we were walking down the aisle. He knew I was wearing Miss Dior and proceeded to tell me it was all wrong for me."

"Any… way…" Cassie once again popped in to explain. "We said his girlfriends must love that, and he said he doesn't do girlfriends." She waved her hand toward me. "Hence, your name came up."

Knowing he felt the same way about relationships as I did, in addition to his sexual skills, only spurred my desire to see him again. Why couldn't we casually hook up when we wanted to? The thought of another train wreck of a date like last night didn't appeal to me in the least.

During the wedding weekend, things were effortless with Kyle and me. No tense moments, no awkward pauses in conversation, and no cringing sexual encounters. I allowed the memories of each time to play in my mind, drowning out Des and Cass's conversation. When Cassie said, "So, they'll be joining us tonight at Brae and Jude's place," a new visual popped into my thoughts of Kyle and me sneaking away to have sex somewhere in Jude's posh building.

And just like that, Cassie's tidbit and the delivery of my cheddar, bacon, and sausage frittata erased the foul mood Yogi Wan put me in.

Kyle

FOR CHRIST'S SAKE, IT WAS fucking freezing. I lifted the collar of my jacket to protect me from the punishing wind. Damn. I loved New York, but I hated the way the seasons crashed into each other instead of easing in with mercy. Just a few weeks ago, we were enjoying Indian Summer temperatures that afforded shorts and T-shirts.

I turned the corner, my eyes noticing the tall Italian approaching from the opposite corner. "Good timing," I said when we met in front of Jude's building. Lifting my chin toward the paper sack he carried, I asked, "What did you get?"

"A few bottles of wine and Belvedere for Soren." His eyes focused on the huge plastic bag I held. The iconic bright turquoise typeface, The Pleasure Chest, announced to every respectable hot-blooded New Yorker just what was inside. "You were serious."

"Of course I was serious," I quipped with an exaggerated eye-roll. "Picked a few things up for myself as well." Side by side, we entered the building.

"I'm sure you did, you hornbag. Nothing says romance like a twelve inch dildo." His voice echoed in the lobby, bouncing off every hard surface without apology. I followed him past the doorman who looked up with narrowed eyes. The man knew who we were, and I wasn't entirely sure it was the word dildo or the sight of us that caused his disdain. We stepped into a waiting elevator when Luca said, "Why do I feel like this is a bad idea?"

"What's so bad about getting newlyweds a few new sex toys? When did you become such a prude?"

His head twisted to mine, and he blinked a few times before sighing. "Not that, jackass. The fact we are sabotaging Jude's return to New York."

"He'll get over it. You give him the Belvedere, I'll give him the butt plug, and all will be forgiven. If not, it was all the girls' idea."

Cassie opened the door a few seconds after Luca's hard knock. "Hey, come on in. They should be here any minute."

"How did you guys get in?" Luca asked, always the practical one. It took us years to get the hardass doormen who worked this frou-frou building to finally trust us.

"Vanessa," Cassie said, as if it was obvious.

From the foyer, I could see Desiree lighting candles around the living room and the back of Vanessa's head. She sat on the couch looking down at her phone. Her thick chestnut hair hung in a straight and inviting ponytail. There was nothing hotter than wrapping a hand around a woman's ponytail as you fucked her from behind.

As Luca and I dumped our jackets on one of the barstools, Cassie snatched them up and reported it was just us and not the lovebirds. At that announcement, Vanessa's head twisted, her eyes immediately connecting with mine. A devious smile spread across her gorgeous face, and I responded with a wink.

Just as promised, the apartment was decorated with flowers, candles, and a huge *Welcome Home* banner that hung from corner to corner across the floor-to-ceiling windows. They had an assortment of appetizers on the granite island and champagne chilling with crystal flutes waiting patiently to be filled.

"This is impressive," I said, giving props where props were due. Speaking of props, I reached into my plastic sack and pulled out a flogger, sticking it into the floral arrangement that sat on the coffee table.

"What the heck is that for?" Cassie asked, her tiny fists hitched to her narrow hips.

"It's for hours of fun," Vanessa answered for me. She leaned forward and ran her fingers across the smooth leather strips nestled between the pink roses. "This is a nice one, Kyle."

"Thanks. I'm sure Jude won't mind if we test it out." Our eyes connected, held, and… something passed between us. Promise? Possibilities? Much more than a BDSM flogger could supply. *Shit, I should have bought two.*

Cassie quipped, "Oh my God, Kyle," effectively killing our moment.

"Is that a yes, Cassie?"

"Definitely not."

When my eyes cut back to Vanessa, the moment had passed. Back was the almost bored expression she perfected so well. Funny, I barely knew this woman, but I knew it was an act. The reason, because the look on her face just a few seconds ago was the same she had when I made her come in the barn… and in the laundry room.

Moving my attention back to Cassie, I took the opportunity to tease her, pulling the flogger from the vase and running the fronds through my fingers with a raised brow. One look at the toy in my hand, and she bolted behind Desiree for protection.

"Aww, come on, Cass. I'll be gentle the first time."

She emerged with her hands on her hips in a threatening way. "You're such an ass, Kyle. Flirting will get you nowhere, especially while holding that thing."

"First off, I've been called worse. Second, don't knock it until you try it," I quipped while wiggling my eyebrows. Vanessa's groan and eye-roll caused me to laugh.

Cassie didn't have time to respond. The door swung open, and two groping adults with frantic hands and connected mouths, clamored through completely oblivious to their audience.

Chapter 6

Vanessa

JUDE HAD ONE HAND UP Brae's jacket and the other on her ass. He lifted and pushed her against their door, never breaking their connection. I was impressed with the choreography, not to mention how unaware they were of the five sets of eyes witnessing every tongue flick and pelvic thrust. With Jude's back toward us, we could only assume the sound of a zipper lowering meant they were going for it, yet no one moved or said a word.

Taking matters into my own hands, because my friend would be mortified if her husband dropped his jeans as we all watched, my slow steady clapping snapped their attention toward us.

"Surprise!" We all yelled. It took a second for them to focus, see us, and realize what almost happened before our very eyes. Kyle blew a party favor horn, and I snorted when the colorful paper roll shot out from the end of a plastic penis with a squeal sounding like someone stepped on a cat's tail.

"Oh my God!" Brae dropped her legs in haste.

A rosy tinge colored her tanned cheeks just as her

husband barked, "What the fuck are you all doing here?"

"Um… welcome home," Cassie said tentatively, raising her arms like a cheerleader.

"Nice moves, Soren. That takes control," Kyle complimented with a huge grin. Jude adjusted himself and mumbled something that no one understood.

"Ah, shit." Luca grimaced. "He's breaking into his native tongue."

"Wow, this is such a nice surprise." Brae smoothed her hair and grabbed Jude's arm. "Isn't this wonderful, honey?"

Jude's glare didn't match his voice when he said, "Yes, it's fantastic."

"You can resume after we leave." Kyle leaned forward and patted his friend's shoulder. "I brought presents. You'll thank me later, Soren."

"A gun?"

"No, but there is a bullet involved," Kyle responded without missing a beat. The way he shrugged, Brae gawked, and Jude raised a brow in interest elicited another laugh from me. Kyle looked my way and did the same. He was a very handsome man, but when he smiled or laughed without abandon he was even hotter.

His sky-blue eyes looked like they were backlit. And I didn't really notice that until he directed them to me. I also never paid attention to scruff on a man before, but on Kyle's jaw it acted as an accessory to his boyish good looks. It announced, he may have an adorable smile, stunning eyes, and a devilish charm, but he was all man.

Normally, my type was more tall, dark, mysterious— like Luca. Kyle's sandy brown hair, light eyes, and open-book personality were new for me. The attributes I did find attractive were his insatiable appetite for sex, his tall lean frame, and the way his mouth could make me wet when it wasn't even near me. He had pretty lips—kissable, bitable, and sexy all in a perfectly proportioned way.

I also never studied a man as much as I did Kyle. That alone sent smoke signals to my brain. But that damn mouth of his. Beyond the talent it possessed, it was the humorous comments that flew out from it. There weren't many men who could make me laugh at a drop of a dime. His sarcasm, sexual innuendos, and crass remarks had me biting my lip on more than one occasion.

Once the shock of us being there wore off, we all settled in the living room with drinks in hand and fell into the comfortable banter. I was on the couch facing Jude, Brae, Luca, and Cassie. Beside me to the right was Kyle, to the left Desiree.

For some reason, a surge of anxiety coursed through me. Hearing all about the romantic honeymoon, while sitting beside a man who did all sorts of dirty things to me, started to make me uncomfortable.

"Oh, before I forget," Cassie blurted out. "There's a big Halloween party at Dispatch. Prizes and everything. We're all going. Kyle and I sort of made a bet."

"What kind of bet?" Jude asked, narrowing his eyes at Kyle.

"Don't worry, this one only involves you putting on a costume. You don't have to shack up with a gorgeous chick for six weeks."

"There will be no more shacking up in his future," Brae announced, pointing a finger directly at Kyle.

"For the Swede… no more shacking up for the Swede," Kyle quipped, pointing a finger right back at Brae.

"Really, Cass?"

Her enthusiastic expression swung my way. "Oh, come on, V. It'll be fun! If any of us win, the drink tab at Dispatch is on the opposite sex for a month."

"Oh, that does sound like fun! We're in." Brae's face lit up as Jude's scowled.

"Babe, really?"

"Remember the night in St. John we ended up locked out of our cottage?"

She leaned in, whispered something in his ear, and he said, "Fine," with no hesitancy whatsoever. "But... only if Benedetto is in charge. I don't trust Cleary."

"Wow, that hurts." Jude showed no sympathy toward Kyle. "I must say, though, I'm impressed you got him to agree at all, Brae. That must have been some night from the look on Soren's face. Details." Kyle fished for more, but Brae didn't bite.

"Nope, our secret. But I will tell you we had such an amazing time," she said with a demure smile before recounting G-rated highlights of their two-week stay. The entire time, Jude's eyes were on his wife. It was as if he needed every word she spoke, every smile, every blink, every breath to function. From where I sat, she was his battery and without her he'd be lifeless.

The way Kyle's arm lay behind me on the back of the couch seemed innocent enough until his fingers started twirling a piece of my hair. Out of the blue, I was transported back to my dorm room when my boyfriend Robert played with my hair in the exact same way.

It'd been years—actually nine years ago tomorrow to be exact, since I lost him. My chance at settling down and spending all of eternity with one person vanished in a flash, and I had zero control over it happening. I believed in love and soul mates, but I also believed it came once in a lifetime. Witnessing Jude and Brae's love for each other, combined with the anniversary of the day I lost him, caused bile to rise in the back of my throat. I was so very happy for my friend, but at the same time so very envious.

Kyle listened intently as Luca filled Jude in on the torturing lunch meeting he had to endure while he was off frolicking in the Caribbean. I wasn't even sure Kyle was aware he was touching me.

I was very aware... also very aware of how my throat constricted from the memories that suddenly haunted me. The fact that my body reacted to his touch caused guilt, but the way my insides clenched from my loss caused me to want to run. All the emotions suffocated me, and it was all too much to handle.

When his hand skimmed over my shoulder and settled on the back of my neck, I stiffened. But when he began drawing circles on my over-sensitive flesh, the intimacy of the act caused me to fly off the couch and loudly announce, "Who wants to do shots?"

My friends looked at me like I was deranged, and fuck if I didn't agree with them.

"Oh, hell yeah." Kyle jumped up and followed. The man looked like he didn't have a care in the world or a romantic notion in his mind. My brain misread his actions, and I had no idea why.

Kyle moved toward the liquor cabinet with Jude and Luca behind him. Desiree's eyebrows bunched together. "What's wrong with you, Vanessa?"

Wasn't that the question of the night? If I only had an answer. "Nothing is wrong. I was just thirsty. Can't a girl be thirsty?" Each of my friends stared at me with narrowed eyes. Fine, they didn't believe me, but that was the best excuse I had to offer.

Brae, who was still in honeymoon oblivion, threw her arms around the three of us for a quick hug. "I missed you girls. Brunch tomorrow?"

"Well, since you missed brunch and yoga today, that sounds great," Cassie said with a rueful smile. Des and Cassie's eyes darted to me with shit eating grins on their faces, but they didn't tell her that we needed to find yet another yoga studio.

"Girls!" Kyle called as he stood at the island with Luca and Jude. The shots were all poured and lined up ready to be consumed.

"What is this?" Cassie asked, sniffing it before scrunching her nose in disgust.

"It's the only shot Soren will do," Kyle responded, lifting the bottle of Belvedere with a flourish. "To the happy couple!" He lifted his tiny glass and slammed it back. One by one we all followed his lead, and the moment our glasses were emptied he refilled them without asking.

The expensive vodka rekindled Jude's fire, and unapologetically he announced, "Lock up on your way out," as he grabbed Brae's hand and dragged her toward their bedroom. Her giggling protests did nothing to deter him, and a few seconds later we were left standing around the island staring at each other.

"Well, on that note," Desiree said, grabbing her bag and jacket and heading for the door. Cassie followed, as did Luca.

Kyle's eyes connected with mine. "My place?" His whispered invitation held so much promise.

"V, are you coming?"

My gaze spun from Kyle to my friends at the door and back to Kyle. My head was too fuzzy from alcohol—or so I wanted to believe it was the booze, to agree to spend any time alone with him. I needed away from all the lovey dovey shit that suffocated me all night. I needed air, and before I could change my mind I stared back at him and responded, "Yes, I'm coming."

The only sign of disappointment I witnessed was the way he clenched his jaw as I walked away.

Families, couples, and friends just like us enjoyed their meals in the small comfortable restaurant. When the cute waiter came by with our mimosas, we placed our breakfast orders. Brae lifted her glass initiating a toast. "To us. May our friendship always be as strong as the shots we drank last night."

We gently tapped the glasses together before taking a sip. Well, my friends took a sip, I downed mine in one swallow. Last night's events still ran rampant in my brain. This wasn't like me. I didn't let a man consume my thoughts.

I wiggled my finger at our waiter, indicating I needed another drink.

Brae's elbows were on the table, her head propped up on her hands. "So, what did I miss?"

Cassie and Desiree looked at me. "What? I'm not the only one who did anything."

A sweet laugh came from Brae. "Tell me about Kyle." She waggled her eyebrows.

"There's not much to tell. We had fun together, that's all."

"Hmm…"

"Brae, there's no hmm."

Cassie chimed in. "I don't know, V. The way he looked at you last night, and don't think I didn't notice the way he touched you, I'd say the man has it bad."

I shook my head. "No, you're wrong. We aren't like that."

"Could have fooled me," Cassie said with a shrug.

This felt more like an episode of Dr. Phil, or worse, Judge Judy.

"It is what it is, great sex—nothing more, nothing less. The man is an orgasm wizard in the way he yields his magic wand."

An older woman sitting at the table next to us, with who I'd guess to be her grandchildren, clucked her tongue and glared at me. What was her problem? Like she had never had sex before. Where did those rugrats and their parents come from? The stork?

Desiree smiled at the woman and apologized for me. "Can we please change the subject?"

Changing the subject was fine by me. I woke up horny, which wasn't in itself unusual. The dreams starring a certain wisecracking Canadian were what had me freaked out. Sex dreams were normal occurrences for me, as was the method on how I handled them. But the men who came to life through my vibrator were always faceless.

"Cassie, why don't you start? How's school going?"

Our sweet friend let out a sigh just as our waiter brought our meals and my second mimosa. Before he could retreat, I snagged his wrist and whispered, "Honey, keep them coming." He nodded with a huge grin and walked away. Three sets of eyes stared at me and forced me to ask, "What?"

Des spoke up. "Keep them coming?"

"They're mostly juice. Relax, *Mom*," I said knowing damn well the reason I hoped to catch a buzz was to stop thinking about a certain Canadian for a while.

"Anyway…" Cassie said in a sharp tone at my interruption. "It's great. You know I love my kids. They're like little sponges waiting to soak up every bit of knowledge I'm willing to share with them. In a way, I envy them. Their lives are a clean slate, ready to be shaped into whatever it is they want to be. They haven't been tainted." She beamed. "One student told me he wanted to be a teacher one day. Who knows what he will do, but just hearing that makes all of the stress worth it."

"That's wonderful, Cass." Brae smiled at her. "What about you, V? Is your scrooge of a boss any better?"

"No. He's still a Grade A douchebag." I glanced at grandma sitting next to us and shrugged. "Enough about me today, trust me when I say my life isn't exciting. What about you, Des? Any juicy stories?"

She placed a strawberry in her mouth and rolled her eyes. "Your boss has nothing on this loser that's divorcing one of our clients. Married men suck." Brae's eyes popped open. "Please, this man is nothing like Jude. No, this guy, has a five-strand comb-over, a keg rather than a six-pack, and is shorter than I am. And get this, he filed for divorce after twenty years of marriage because he felt his wife was hindering his love life." Cassie snort-laughed. Des waved her fork in the air before piercing a grape with it. "It gets better. When we left court, this jackass drove away in his little red sports car with a vanity plate that read, D-O-U-L-8-R."

The three of us sat there and mouthed the letters trying to figure out what the hell it stood for. Then Cassie snapped her fingers in the air. I swear if there was a game show buzzer on the table, she would have pressed it. "Do you later!"

Brae's nose crinkled. "Gross."

"Right?" Des mimicked Brae's expression. "Trust me, his wife was a warrior sticking with him for as long as she did."

Cassie snickered and in a breathy voice said, "Aaand Warrior One." I shook my head, wondering where my third mimosa was.

"Oh, Cass, you sound just like a yogi. Speaking of, how was class yesterday? I can't wait to go next week." Brae beamed.

I wanted to smack the enthusiasm right out of her right after I smacked Cassie and her big mouth.

Des laughed. "Well, since you asked." She glanced at me. "Would you like to explain, Vanessa?"

"Sure." Cutie came back with my cocktail. After a long steady stream flowed down my throat, I smiled. "We need to find a different yoga studio."

Brae's eyebrows drew together. "Wait, why? I loved it there." Her eyes cut to me. "V, what happened?"

"Ready? Keep up." I drained the rest of my mimosa and ticked off on my fingers, starting with my thumb. "Date with a cheating, lying bastard." Movement beside us had our heads turning toward Grandma as she dragged the kiddies out of the booth and away from us. My pointer finger joined my thumb, and with each statement the other fingers followed in concession. "Condom packet sent his wedding band flying in the air and landing at my feet… I recapped how I kicked him out to these two… Cassie swore… the sound of a gong… then Des swore and fell on her ass… another gong, co-eds shushing us pissed me off… I told them all to fuck off.

Grabbed my mat, shouted namaste, and parked my ass on the curb and waited twenty minutes for these two to come out." Twelve fingers later, I glanced at Brae who was staring at me open mouthed while blinking. "So now you know why we got kicked out."

"I've been thinking about this, Brae." Desiree paused for effect. "We know you love your yoga, but maybe for the sake of V's sanity, we switch to kickboxing?"

"Yes! I would love to kick someone's ass on a weekly basis. Let's do that!" The mimosas caused my voice to amplify, and soon enough the rest of the restaurant was glaring at me much like Grandma had earlier.

"Absolutely not." Brae shook her head adamantly. "I can only imagine the havoc that would ensue putting you in a kickboxing class."

Whatever.

Chapter 7

Vanessa

A S I HAD DONE FOR the past nine years, I spent my morning flipping through the pages of a scrapbook that commemorated our life together. At the time I made it, I had no idea it would be all I had left of him. Concert tickets, photos of us together, his pledge pin, a few goofy notes that he'd tucked into my textbooks or left on my pillow all caused the flood of sorrow to hit like a ton of bricks. Once I studied the last page, I slammed it shut and shoved it back into my drawer, not to be looked at again until next year.

Besides my memoriam, my only other mission today was to ignore the date and what had happened that night that forever changed my life. Although I pretended to be annoyed at my friend, Cassie's idea for Halloween provided the perfect distraction.

The costume shop was packed with last minute Halloween procrastinators. I stepped out of the dressing room, and a small pack of college-aged guys swung their gazes my way.

"How's this?" The short black skirt lifted and fluttered

around my toned upper thighs as I gracefully twirled in my stilettos for the audience watching me.

"A French maid?" Cassie's eyes narrowed. "I thought we were going as a group? We can't all be maids, that's not fun."

A few of the handsome faces lifted their brows and nodded in approval. "They seem to like it," I quipped, wiggling my fingers in a flirty wave.

Cassie turned and only then realized we were being watched. "Focus, V. We don't have much time. What other options do we have?"

Noticing the pale pink satiny ears that poked up among the other costumes, I snapped my fingers. "I got it! How about we all go as a different color Playboy Bunny? We'd look really Hefner-worthy in those."

"I second that." A deep, Italian voice came from behind the stand of Star Wars costumes. Like a magic trick, the appearance of his tall frame sent the gawking frat boys in opposite directions.

"Hey. You're cheating," Cassie accused Luca as he stepped closer holding a rental agreement in his hand.

"I was here first. Maybe you're the ones who are cheating." His eyes darted around us. "Where's the rest of your clique?"

"After having a few mimosas, Vanessa announced she would be point person in charge of costumes, they elected me as a chaperone. Why are you the only one here?"

"You heard Jude. He doesn't trust Kyle." Luca thumbed toward me. "No more than you guys trusting her."

My fists went to my hips. "Excuse me, I'm right here." These two were killing my buzz. "And now that the

Italian Stallion saw this costume, and heard about the bunny option, they're a no go."

"Don't change your mind on my account. Plus, if Kyle sees the four of you as Playboy Bunnies, I think he'd bust a nut." His eyes connected with mine, but it was his smirk that suggested his comment was meant for me. "Actually, if he saw you in this, he'd bust more than a nut," he added, confirming my suspicions.

I looked down, imagining modeling my sexy costume for him. His hands would travel up my legs, reach the ruffled bloomers, and tear them off with one swift yank. The visual sent a jolt zipping through me.

"Anyway, I'm out of here. This place is giving me a headache." Luca flipped his free hand in the air. "Ciao, ladies, and choose wisely because our costumes kick ass. Mmmm. I can taste those free drinks already."

"Why? What are you guys going to be?" Cassie smiled coyly at Luca.

"Nice try, but my lips are sealed. I will leave you both to it."

We waited until Luca was gone. "Seriously, V. What are we going to wear? We need to win. I refuse to lose to the guys. They will never let us live it down."

Cassie had a point. Plus, I hated to lose. "Be right back, I got this." With a purposeful stride and the perfect sway in my hips, I started for the registers. Ignoring the small line of customers, I focused on the nerdy looking cashier.

"Excuse me." I leaned forward, resting my elbows on the cool glass counter. He glanced up in annoyance until he saw my ruffle framed cleavage. I waited until his eyes came back to mine and gave him a seductive smile.

Before I had a chance to ask my question, a woman

behind me barked, "There is a line, you know."

Not giving her my attention, I reached out and placed a hand over his. "You just helped a friend of mine. Do you remember that tall man with an accent who was just in here?"

"Yes," he replied quickly.

"Can you tell me what Star Wars character he decided on? I want to surprise him and pick one that will complement his."

A confused look crossed over his face. "Star Wars? I'm pretty sure he decided on superheroes."

"Oh, so maybe you have a Mary Jane costume? Isn't that who Spiderman shacked up with?"

"You'd be better off choosing Lois Lane. I think we have one left." He completely forgot the line that stretched to the right and started to move around the counter. "I'll show you."

Grumblings and cursing forced me to say, "Oh, no worries. I'll find it. Thank you."

Feeling all eyes on my bare legs when I walked back to Cassie, she smirked knowingly. "What did you find out?"

"Superheroes, the cool ones." Cassie nodded, reading my mind. "Game on."

Kyle

LUCA RUINED MY AFTERNOON.

By texting a picture of a certain brunette in a French maid's costume, my prick of a friend managed to capture my attention while pissing me off in the process.

The words—*look who I ran into*—along with the perfect shot of toned legs in fuck-me heels, and tits that were barely contained in the small dress, caused my frustration to grow along with my dick.

When my cell rang, I debated not answering. Curiosity forced me to hit that fucking accept button.

"Dude, you should have been there." The more descriptive he got, the more my ire worsened. I was well acquainted with those legs. The memory of the way she wrapped them around my waist as I plunged into her was still fresh in my mind. Hell, I could still feel the weight of her perfect tits in my hands.

"Did she know you were taking pictures of her, you pervert?"

"I took it for you, asshole. You're welcome."

"Is that all you needed to tell me?" Luca was totally onto me when my tone failed to hide my envy. His deep chuckle prompted me to end the call without a good-bye.

I had to appreciate his voyeurism in the way he captured her assets so perfectly. That picture would provide me hours of entertainment when I didn't have the real thing available to me. Why I didn't have the real thing remained to be a question that had irked me since leaving Jude's place last night.

I was sure we'd end the evening in the position we both seemed to favor. Yet, there she went out the door without so much as a backward glance. She left me confused, in need of an alternative method, which turned out to be a very poor substitution. Afterward, lying on my back while staring at the ceiling, I spent too much time wondering why the sudden change in attitude on her part.

And now, thanks to that Italian prick, I was again

consumed with thoughts of Vanessa Monroe. Not wanting my day to end like my night had, I picked up my cell and texted her.

> **Me:** My apartment could use a good cleaning. Are you free to come do the job?

A smile I couldn't prevent lifted the corners of my mouth when the little dancing dots appeared on my screen and her nickname popped up with a response.

> **Nessa:** Cleaning is not where my talent lies... getting dirty is.

Well, damn.

> **Me:** I can work with that. Are you free to get dirty?

No dots danced. A full ten minutes passed and no response came. Rather than send another text, I dialed her number. I wondered if she would pick up, and then a breathy, "Call me later," came over the line before she added, "Hi."

"Bad time?"

"Yes."

Ignoring her, I asked, "So, are you?"

"Am I what?"

"Free to get dirty?" In the background, the sounds of traffic replaced her voice. "Hello?"

"I don't know."

"You don't know if you are free to get dirty? Or if you want to?" More silence came. "Do I need to remind you how good it was the last time we got dirty?"

"I remember. I just don't..."

"If you change your mind," I interrupted. "I'm in Lenox Tower... 72nd and 2nd... apartment 18D. I'll leave your name with my doorman." I hung up and said a silent prayer, hoping the Vanessa I spent a weekend having a good time with appeared at my door. But with each passing minute, as they piled up like little dominos, what turned out to be an hour later caused hope to fly out the window.

While waiting for my takeout to arrive, I grabbed myself a beer and stepped toward my balcony door in my living room. The view was spectacular. Stars started to dot the sky alongside the pale moon, creating the perfect dusk skyline.

In unison with the growl coming from my stomach, my buzzer sounded. I snagged cash off the table and pulled the door open to hear Vanessa announce, "Yeah, so I came to get dirty." After a pregnant pause, Vanessa's brows lowered. Her eyes focused on the cash in my hand. "Were you expecting someone else?"

"I was waiting for Suzie Lu."

"You hired a hooker?" She glanced at the twenty in my hand with a sideways smirk. "And not a high-class one at that."

"Funny. Suzie Lu is bringing dinner, but I would rather have you than Kung Pao chicken."

"Good call. I'm spicier."

Vanessa had a certain way of looking at things. Plus, the sparkle in her eye and the fact she was undeterred, prompted me to ask, "Would you like to stay and join me?"

"Are we still talking about Kung Pao chicken or sex?"

Rather than answer, I pulled her into my apartment and slammed the door shut before pinning her up against it. With our bodies aligned from head to toe, I crushed my lips against hers needing a taste of that spice I craved.

Forgotten was my dinner, or the fact it would be arriving soon.

She pushed away breathlessly and gasped. "Do we have time?"

"If we stop talking." I lifted her and those stunning legs wrapped around me just as I wanted. Carrying her over to my island, I laid her down and removed her shoes, jeans, and panties in rapid speed. The upper half of her body was totally clothed, making it all that much hotter. There was no need to pretend I wanted anything other than her coming all over my face.

She was on the same page, no questions asked, and no attempt to slow things down. Instead, she relaxed as best as she could on the cold hard granite and enjoyed every stroke of my tongue.

Her fingers gripped the ends of my hair and tugged, forcing a hiss to escape from my lips. The burst of air on her clit brought her that much closer, and it only took a few more demanding sucks to steal her first orgasm of the night.

Just as I lifted my head and licked my lips, my buzzer sounded with what I assumed was delivery of my dinner. Having just had the best appetizer, I demanded she stay put while I answered the door.

Blocking the view into my apartment from the deliveryman's gaze, I shoved the cash at him, grabbed my takeout, and stalked back to where she still lay on my kitchen island. I loved how she hadn't moved, and instead reveled in the aftershocks of her release. No embarrassment, no awkward moments on her part, just complete confidence.

Such a fucking turn-on.

What was even hotter was how I then stood between

her spread bare legs, feeding her Kung Pao chicken out of the white paper carton one piece at a time. With each drag of her lips over the thin wooden sticks, my cock reminded me to move things along as he was still waiting for his turn.

"This was what I imagined doing last night after Jude and Brae's party," I said but stopped when her eyes narrowed.

"You imagined feeding me bad Chinese takeout?"

"No, I imagined me in between your naked legs just as I am now." I pushed forward and kissed her lips, the combination of the Kung Pao heavy on my tongue with just a hint of Vanessa lingering. "Can you taste how much better you make bad takeout taste? It's a taste I'll never tire of."

She pushed away the carton and said, "I think I've had enough."

"Of food or me?" I took her hand and pressed it to my crotch. "Because he needs dessert." A quick flash of the look she had given me last night at Jude and Brae's crossed over her beautiful features. "What?"

"Nothing."

"Don't lie. You have the same expression you had last night. Why did you blow me off, Vanessa? I hoped we could come back here and have a good time with my purchases from the Pleasure Chest. I had us in mind when I bought them."

"*Us?* We're an us now?"

"Really? We're pulling hairs over a pronoun? Okay, I wanted *Kyle and Vanessa* to have a good time? Is that better?"

"Provided that's just what it is… a good time." She bounced off the island and moved to the other side of the kitchen. "All the lovey dovey shit last night, not to mention the shots, got to me. I needed to go home… alone."

"What the hell? What lovey dovey shit? You *just* came over for dirty sex based off my suggestion. This isn't exactly the making for a Hallmark movie." I closed the distance between us and forced her to look directly into my eyes. "If you think I'll be professing eternal love tomorrow, it won't happen. I'm not looking for a wife, Vanessa. I'm not even sure I'm looking for a fuck buddy. What we stumbled on needs to continue. It'd be a damn fucking shame if we let our chemistry go to waste. Trust me, that shit doesn't come easily. Sexually, we're good together." I kissed her firm and hard. "That's just what this is. No more than that. Are we cool?"

I thought I saw skepticism in her eyes, but then she quickly nodded and said, "As a cucumber." Her hands traveled down my abs and popped the button of my jeans. "Speaking of…"

In the way she dropped to her knees should have validated the little spiel I made a few moments earlier, yet something about the gesture caused more than just lust to course through me. What that was, though, I didn't have a clue. Plenty of women had been in the same position Vanessa was in, looking up at me, perfect lips parted and ready to take me. Yet, the only thing on my mind at the time was how hard I'd come down their throats.

The difference was now I felt a pang in my chest that I didn't understand. Based on her one-eighty last night, and again today, it was obvious there were many complicated layers to Vanessa Monroe. The sudden urge to find out what they were started to consume me.

Chapter 8

Vanessa

WE STOOD IN MY BEDROOM, staring at ourselves in my full-length mirror. "We are so going to win tonight," I purred.

Cassie tightened her red Supergirl cape around her neck. "You better believe we are. I can't wait to see Brae as Wonder Woman. And from behind, with the two of you in head to toe black latex, I can't even tell you two apart. Meanwhile, Brae and I are practically naked and it's freezing outside."

Des smiled through her Batgirl mask. "Use your cape to keep you warm, and your legs look amazing."

Cassie cocked her hips back and forth. "They do, don't they."

She really did look amazing. Hell, we all did. "Plus, the cold does wonders for tits." I cupped my boobs for emphasis. "Unlike the male anatomy that needs to worry about shrinkage."

The three of us laughed. "We can't lose. Do you hear me, ladies? I refuse to buy the guys drinks for a month. Do you know what our bar tab would be? Between Jude's

Belvedere and Luca's Macallan, we'd be in debt in one night," Des spouted. "The only one who would be our saving grace would be Kyle and his cheap Canadian beer."

"Well, I don't give a shit what they drink, like Des said, we can't lose tonight. Flirt with the judges," I suggested. "We have tits, the guys don't."

"What if they're female judges?" Des asked.

"Always need to throw a wrench in things don't you, counselor." My phone pinged with an alert, ending our conversation. "We'll worry about that later. Right now, our Uber is waiting downstairs."

As soon as we stepped outside, a gust of frigid wind blew Cassie's cape in the air. "Holy shit!" she screeched, reaching behind her for the red satin material.

Hoots, hollers, and whistles came from costume clad New Yorkers clogging the streets of SoHo. *Yeah, we so got this.*

The heavy base vibrating outside Dispatch was a good indication that the party was in full swing. Cassie pulled our tickets from her utility belt and presented them to the bouncer who stood next to a man dressed as a cop.

With an adorable smile and a flutter of her eyelashes, she ran her index finger down the officer's arm. "I love your costume." She used the same finger to trace over his nightstick. "This is so big… and hard. It's so realistic." Cassie flattened her hand over his badge, and in her best Jessica Rabbit impression finished with, "Officer Johnson."

Des and I stared at her in awe. What the hell was she doing? The NYPD blue did not look amused as he crossed his arms, and in an authoritative tone said, "It's department issued."

"Holy shit, you're a real cop?" Cassie's eyes grew wide. "Um… thank you for your service, Officer Johnson?"

I wrapped my fingers around her wrist and pulled her away from the door and through the dimly lit room. "Seriously, Cass, just because we're with an attorney, we don't need legal trouble."

She shrugged. "I thought he could be one of the judges."

"We need drinks, STAT. If that's your idea of sexy flirting, you need to work on your delivery."

Des added, "Good call. Brae just texted me and they're on their way."

The sea of costumes parted as we made our way to the bar. Roaming eyes followed our path with more whistling like we had heard earlier echoing around us.

"Everyone is staring at us," Des shouted in my plastic-covered ear.

"Good." I turned to witness for myself the many eyes shamelessly ogling over our bodies. The black latex left nothing to the imagination, showing every one of our curves for all the world to see. My eyes connected with those of a tall gorgeous cowboy. He lifted his beer with a tip of his hat and a seductive wink.

I smiled back, my attention then stolen as a Batman and a Riddler crossed the crowded bar, coming right for us. That was most definitely Kyle, I'd recognize that walk anywhere. Turning back toward the bar, I said, "Girls. I think I see them. Let's have fun and see if they recognize us."

With purpose, I leaned over the bar knowing damn well my black shiny ass was on display. Catching the bartender's attention, I ordered us a round of lemon drop martinis just as Luca's deep voice said, "You cheaters."

Cassie giggled and turned while Des and I remained facing the bar. "We have no idea what you're talking about," she responded with another giggle.

"Sure you don't," he said in a snide tone.

"Anyway, how did you know it was us?"

"Cassie, it's you in a Supergirl costume," Luca teased. "But those two look pretty identical from behind. We know it's not Brae, so one is Des and the other is Vanessa."

"But who is who?" Des responded without turning. The urge to turn around consumed me, but I remained still, ignoring the conversation behind us.

A firm hard chest suddenly pressed into my back, one hand settled on my hip, and pulled me harder against a firm bulge. I should have pushed him away, resisted him... but I didn't. When warm lips rested on my covered ear and said, "Hello, Catwoman," I held back a moan.

I could feel every inch of him against every inch of me. "You're sure I know you?" I purred.

"I could pick this ass out in a line-up," he admitted into my latex-covered ear. His hand moved around and up the center of my torso until it rested right under my boobs. In spite of the constricting latex that had my internal temperature elevated all night, goose bumps broke out all over my body. "I couldn't wait to see what you were going to be wearing tonight. But damn, never could I have imagined you looking just as hot in an outfit than you do out of it. Turn around." When I hadn't moved, the hand flat on my abs slid down and settled with a pinky resting on my clit causing it to pulse beneath the plastic fabric.

Only then had I turned until we were nose to nose.

The slippery nature of my costume allowed his hand to smoothly slip around me and come to rest right on my ass. My crazy platform heels bringing me closer to his height. "Is that a cup I feel over you?"

"Knowing you were here tonight, and me walking around in nothing but a green leotard, would be asking for trouble."

My eyes held his for a moment before I dragged my line of sight down his torso, stopping at the bulge, and moving back up. "The Riddler is very apropos for you."

"What Riddler? I can assure you nothing about me tonight is a joking matter."

"So, how did you know it was me?" I repeated what Cassie had asked earlier.

"Like I said, I recognized your perfect ass." He kissed my exposed jaw before resting his lips over where my ear was beneath the mask. "Then I recognized your scent."

"I'm not wearing perfume tonight."

"I'm not talking about the kind that comes from a bottle, Catwoman. Remember, it's what I do." He pushed his pelvis into me. "My body seems to have a specific reaction to the pheromones you release… not to mention you look fucking hot, Vanessa."

"Thanks, Riddler."

Luca cracked up behind Kyle. "Haha, The Riddler."

Kyle twisted his head and deadpanned, "You're an asshole. I told you this would happen." He focused his gaze back on my face, specifically my lips. "Do you see question marks all over me? No. Want to know why? I am the Green Lantern. Proud member of the Justice League."

"Who?" we all said in unison.

Luca chuckled once more. "I told you to say you were The Hulk."

"Fuck you," Kyle said just as I spotted Superman towing what could only be described as Laura Ingalls sporting a Wonder Woman costume. The royal blue skirt she wore hung to her knees.

What the fuck? Soren!

"Oh my God. You guys look so awesome!" Brae exclaimed over the amplified sounds of chatter around us. The smile on her face fell when she saw my livid expression as I stepped around Kyle. "What?"

I grabbed her wrist in the same way I had Cassie's, and through clenched teeth said, "We need a picture before they start judging costumes." Brae had to practically run to keep up with my stomps through the crowd. "Des, get me a pair of scissors and meet us in the ladies' room."

"Scissors?"

"Shut it. We need to do emergency surgery on that ridiculous outfit you're wearing."

Her head dropped as she surveyed her costume. "Why?"

With a purposeful huff of pissed off air, I let go of her wrist and fished my cell out of the top of my boot. My fingertip practically cracked the glass as I jabbed until I produced an image of the actual costume I had ordered. Thrusting the phone in her face, I said, "This. This is what you were supposed to be wearing."

Her eyes sprung open. "Oh, that's hot."

"Yeah, you goob! I told you we were hot superheroes. How did you end up wearing this 1950s version of a Wonder Woman costume?"

"Jude," she said with a firm shake of her head. "Ugh, that man. I knew I should have gone with him to pick it up."

"Asshole!"

Des appeared, yielding a large pair of scissors. "Scalpel?"

I snatched them from her and continued our journey into the ladies' room. "Out!" I barked to a cheerleader and a Minnie Mouse loitering in front of the mirror.

"Bitch," one of them said, but followed my demand upon seeing the huge scissors.

Wordlessly, I sliced the skirt up the seam and assessed how high I should go. When I ducked my head under her skirt, Brae said, "What the hell are you doing?"

"Hush." I ran the scissors around her utility belt, leaving her in just the leotard. *I'll show you to mess with me, Soren.* The top half still remained the same in a customary Wonder Woman bustier. But instead of that ridiculous tablecloth she had around her hips that hung to her knees, she was now left with the tiny royal blue star-covered brief.

The scraps of satin pooled around her red fuck-me pumps. At least she wasn't wearing frumpy flats. "Why don't you have on the red boots?"

"It looked stupid with the skirt. I thought these shoes were better."

"Well, duh." I stood back to admire my handiwork with a devilish grin. At seeing it, Brae twisted to look in the mirror.

"Oh my God! I can't go out there looking like this!"

"The fuck you can't. This is better than that circus tent you had on as a skirt. You could have sheltered the entire Justice League under that thing. Your husband just made things worse for you. The costume I picked out at least had a tiny skirt on it. Now you're as clothed as a

Rockette."

"Jude is going to kill you."

"He'll get over it. You match his star tattoos. Besides, all I have to do is remind him that life in prison means no Brae."

Her scowl softened. "Aw, that's so sweet."

"I have to say, Brae. You have a great ass," Desiree said enviously. Three pairs of eyes focused on her butt. "Seriously, have you been doing squats?"

"Yoga… and Jude's strict regimen of sex, sex, and more sex."

"You poor thing." Cassie placed her hand on her chest in a dramatic fashion. "Although, all the guys looked as though they're doing something right. Did you notice the muscles protruding from their costumes were not of the foam variety?"

Des used her hand to fan herself. "I will say, they don't lack in the looks department."

"Enough talking. We have a contest to win." The four of us created a circle, each with a hand in the middle. "Use your tits and asses in the way God intended."

We walked out, spines straight, shoulders back, and didn't get very far when a shirtless fireman stepped into our path. "I found my winners right here," he shouted, drawing the attention of every male in the vicinity.

"Be sure to write us down on your ballots," I responded. "We sure would appreciate it."

Many others added their opinions as we made our confident journey back to the bar. Well, except for Brae, who looked nervous. That was until she saw the circle of harlots surrounding her Superman.

"What the hell?" Her hands went to her hips, she

stuck her boobs out, and in my head I heard the Wonder Woman theme song.

Upon seeing us, Jude turned into Superman before our very eyes as lasers shot from his eye sockets to Brae's bare legs. He grumbled, "Where the hell is the rest of your costume?"

"Look here, Clark." I poked my finger at the S logo on his muscular chest. "This is your fault. If you stuck with the costume we ordered, your wife wouldn't be practically naked. Besides, she looks beautiful."

"She always looks beautiful," he said, staring directly into her eyes. My heart flipped at their lovebirds display, yet again. *What the hell were these two doing to me?*

Ignoring how Soren just managed to make me swoon, I quipped, "You're now the proud owner of a Wonder Woman costume. You're welcome."

"So, we get to keep this?"

Brae looked down and smirked. "Considering she massacred it, yeah."

A devilish grin spread over his face. "I like that idea." Suddenly, his expression turned livid as he focused on something behind us. "Fuck this," he grumbled. Without warning, he lunged for her wrist, pulled her into the space between his spread legs, and wrapped his cape around his wife. His eyes then connected with a poor sap dressed in a skeleton costume and he barked, "Move along or I'll break your bones."

"Jesus Christ, Jude. Instead of causing a scene, why don't you, Batman, and The Riddler buy us a drink?"

"I'm not The Riddler!"

A scantily dressed platinum-blonde whore rushed over to him. I had no idea what this bitch was supposed to be with a white corset that barely covered her fake boobs, thigh-high stockings, and a frilly skirt. The ridiculous large cane she held in one hand could have meant she was Little Bo Peep.

"I love the Green Lantern," she announced, running her hands over his pecs. "Green is my favorite color."

"Well, today is your lucky day." Kyle threw us a sideways snarky smirk before focusing on Little *Ho* Peep.

She took his hand and said, "Let's dance." And as she pulled him onto the dance floor, I wanted to beat her with her *Ho Peep* cane.

Chapter 9

Kyle

LESS THAN A MINUTE INTO the dance and I wondered why the hell I accepted. I actually considered apologizing, admitting I made a mistake. *I'd rather be dancing with Catwoman.* Until in my peripheral I saw Catwoman being led onto the other end of the dance floor by a tall cowboy.

Instead of soft ruffled material beneath my palms, I should have been gripping smooth rubber. And not the kind that went over my cock, although that would be later. What I desired was the kind of latex used for a Catwoman costume. The kind that showcased every curve, every crevice, and every dip of one of the most perfect bodies I'd ever been balls deep in.

Oblivious to my thoughts, Bo Peep seemed content as we swayed to the slow music the DJ provided. Every time I looked down, my eyes were met with an abundance of cleavage. She had the type of tits men dreamt of fucking, and yet they weren't having any effect on me.

"I'm Amber." Bright blue eyes stared up at me.

"Hal." I blurted out The Green Lantern's real name.

"It's nice to meet you, Hal..." When she repeated my name, I had to fight the urge to laugh. Inching her body closer to mine, her seductive drawl accompanied by her hands roaming up my chest should have turned me on. Instead, I saw the *pussy* I wanted dancing with a cowboy.

My eyes tracked his hands traveling up and down Vanessa's body. With each passing touch, his fingers got closer to parts of her I had enjoyed on several occasions. It was when his thumb skimmed close to her tits that I saw red. Various scenarios on how to stop him played in my mind. *Dammit!* I shouldn't care. Why did I care? I had a hot blonde ready for the taking, but all I could think of was that I didn't want that asshole's hands on Vanessa.

Right before Tex's hands curved around her ass, I twirled Amber with an outstretched arm, catching Catwoman's attention. She turned and looked at my dance partner with disdain. That had to mean something, right? What—I didn't know, but fuck if I wasn't going to find out.

Vanessa's eyes then caught mine and held. Our partners forgotten, the bar noise went unheard, while a silent battle of wills continued. She was the first to look away because the prick dancing with her said something. It was then I realized my partner had also said something to me.

"I'm sorry, what did you say?"

Amber's gaze ping-ponged between Vanessa and me. Her brows scrunched up right before she patted me on the arm. "Thanks for the dance, Hal," she said and walked away without an explanation. It didn't take a rocket scientist to figure out what it was that miffed her ruffles.

So, there I stood on the dance floor, alone and the only one not moving. *Fuck it,* I thought, and a few steps later tapped Tex on the shoulder. Vanessa's green eyes narrowed just as the cowboy looked back at me. "Cutting in."

"Get your own partner, Peter Pan. The lady is with me."

Peter Pan? Vanessa laughed, and once again I was ready to punch Luca. But first, I had to deal with this dickhead. Rather than put the ball back in his court, I held my hand out to Vanessa. "Dance with me."

"You can't be serious," the cowboy responded before she did. "I'm not done with her yet."

"Done with me?" Vanessa moved her fiery glare to the prick who had just made a huge mistake. A smug smirk automatically spread on my face when she stepped out of his hold. It was short lived when she said, "I got an even better idea. You two can dance with each other."

She pivoted on her spiked heel and gracefully walked away from the two of us. The cowboy cursed at one of us, or maybe both of us, and neither she nor I cared. Her retreat proved as much, and my chasing her did as well. Before she even reached the end of the dance floor, I grabbed her arm and spun her around to face me. "You should be dancing with me."

Fury darkened her green eyes as she leaned closer, getting right in my face. "You didn't ask. Besides, I like cowboys."

"Yet, he's standing over there holding his dick, and you're here arguing with me."

"I can solve that problem." Her body attempted to move away, but my grip on her bicep prevented it from happening.

"Give me ten minutes. I have a proposition for you."

Vanessa firmly placed her hands on her hips. "I'll give you five."

Not wanting to waste a second, I grabbed her hand and led her to the small hallway in the back of the bar.

"Look, I'm going to make this simple. I want you." Her eyes widened. "You already know I'm not looking for a labeled relationship. I like my freedom and messing around, but what I really want is to mess around with you. I have no interest in having a girlfriend, and that's not what I'm suggesting."

"What do you want, Kyle?"

The best thing to do was to come right out and say it. "I want to fuck you and only you. We fuck each other and no one else."

"Sounds like a commitment to me."

"We're committing to screwing around, yes. But, no expectations other than—you can expect to have at least one orgasm each time we're together."

She looked away as she contemplated what I had just suggested. When her gorgeous green eyes came back to mine, she said, "We need rules."

"I agree." I stepped closer, leaving no space between us and no room for her to change her mind. "Come to my place tonight and we can iron out the details."

"We go to my place, and you have a deal."

"I'll go anywhere you want." Little did she know I'd go to Newark, New Jersey to talk to her. I couldn't help the pull at the corners of my mouth.

"Stop smiling, I haven't agreed to anything yet."

"Yet," I repeated. And since I still had a minute on the clock, I pushed my cup-shielded cock against her black latex covered pussy and spent it with my mouth on hers. She opened eagerly for my tongue, the taste of sweet lemons and Vanessa making me wish we were already at her apartment.

Our kiss was interrupted by the DJ's voice that the ballots had been tallied, and all winners of the costume contest were about to be announced.

"To be continued," I said when I pulled away. Her eyelids hung heavy with lust when I took her hand and led her down the hallway.

As we approached the bar, Cassie grabbed Vanessa's other hand and yanked. "There you are. We need to stand together so we can collect our prize."

Supergirl was mighty confident. Luca called me over, "Get ready my friend. We're about to hear our names called."

Cassie shook her head, and I leaned down to her. "I hope you didn't practice your acceptance speech." She glared at me. "By the way, I'll have a double Crown on the rocks."

"Shut up. You aren't winning. We are. Didn't you hear the cheers for us? Hell, Brae has been getting looks all night."

When I glanced at the newlyweds, Jude still had Brae in the same hold while brooding. The only difference was frayed threads and tears circled his neck, and his cape was now tied around her waist in a makeshift skirt.

Winners names were called, then our ears perked up when the DJ said, "The winners of the group costumes are…"

Cassie turned to me. "Get ready to go down, pretty boy."

"Is that a proposition?"

She tsk'd and slapped my chest. "No. It's not."

Vanessa chimed in, "Proposition seems to be the term of the night."

I shot her a wink. "Only for you. By the way, we need to stop at my place so I can change out of this get up."

The DJ held up a gaudy, cheap as fuck, plastic trophy. "The winners are… The Justice League!"

Supergirl threw her arms up in the air claiming victory and shouted, "Yes! We won!"

I started toward the dance floor. "Sorry, but we won."

The DJ went on to mention the members of the Justice League, both male and female alike. Cassie's expression changed from elation to one that looked like her puppy just died. "Well, that sucks. We aren't a group."

"Looks like we are, but if you don't want to claim the title, I'll be happy to do it."

Her cape lifted as she practically took flight racing me to the dance floor. The DJ handed us the trophy, which I pretended disappointment but gladly let her have. Once we got back to the bar, Jude stood from the barstool his ass occupied all night, waved, and left with his wife.

Luca tossed a hundred dollar bill on the bar, catching the bartender's attention. "The ladies' drinks are on me."

"What the fuck? I'm thirsty," I said to my generous friend.

"Fine. The Riddler's drinks are as well."

We made a detour to my place for me to change, and then headed right for hers. Once through her door, an awkward silence stretched for a few seconds that felt like a few minutes.

"I need to get out of this thing; I'm dying of heat."

"Go ahead."

The mask of her costume and her keys landed on a small half-moon shaped table in the foyer. She bent at the waist, yanked off one platformed boot and then the other. When she chucked them toward the corner and knocked over a decorative umbrella stand, I laughed out loud.

"What?"

"You're a slob." The place was small and a mess to my standards. A red lace bra sat on her coffee table. A few pairs of shoes littered the hardwood floor and the orange shaggy retro area rug. Dishes in the sink, makeup on her counter, and a hairbrush on a side table all seemed perfectly in place for someone like Vanessa.

"Shut it. I wasn't exactly expecting company when I left earlier," she quipped defensively. "Make yourself comfortable. I have beer in the fridge." Instead of walking away, she stepped directly before me and turned. "Can you unzip me?" Her hands gathered her chestnut hair and she waited.

The clicks the metal tab made over the teeth of the zipper taunted me. Every inch that I lowered it goaded me to follow its path with my tongue. With each clink, her smooth skin I exposed tormented my lips like a piece of metal tempting a magnet.

Leaving me behind in the foyer, she walked toward a closed door and disappeared behind it. I wanted nothing more than to follow her, but we needed to talk. If I started something like peeling her out of that Catwoman suit, talking would not be happening in the near future.

It only took a few steps until I was in her small living room. I could smell her perfume lingering with a faint hint of vanilla from the candle she must have recently lit.

I really didn't know her all that well, but the way her apartment was furnished and decorated spoke volumes. The furniture was as bland as bland could be. Beige couches, pale woods, neutral everywhere.

Besides the disarray, hints of a personality that was all Vanessa came from the artwork she had on her walls. They weren't expensive paintings or even lithographs, but in those framed prints that could be purchased in any mall in America, her story could easily be told.

At one glance, it made me wonder if she wanted to see the world, experience passion in the most passionate of places, and live. Was she starving for culture and craving experience? My eyes scanned the different landmarks on the landscape she painted in her living room.

Paris, Rome, even Sydney, Australia were places I visited over the years, and until then I had no desire to return to any of them. Seeing them laid out as they were on her wall felt intimate in a strange way. I couldn't help but be confused by the sudden urge I felt to want to go back there… but go back there with her.

The sound of her shower meant she was not merely slipping into something more comfortable. Taking her advice, I helped myself to a beer from her fridge and relaxed on her couch to wait for her.

I planned to reiterate what I already admitted to at the bar. We were good together; to pretend we weren't or ignore how good we were was plain stupidity. But now being so close to this *come to Jesus* moment, I worried I wouldn't sell myself or my plan successfully.

Even in my own head I knew it sounded ridiculous. Neither one of us were interested in any kind of a relationship. So why would I think suggesting one was a good idea? Yet, how could we not pursue the amazing sexual chemistry between us? If we called it nothing more than good fucking, it still needed to be explored.

While I rehearsed my spiel in my head, she appeared in the living room looking beautiful. In spite of the freezing temperatures outside, she wore a pair of knit athletic shorts and a form fitting tank top. Those bare legs begged for my hands, and coincidentally my hands begged for her.

Her eyes noticed the beer in my hand, and she backtracked to her kitchen to get herself a bottle of water. There weren't many places to sit in her living room, so she planted her ass beside me on the couch with a sigh.

"Sorry it took so long. I needed a shower. I think I lost five pounds in that thing."

The space between us couldn't have been more than a foot, and with her so close her scent assaulted me. "You smell phenomenal."

"I know, right?" She stretched her arm so her wrist came right below my nose. "I love it. Don't tell Brae. When we were at their place last week, I spotted it on the vanity. One sniff and I instantly fell in love... so I swiped it. Brae will think her cleaning lady stole it. They hate each other."

"Modesty."

Vanessa's eyes widened. "Yes. Wow, you weren't kidding when you said you had a great nose." She lifted her arm and gave herself a long healthy sniff. Her cheeks flushed. "Your competition?"

"No. It's mine."

She looked impressed, and fuck if that didn't boost my ego. I think besides making her come as expertly as I had, knowing she loved one of my products made me equally as proud. Especially since she had no idea it was mine.

Though it wasn't my skin touching hers, in a way, I was all over her body. The image of her smoothing that luscious white cream over her arms made me want to have this conversation even more.

"So," she curled her legs under her ass, "let's discuss this proposition of yours."

"Like I said before, I want to fuck you and only you. And in turn, I want you to fuck me and only me." Her eyebrows furrowed. "With rules, of course." I angled my body toward hers. "The thing is, it's hard to find a compatible partner without the chance they'll become clingy or want more than orgasms."

Vanessa raised her hand up, palm facing me. "All good points, but like I said at the bar, that sounds a lot like a commitment. I'm not interested in a commitment."

"Can you please just hear me out for one second, and then you can chime in with your negativity?"

She crossed her arms. "Fine. The floor is yours."

"Thank you. Here are the rules…" Vanessa nodded. "No commitment other than the fact that we just fuck each other." Another nod. "Once we prove we're clean and protected, no more condoms." She arched an eyebrow. "I've never gone without, and I get tested yearly. My last results came just before meeting you. Can I assume you're on birth control?"

"Yes, and I get tested as well. I can give you my results right now if you want. And, like you, I've never been with someone who was bare."

Fuck if that didn't have my dick turning to stone. "If we want to be with someone else, we break off our arrangement. No questions asked, no hard feelings."

Vanessa once again nodded, then added, "If one of us wants it to end, even without someone else on the sidelines, same rule applies. No hard feelings, no questions, no explanations."

I loved that she added to the list. This meant she was warming up to the idea. "Fine, rule number five, no falling in love."

"Absolutely not." Her pink tongue wet her lips. "So, we're basically going to be friends with benefits?"

"We are friends, and sex with you is definitely a benefit." I winked at her.

"True. So, you won't start courting me and being all lovey dovey when we're out?"

"Nope. Unless you think me wanting nothing more than being buried balls deep inside of you lovey dovey, then we should be good. So, do we have a deal?"

Vanessa smirked and extended her hand. "Deal."

Chapter 10

Vanessa

THAT PROPOSITION SHOULD HAVE HAD me asking him to leave, but on a certain level it all made sense. Kyle's claim that we had great sex was true. The man knew my body better than any other I'd ever been with.

Kyle released my hand after giving the back of it a chaste kiss. "You're something else, Nessa." He pulled my feet onto his lap and started rubbing the arches. With each pass of his thumb I groaned.

"Nessa?" My back settled into the soft cushion.

"Since you're fond of nicknames, that one is mine for you."

The term he chose was endearing if I was into that sort of thing. "Do I have a choice?"

"Nope. Unless you want to be called Kyle's bitch or KB for short."

"Nevermind, Nessa is fine."

"Thought so."

The pressure of his fingers intensified. "Mmm, that feels so good. Those shoes hurt like hell tonight."

"If it's any consolation, you were the hottest woman

in the place. No one held a candle to you."

My red-tipped nails wiggled beneath his fingers. "Not even Bo Peep?"

He let out a chuckle, slid his arm under my knees, yanked me down the couch, and angled himself until he hovered over me. My breath hitched when his eyes met my own. "Were you jealous?"

Yes. "No, of course not. She just didn't seem your type, that's all."

"She wasn't." My chest brushed against his with each breath we took. He tucked a loose tendril behind my ear. "You're my type. You know, if I had a type."

Something dawned on me. Was this arrangement we agreed on the first one he'd been in? Had he done something like this before? If so, why did it end? Was it his idea? Hers? Shit. No, I didn't care. It was no big deal. Just sex.

"I see your wheels turning. Care to share what you're thinking?"

"Just wondering if you've done this before. You know, sex with just one person." Even saying that phrase felt foreign to me. How this wasn't a commitment still confused me.

"Nope, never wanted to."

Hmm… interesting.

Knowing he'd never wanted to do this before both excited me and scared me. But, the excitement won out. I was so tempted to rip off his clothes and seal this deal of ours with amazing sex, but everything seemed to be happening so fast. Granted, slow had never been part of our vocabulary, but casual sex and sex with rules wasn't the norm.

"I'm tired." I let out an exaggerated yawn. "Would

you mind if we called it a night?" Considering how badly I wanted him since he dumped Ho Beep, my request seemed dumb as hell. Something inside of me felt I needed to set the tone here or he would and could ruin me. Surprisingly, Kyle didn't argue. He pushed himself off of me and headed toward my door. "Wait. I think there is one more rule we should put in place."

Before he opened the door, he turned to look at me. "What's that?"

"No sleepovers. Waking up with someone is way too intimate."

He gave me his mega-watt smile. "Noted. No sleepovers." Kyle placed his palm on the nape of my neck and tugged me toward him until our lips were a breath away. "I'll call you. Sleep well, Nessa." His strong lips met mine in a brief kiss.

"Bye, Kyle."

"Wait, he wants what?"

Cassie was the only one available this morning to have breakfast with me. Des was hungover and Brae was still in post-honeymoon mode. We had returned our costumes, less the Wonder Woman since that was now a purchased item along with Superman. Apparently, returning damaged goods was frowned upon.

"Just sex, no strings."

Cassie took a sip of her coffee. "Well, that doesn't sound awful. I mean, the man is super sexy. Plus, didn't you say you already agreed?"

"Yes, I did. Am I overanalyzing this? I mean, it's a great plan, right? Neither of us want a relationship, so it's just safe sex all the time, no strings, no bullshit."

She set the cup on the saucer. "So, did you start your pact last night?"

"No, we didn't. I said I was tired, and refreshingly enough, he left without argument."

Cassie studied my expression and said, "Isn't that what you wanted?"

"Yeah," I blurted out, but wondered why I felt so alone after he left. I thought about it a long while and decided if it was as easy as—ask, receive, no arguments, then it would be the perfect arrangement.

Reading my mind, Cassie smiled. "Well, it sounds perfect for you. Is he good in bed?"

The memory of what it felt like to have Kyle inside me had the lower half of my body reacting. "No, he's better than good." I leaned in toward her, remembering the last time we discussed sex in a restaurant. With eager eyes, she moved closer. "The man knows his way around a woman's body. I'm really not sure which is his best asset, his fingers, tongue, or his dick."

Cassie started laughing. "Don't hold back, V. Really, do tell."

I glanced around like a covert operative ready to disclose a major government secret. "Well," I said in a hushed tone as I brought myself even closer to Cassie, "I've never had to worry about not having an orgasm when we've been together. The man's tongue and fingers are talented beyond any other lover I've had."

Cassie bit the corner of her mouth and squirmed a bit in her seat.

"But, his dick. Oh my God, he does this thing where..." I sat back and fanned myself. "Well, I'm sure you can fill in the blanks."

"Are you even kidding me right now? Tell me!" She

smacked her hand on the table, rattling the dishes and flatware. She also managed to garner some attention from the other customers. With gritted teeth, she stressed, "You need to tell me. It's been a while for me, and this is the most action I've gotten in months."

My eyebrows shot up to my hairline. "Months? Sweetie, you haven't been with someone in months?"

Cassie rolled her hand back and forth. "V, don't worry about me. Tell me... his dick what?"

Just as I was about to disclose one of Kyle's talents, my phone rang. "Speak of the devil. Do you mind? All this talk has made me horny." Cassie grumbled something incoherent, making me laugh before she told me to answer it.

"Hi."

"Hi, I need to go into my lab and wondered if you'd like to join me. I'm working on a couple new fragrances, and since I know you like my products, you can give me your opinion."

Without thought, I brought my wrist to my nose and inhaled. "That sounds like fun, okay. I can meet you there in about an hour. Text me the address."

"I will. And Nessa, since I forgot it last night, bring your paperwork." He ended the call, leaving me pulsing over his suggestion. That one command meant Mr. Cleary had plans for us besides playing with fragrances.

With Cassie's eyes on me, I nonchalantly speared a breakfast potato before popping it into my mouth. "Hello! What did Mr. Friends with Benefits have to say?" she asked, waggling her brows.

She enjoyed this way too much. Truth be told, so did I. "He's going into work and wants my opinion on something."

"His job is totally cool. I'd never imagine him the type who created perfume. It makes him sexier, don't you think?"

I nonchalantly lifted my right shoulder to meet my ear. "I suppose it does." It most certainly did. All I could do was picture Kyle sitting at a table full of beakers, wearing nothing but a lab coat.

Cass and I finished our breakfast and headed in separate directions. Before we split apart, I told her not to mention my arrangement with Kyle to anyone. We never kept secrets from our friends, but there was something about what I had agreed to with Kyle that felt very personal. The only reason I even mentioned it to Cassie was to make sure I wasn't losing my mind.

I headed home to get the paperwork he requested, and less than an hour later the cab pulled up to the address Kyle texted me. If his name weren't on the sign outside, I would never have guessed this industrial style building housed a fragrance lab. Once through the black glass doors, the brick facade on the outside was in complete contrast to the luxuriously modern interior.

The security man at the desk looked up and smiled. "Ms. Monroe?"

Surprised at the efficiency Kyle managed his staff, I offered a quick nod. "Mr. Cleary is expecting you on the sixth floor."

The elevator doors opened to a square foyer with each glass wall housing a different lab. Directly in front of me was the largest, where Kyle sat at a long table, much like I had pictured him.

Except, instead of the white lab coat, he wore a light blue T-shirt that stretched across his broad chest and enhanced the color of his eyes. The cotton fabric molded over his muscles, almost defining them. Rather than go right in, I stayed in the hallway and watched for a moment through the glass window.

He wore black-rimmed glasses, which made him look even sexier. Kyle picked up a colored liquid, added it to another, sniffed, and then tapped something out on his keyboard. His eyes must have caught my movement because when he looked up a grin appeared.

I pulled the door open and hovered at the entrance of the lab. "Hi, you looked deep in thought, I didn't want to disturb you."

He walked closer, gave me a kiss on the cheek before taking my jacket, and motioned for me to sit on a stool next to his. "Welcome to my home away from home."

I took a moment to appreciate my surroundings. It wasn't what I had expected, not that I'd been in many labs before. Of course it was sterile; you could probably eat off the floors as clean as they appeared. There had to be about six long tables, each had a computer and what you'd see in a chemistry class—less the Bunsen burner.

"It's a great space, Kyle, much bigger than I thought it would be."

"Thank you. I'm glad you're here."

I pulled out the folded piece of paper giving me a clean bill of health before placing my bag on the table. "Here you go." With a salacious grin, he accepted it and handed me one he pulled from his back pocket in return. I unfolded and read the one line that proved he was clean. Kyle watched with that same grin, but made no move to do the same. "Aren't you going to look at it?" I asked when he shoved them both in my bag.

"Nope. I trust you." He plucked a thin glass tube from a wooden rack and held it beneath my nose. "What do you think of this?"

Floral tones immediately hit my senses. "It's nice but too flowery." When I realized this was most likely something he'd been working on, I added, "For me."

He nodded. "I thought so, too. Sniff this," he instructed while holding up a glass jar filled with what looked to be coffee beans.

"Why?"

"It's to cleanse your olfactory palate." He set the liquid aside and picked up a different container. This one looked like floral soup. Different flower petals sat in what I assumed to be water. Kyle strained some into a glass container, dipped a testing strip in it, and waved it in the air before bringing it under my nose. "What about this one?"

My senses took flight, and I was immediately transported. It was fresh, with just a hint of the floral note that the other one had. Almost like a breeze quickly blew through a garden. It was just enough, but not too much.

"Yes, I really like that one." Kyle smiled and typed into his laptop. When I glanced at the screen, it looked like hieroglyphics. "What language is that?"

He chuckled. "Believe it or not, it's English. But, it's just chemical equations. Here, hand me your arm." He held out his hand waiting for me to follow his direction. When he saw me hesitate, he confirmed nothing would happen to my skin.

Kyle took a dropper and dripped the smallest amount of the liquid on the inside of my elbow. He blew on it and his warm breath sent a tingle up my arm starting from the inside out. A smile tugged at the corners of his lips before he brought his nose to my arm. Never had a man smelled the inside of my elbow, and the act caused a strange pull within me.

"Just as I thought," he said. "Smell it now."

"Wow, it smells even better. I would love to just play like this and create things people fall in love with. How did you do that?"

He tapped his temple with his right index finger. "I'm a genius."

"Do you always work on Sundays, Mister Genius?"

"Sometimes. I enjoy being in my lab when it's just me. But after I smelled *Modesty* on you last night, something triggered in my head and I wanted to capture it."

"Why did you put it on the inside of my elbow?"

"It's a pulse point, much like the wrist, but my favorite place to test fragrances is there and here." Kyle dragged his finger up my arm and across my collarbone until he reached right between my breasts. "Cleavage is one of the best places for perfume placement." He didn't remove his finger as he explained. "Bodies emit heat at the pulse points, but right here..." He slid his finger lower and then around the curve of my breast. "Is where I love to smell my scent."

I glanced up at him, his eyes were on mine as he moved his finger up and down, stroking my sensitive flesh. My chest rose and fell with each of his movements, my panties dampened, my nipples hardened, and I wanted him. The combination of his sex appeal, along with his touch, turning him down last night, and my surroundings all had me in a state of anticipation.

He removed his finger, and my breath hitched. Our eyes never left each other's. Kyle was sex personified. With one tug at the corner of my V-neck, he pulled it down exposing the left side of my bra. He cupped my breast with his large palm, brought his lips to it, and sucked my nipple through the thin fabric.

My back arched, pushing myself further into his mouth. He lifted me off of the stool, took a few steps, and set me down on a table adjacent to where we just were. "I need to be inside of you, feel your wet heat surrounding my cock. Smelling my creation on you is doing heady things to me, Nessa."

"Then do it, Kyle. I want you, too."

"Lay back." Without hesitation, I followed his command. He unbuttoned my jeans, pulled the zipper down, and said, "Lift."

Before I knew it, my jeans slid down my legs along with my panties. Both pumps came off as well, and they all landed on the concrete floor with a thump. He wrapped his hands around my ankles and brought my feet up to the edge of the table. There I lay, much as I had been on his kitchen island. Completely exposed from the waist down, I propped myself up on my elbows to look at him.

He stood about a foot away, his left arm supported his right elbow, chin propped in his right hand. Kyle's eyes were transfixed. Without conscious thought, I brought my knees together.

"Spread them. I want to look at you." Kyle stayed rooted in his position. He didn't come closer, and it made me crazy. When I didn't move, his voice deepened. "Now. Open your legs. Drop your knees to the sides."

His crude orders caused my pussy to clench. The glasses, the look in his heavy-lidded eyes, caused butterflies to take flight in my stomach. Every inch of me responded to this man, both inside and out. I swore my nipples were going to pierce a hole in the satin fabric of my bra. I did as he asked. His Adam's apple bobbed and the muscles in his arms looked corded as if he refrained himself from touching me.

"Touch me, Kyle."

As if in slow motion, he shook his head back and forth. "No, I want you to do that. Show me, Nessa. Show me how you touch yourself. But don't make yourself come. I want that pleasure."

Fuck. I bit my lower lip as I brought my middle finger down the tiny strip of hair before feeling my own heat.

"Tell me why you're so turned on." His eyes tracked every movement. "Why are you so wet for me, Nessa?"

"It's your eyes. The way you're looking at me."

"How am I looking at you?" He paused. "Slide your finger inside and tell me."

Doing as he asked, I slid one finger in and moaned. Kyle's reciprocating moan, spurred me on to add another finger. "Like you want to devour me." I methodically pumped my fingers, eliciting another moan.

"I do want to devour you. I'm so fucking hard right now. Watching your slick fingers move in and out is the biggest fucking turn-on. Your pussy is the prettiest shade of pink, the way it's glistening, begging for more. Begging for me. That's what you want, isn't it?"

My voice caught in my throat. Want, need, and everything in between. I could feel myself getting close.

"Tell me, Nessa. Isn't that what your pussy is begging for? My cock so deep into you, my thumb on your clit, and my lips tasting your skin?"

Between the way he shortened my name, to his dirty talk, I knew with a crook of my own finger, I'd be done. But he was right, that was what I wanted. All of what he said.

"Take me, Kyle."

Chapter 11

Kyle

THERE WAS NOTHING MORE I wanted than to take her, as she put it. My dick practically screamed for me to set him free, but I wanted to savor her. Having her laying there as I intensely eye-fucked her was the ultimate exercise in restraint.

Whenever around Vanessa, I had to have her. This was nothing new and had been my M.O. since the day we met. But there was something about her that turned me on more than anything I thought possible.

After my willpower tapped me on the shoulder and said, *"Get the fuck on with it,"* I took two steps forward. I removed my glasses and tossed them on the table beside her. Pulling her fingers from her slick heat, I shoved them in my mouth. Vanessa's eyes grew heavy. My tongue swirled to lick them clean and savor her taste. Without hesitation, I released her hand, grabbed the back of her neck, and crashed my lips onto hers.

Our tongues glided, twirled, and licked. She wrapped her ankles around my back, tugging me closer to her. Her naked ass scooched forward, her wet pussy mere inches away from my denim-clad dick. All of this needed to be rectified. Both of us needed to be naked.

My eyes cut to the glass wall since we were essentially in a fishbowl. It wasn't that I expected anyone to come waltzing in, but it could happen… and right now, she was for my eyes only. In a swift motion, I slid my hands under her naked ass. As I bent at the knees, Vanessa grabbed her things off of the floor before I carried her into my office. My first thought was the couch, but then my desk turned into a beacon.

I set her down for a minute to close the mechanical blinds in my office while she tossed her things onto my chair. Once we were shielded, I stripped her top half naked and shed my clothes. My eyes pinned to hers, I pulled a condom out of my back pocket and then remembered the paperwork we swapped. "Oh, right. We don't need this," I said, tossing it aside with a grin.

My hands went right for her. Starting at her shoulders, moving down every part of her gorgeous body. Her skin was smooth, firm, and still as soft as a woman's should be.

"Turn and bend over. This one is going to be fast, but I promise you, it will still be phenomenal."

She wet her lips with the tip of her tongue. "I have no doubt."

The term sex goddess didn't hold a candle to this woman. Vanessa had confidence in spades, which was hot as fuck. Without pause, she turned, grabbed the sides of my desk with her hands, and wiggled her ass back until it just grazed the tip of my dick.

Before I fucked her, I touched her. One finger slid in, then two, and then I added a third, causing her ass to lift. I gave her a gentle tap, but I'd never hurt her. "You know… spanking turns some people on. I'm not into it, at least not with my hand. Maybe one day I'll mark this fine ass with a crop, Nessa."

"I prefer a flogger."

"That's the only toy I don't own. I'll have to get one, then."

"Promises… promises."

My response was to curve my entire body over hers, kiss her neck, and thrust hard and deep inside of her. "Fuuuck," I said as my balls came to rest on her clit. Holy shit, I never wanted to remove myself from her. Maybe I shouldn't have gone so fast because I wasn't at all prepared for what she felt like. Tight, smooth, warmth surrounded me in such a perfect way, I literally stopped in my tracks forgetting how to perform simple motor skills such as thrusting.

She pushed back to get me to move, wanting more, needing more. I stood and gripped her hips, holding her in place as I watched my dick slide in and out of her.

"Holy Christ, Nessa. You have no idea what I'm dealing with right now. Fucking you raw is indescribable." I pulled out to my tip, only to quickly piston back inside her. A tiny gasp meant Vanessa enjoyed my method, and I couldn't stop even if I wanted to.

"Your ass is perfection." I clutched her right cheek with my hand and gave it a squeeze. "One day, I want to make it mine, just like I made your pussy mine."

In a rushed breath, she said, "I want that, too."

What? Did she just agree to anal? *Holy fuck.* I was green-lighted, and even though it wouldn't be happening today, it would happen. I planned to take her every way possible.

Those four words turned my cock into a jackhammer. There was no way of slowing down. I straightened and watched my cock slide in and out of her. Papers that I had in a neat pile were now scattered. With each pump, my desk shifted slightly from where it had been. Jesus Christ, I'd never be able to work again without picturing this moment.

"I'm so close, Kyle. Don't stop."

"Never."

Her wet heat pulsed, tightened, and milked my cock dry as we came together while yelling each other's names.

"Holy fuck, Vanessa." I flashed her a grin. "Amazing. Admit my idea was genius."

Still in her post-coital bliss, she easily agreed. "Brilliant."

Grabbing her chin, I curved my body over hers and kissed her hard on the lips. "I know. You and I could be onto something." She accepted my offered hand and straightened. I reached into my desk drawer and pulled out a few tissues. While wiping her clean, I went on to say, "Just think…"

"What are you doing?" Her hand gripped my wrist as her cheeks flushed a deep rose hue.

"I just fucked you bareback, Nessa. I'm cleaning you up," I stated the obvious. Removing her hand, I continued and then tossed the tissues into the trash. "Anyway, I was saying. Just think of all the angst and stress so many could avoid if they signed up to an arrangement like ours."

The awkwardness slipped away as quickly as it came. Side by side we added clothes in the reverse order we removed them.

"Fuck all the dating services making millions, we

should start our own for people just like us who want great sex without the hassle of dating. Call it something like, *No Strings Attached* or *E-Fuckery*."

She laughed and shook her head. "*E-Fuckery?*"

"Yeah. It takes out all the awkward unanswered questions of when and how."

"Before you go sinking all your money into your idea, why don't we take some time to see if this so-called arrangement even works out?"

"Why wouldn't it work out?" Once we were dressed, I pulled her into my embrace. "I'll even make you vice president."

"Why am I vice president?"

"Because it was my idea," I responded with an obvious eye-roll.

"It was because of me you came up with the idea." She pointed over my shoulder. "Just like that sinful fragrance you worked on." Her finger then tapped her right boob. "All me."

She had me there.

It was all her.

Since meeting her, the creative juices within me flowed in abundance–almost as much as my sexual ones did. I pretended to ponder her point. "Fine. Your title can be over mine on paper, but I'm over you everywhere else."

"I can live with that."

A phone ringing in the lab reminded me where we were. "Want to hang out for a bit while I finish up? We can grab dinner afterward."

"Dinner?" The one word question seemed heavy enough to halt the movement of her hands as she finger-combed her hair.

"Uh, yeah. Dinner." I closed the distance between us to fix a thick strand that stood straight up on the top of her head. "You know that stuff you shovel into your mouth to fuel your body every evening? Otherwise known as food." Our faces were only a few inches apart, and up close her beauty overwhelmed me. The tether between our gazes sparked with electricity. In the way her green eyes widened, I knew she felt it, too.

Just as I was about to kiss her, she shoved me, effectively killing the moment between us. I'd been in pretty compromising situations with this woman, yet staring into my eyes freaked her out. I allowed her the distance she needed and took a step back.

Either she was a great actress or I overestimated our connection as she nonchalantly walked out of my office. "I meant, dinner sounds like a date," she called out over her shoulder.

"Why is getting food a date?" I challenged, again following and coming to stand before her. As a test, I cupped her face and forced her to meet my gaze. "Nessa, stop over thinking this so much. We're simply having a meal. It doesn't have to be any major production. In fact, if you want, we can grab dinner and go back to my place. Eat it on the floor, naked. Eat it off each other naked. Whatever you want."

"Okay, fine." She gripped my wrists, pulled them away, and plopped down on a stool at the table where I was working when she came in. "Naked dinner at your place it is." With a wave of her hand toward my current project, she said, "So, show me how you work your fragrance magic."

My test proved correct. She wasn't comfortable with intimacy… and now knowing that, I planned to have some fun with her. "Magic is my middle name," I responded, pulling my stool right up against hers until our hips aligned. With our bodies so close, it didn't take much to lean in and whisper into her ear. "Most of my magic begins with this." Her stiffening at the moment I sucked on her earlobe contradicted her stifled moan.

Oh, yes. This was going to be lots of fun.

Vanessa

THE FIRST AND ONLY TIME I went to Kyle's apartment, I really didn't pay attention to my surroundings. I was too preoccupied with the internal debate on whether taking him up on his offer and showing up at his place was the right thing to do.

That wasn't me. I wasn't the chick who dropped everything and ran because a man told me to. Yet, there I was at his door because of his suggestion.

So, the frou-frou marble lobby, the poor sap in the brass-buttoned navy blazer complete with epaulettes, and the smoky-mirrored elevator went unnoticed on my first visit.

Tonight, with Kyle beside me as we made the eternal trek from lobby to the eighteenth floor, there wasn't a detail I didn't miss. He respected my silence and thankfully said nothing until we walked into his apartment.

He led me from the foyer to the only room I had become familiar with. The sight of that kitchen island caused my vagina to tighten at the memory of what he did to me when I was last on it. How did I not notice the opulence of the connecting family room that screamed

New York success? My entire apartment could fit in that one space.

There were two long leather couches, plenty of tables, and all the electronic necessities every respectful bachelor needed in today's day and age. It may not have been as sprawling as the Sorens' penthouse, but it was just as stunning. I was impressed.

After taking my coat, and removing his own, I continued my perusal of the space. The man was seriously OCD. There wasn't a thing out of place, a napkin on a counter, or so much as any evidence a human even lived there. I felt him before I heard him when his chest pressed into my back. "Why are you so quiet?" he asked with lips directly at my ear.

There was no way I'd admit to being embarrassed that my apartment was a mess, while his was immaculate, manly in all the right ways, a work of art. "Tell me you have a cleaning lady and that you're not just a freak."

"A freak?" He chuckled, causing a warm puff of air to hit my neck. The effect was as sexy as his lips touching me. "Yes, I have a cleaning lady, but I still prefer things clean and organized."

"So, you are a freak then. No one lives like this. It's disgusting," I teased, and another hearty laugh escaped at my insult.

"My apologies. I guess I like things in their place," he said, still standing directly behind me. He moved his hands to my shoulders as he added, "Once I find something that works, I rarely deviate. I'm a man with a plan." The innuendo in his admission had me twisting around in order to see him. Amusement had turned his handsome manly features into adorable boyish ones. "What?"

"What about spontaneity? Winging it? Keeping things exciting?" His eyes narrowed as he searched my face.

"Are we still talking about my apartment? Because if you veered onto a different subject, I've proven that I'm pretty fucking spontaneous, Nessa." And just like that, the fun banter turned more serious. The tone in his voice, combined with the affronted look on his face, forced me to change the subject.

"How about a tour of this place? Last time I never got out of this kitchen, then again I really never got off that island." At the hint of what occurred on the island, a brilliant smile suddenly spread and all of his ire disappeared.

"Sure. I'll start with my other favorite room." Not giving me a choice, he grabbed my hand and pulled me down a hallway to the third and last door at the end. With a flourish, he opened it and said, "Ta-da."

More shades of gray decorated his bedroom. Nondescript white pleated shades covered the enormous wall-to-wall windows. My guess was when drawn his view was of 2nd Avenue. His furniture throughout was more contemporary than traditional, but with an obvious masculine influence. I could feel his eyes on me as I examined the room he dubbed his favorite.

"This is where some of my best magic happens," he bragged shamelessly.

"Maybe you should have gone as Copperfield to the party and not The Riddler."

"You're a comedienne. Maybe I should fuck the hilarity right out of you," he countered. Kyle lifted me with little effort and tossed me onto his impeccably made bed. His eyes seared into mine as he raised the hem of his light blue T-Shirt and flung it on the floor. The feel of silky fabric beneath me, combined with his predatory glare, hindered my breath from escaping without effort. He noticed and gave me a cocky smirk.

While standing at the foot of the bed, and while his fingers worked the button and zipper on his jeans, the *Man with a Plan* informed me of his plan. "I hope you're not starving because dinner is going to be a while."

Chapter 12

Vanessa

MARTHA STEWART HAD NOTHING ON Kyle Cleary. Even the man's cabinets were immaculate. When I pulled open the bleached oak doors, I'd never seen such organization. Not only were the plates of various sizes held in their own racks, but also his breakfast cereal was removed from their original boxes and placed in plastic containers labeled with the contents. He and Brae were separated at birth. I had a feeling he didn't have a junk drawer. *Note to self, clean out kitchen cabinets.*

Kyle walked in with a brown paper bag filled with Chinese takeout boxes. Waving my hand over the set table, I said, "This was why I suggested pizza. Chinese requires too many dishes to clean up, and you're not the type to eat directly out of the containers like I do."

"Yeah, not usually." He placed each white carton down in the center of the dining table next to a bottle of wine before recycling the bag. "And based on the last time I had it, I was suddenly in the mood for Kung Pao again." He wiggled his eyebrows before pulling out my chair, which earned him a glare. "What?"

"Pulling a chair out is definitely date type shit." I sat down, and he chuckled behind me before kissing the top of my head and then moving to sit in the chair next to mine.

"It isn't date type anything. It's called manners. So, don't freak out when I open a door for you, eh? My mother raised me right. That's one thing about us Canadians, we know how to treat a woman."

"So, is that why a beaver is your national symbol, *eh?*"

"Wiseass." Kyle shook his head before opening all of the containers. He ordered enough for at least four more people. "As far as your easy pizza theory, we'll do that the next time. We can even sit on the floor so you don't have to worry about me pulling out your chair."

"Sitting on the floor eating pizza were your original conditions when we were in your lab. Again, you're a swindler, Mr. Cleary."

"Guilty as charged." He served me some of the Kung Pao, and I served him some of the rice. He added an egg roll to my plate. I added dumplings to his. We each cracked apart our chopsticks and dug in. Kyle chewed before working a swallow. "Speaking of my lab, what did you think?" he asked, stabbing a dumpling and taking half of it in one bite. Once again, the image of him wearing just a lab coat popped into my head. I hadn't realized I smiled until he said, "What are you smiling at?"

"Nothing."

"You don't make a good liar." After I let a few moments pass, he added, "I can torture it out of you." He gripped my thigh beneath the table to support his threat.

"No don't, I'm hungry. I'll tell you." The moment I conceded, he removed his hand. "I envisioned you sitting in a lab, kind of similar to yours, but you had on a white lab coat and nothing else."

"*Really?*" He popped the rest of the dumpling into his mouth and grinned around it. "That could be arranged. Do I get to wear shoes in this fantasy?"

"Sure. I guess. But you do have to wear your glasses. Those are important to the visual."

"Done." I felt his left hand slide under my hair to hold the back of my neck. I've come to learn Kyle liked touching me there. Sometimes, such as at Jude and Brae's place, I wasn't even sure he was aware of it. With his right hand he ate his meal, and with his left hand he made it hard for me to act cool.

"Um… so what made you become a mad scientist?" His fingers began stroking my skin, causing an impromptu hot flash to erupt. Opting for the water, I gulped down half of it in an attempt to cool off as I waited for his response.

"Well, it was sort of an accident." He pulled his hand away to take a quick sip of his wine. "In my normal procrastinating fashion, I waited until the last minute to work on my eighth grade science project. I had nothing, and my only option was the local five and dime. Sitting on the shelf was one of those arts and craft perfume kits. Since I was out of time and had no choice, I used my own savings and bought it. I concocted a perfume that won me an A—end of story."

"Just like that?" He shoved a piece of chicken into his mouth and nodded. "Did everything in your life come so easily?"

"Not everything. My finances were a mess before Soren took them over. Algorithms, Table of Elements, or the metric system, I love. Debits, credits, stocks, bonds, and all that shit, I despise."

"Aren't scientists supposed to be good in math?"

"I am good in math," he said in an obvious manner.

I pushed my plate away and sat back. "Regardless, even if you stumbled upon your career, you still need to be smart to major in chemistry."

"It's just the way my brain works. I see things in smells, in textures." At the look on my face, he shrugged. "I know that sounds strange."

"I just guess I figured you more for beauty than brains."

"Gee, thanks."

I realized how that sounded once I spoke the words. "No, that's not meant as an insult. The first time I saw you, I assumed you were very vain. Now, having gotten to know you a bit, I can see your intellect actually adds to your looks. I really don't know you all that well; it's just an observation."

"You know me better than you think." He glanced down at his empty plate and dished out another portion of Kung Pao, plucked a peanut between his chopsticks, and popped it into his mouth. "What were you like in school?" I responded with a casual shrug. Undeterred, he added, "I picture you as the head cheerleader that every guy wanted and every girl hated. Smart, hot, funny—the entire package."

I blushed from his compliment. "I was more of a daydreamer in high school… and very easily distracted. Even in college, I never embraced everything it had to offer. I kind of moved through in a daze until I woke up one morning and realized I was a month from graduating without any real skills to show for it." My shoulders rose in a shrug. "It was my own fault for letting so many opportunities swirl down the proverbial drain."

I wasn't sure if it was my forced blasé attitude or the sadness in my eyes that he picked up on. His otherwise content expression turned to one of concern. "What happened to distract you, Nessa?"

There was no way I was tugging on that thread. I forced a smile and laughed. "Oh, let's see. I had friends who loved to party and have a good time. And I found out pretty quickly that I did as well."

My heart clenched from the look on his face. Going down the pity road with a man I agreed to being fuck buddies with was not an option. Fuck no.

"At first I thought you over ordered, but you ate a ton of food. I'm always getting flak from Brae that I don't eat healthy enough. She'd be lecturing us right now."

"You're in incredible shape, Nessa. I wouldn't change a thing. You're stunning." Hunger was the only way I could describe the look on his face when he said that… and I knew enough to know it wasn't food he wanted.

"Thanks." After a quick pause, I veered the conversation back to him. "How do you stay so fit?"

"I have many methods," he said with a devilish grin. Finally pushing his plate away, he quirked up a brow and added, "Can I show you one of my favorites?"

And like a magic trick, my innocent question managed to derail his thoughts and aim them toward the reason we were sitting in his kitchen eating bad Chinese takeout to begin with.

Sex.

Kyle

"**W**HAT TIME IS IT?" SHE asked, fiddling with her bra.

I glanced at my wristwatch and came up behind her.

Taking the straps from her fingers, I proceeded to fasten them myself. The backs of my fingers ran a horizontal line as I drew the two pieces of black satin together. Her body responded to my touch, and goose bumps appeared over her flesh. I then placed one single kiss between her shoulder blades and responded, "One."

"One! As in one a.m.?" Clarity hit in the way her widened eyes met mine in the mirror that we faced. "Fuck, I have to work tomorrow."

"So do I." I wrapped my arms around her waist and nuzzled my nose in her hair. "Stay. I'll drive you home in the morning."

"It is the morning." Every muscle in her body went rigid from the hold I had on her. She tried to pry my arms from her body, but the more she did the more I tightened my grip. "One day in and you're already breaking two rules, Kyle."

"Two?" I asked before kissing the back of her neck. "What two?" A few more peppered kisses caused her to relax a bit. "Only one rule." The final suck on her shoulder blade had all tension leaving her as quickly as it had appeared.

"Wining and dining," she said breathlessly. Her body grew heavy as I nibbled on pieces of her from neck to shoulder. "Um… and requesting a sleepover… um… that's two rules."

I lifted my head and met her gaze in the mirror. "Just because I served wine while eating doesn't qualify tonight as a wining and dining situation." With our eyes still pinned, I skimmed my hand from her belly to tit and ran a thumb over her pebbled nipple. In our reflection, I watched her eyes slide shut.

The way she pushed her butt into my crotch meant I

was revving her right back up again. The way I hardened in my boxer briefs meant I was right behind her.

"And regarding the sleepover part," I continued, switching from grazing her nipple to pinching it. "Well, that's just me being the gentleman I was raised to be." On demand, she moaned, one of her hands flying down to rest around my bare thigh. "Therefore, you have two choices. It's late, and you can either allow me to drive you home now… or later." I skimmed my hand down to dip into the front of her thong, adding, "If later, technically it's not a sleepover if we don't sleep."

"Oh, God," she whispered so softly I could barely hear it. With one hand around a perfect breast, I skimmed over her pussy from side to side, back to front.

I needed to play this just so, because she could easily go running if she saw through my motives. The truth was I wanted her to be with me tonight. But while trying to convince her to stay, I hoped my plan didn't backfire. Especially since the way she responded caused my own response that would be hard to shut down if she did decide to leave.

Her scent fucking intoxicated me. I couldn't get enough of it and wished I could bottle it. Inhaling, I ran my nose over her smooth skin from ear to shoulder. Just as I sucked a spot at the top of her shoulder blade, she rasped out, "Kyle."

"Hmm?"

"Some of us have to work for assholes. I am one of those people. I have to go." I didn't buy what she said. The tilt of her head, the way her body relaxed against me, and even how her fingers gripped my leg when mine slid into her meant she didn't want to go anywhere.

"Give me this asshole's number. I'll talk to him."

More kisses came as I ran my lips in the other direction back up toward her ear. "What do you do, Nessa?"

"I sit at a desk all day." I pinched her nipple and her clit hard and at the same time, bringing her close. "And I… oh, fuck…"

"And you what?" I asked, applying more pressure.

"Um…" That was the last sound she uttered as she trembled and came. Witnessing every expression on her face, every muscle in her body react when she climaxed, made me hard as stone. Her eyelids rose, and her green eyes met mine in the mirror. As if nothing had just happened between her legs, she continued saying, "And I daydream of places I want to go and ways to kill my boss."

A deep chuckle I couldn't stop erupted against her neck. Gripping her waist, I spun her quickly until we came face to face. "Please don't kill him. I like this little arrangement we have going. I like watching you come." I kissed her lips long and hard. "And please don't go tonight. I need more of you." She stiffened in my arms, and I veered left with my questioning. "What places do you daydream of visiting?"

"Everywhere," she responded, quickly falling for my tactics. "My short list is Paris, London, Rome." All places that hung on her living room wall. I wanted to take her to those places. I wanted to witness the look on her face when she first saw them with her own eyes and not on a poster. "Where's my shirt?"

"By the window." I released her, and she walked over to where her shirt lay on the floor. Her magnificent ass in her tiny thong caused my palms to itch. I fucking loved a woman in a thong. Not fifteen minutes earlier, I had my hands on that ass as she rode me on my bed. But I wanted her again. The woman made me insatiable for her.

I followed to where she stood and just as she raised her arms above her head to put her shirt on, I snatched it away and tossed it back to where it had been. "Hey! Stop that, Kyle. I really need to go."

"I'll make you a deal. If you stay a little while longer, I'll let you play in my lab and create something."

Her eyes whipped up to stare into mine. "You would? Anything?"

"Anything."

She couldn't hide her excitement, and it was really the first time I'd seen her so intrigued over something. Vanessa had a way about her that portrayed a level of boredom with life. As if she moved along the track waiting for a derailment of some kind... and not necessarily a disastrous one, but one that shook her world.

The fire in those green eyes that I just ignited with one simple question meant she needed a challenge at every turn, and I was just the man to give it to her.

Chapter 13

Vanessa

WARM LIPS ON MY NECK scared me to death. I sprung up in a panic, nearly breaking his nose in the process.

"Christ, Nessa! Relax."

It took a few seconds for me to remember where I was and who with. Hazy images of talking well into the night, having sex again, and passing out sometime afterward slowly filtered into my mind. I blinked over and over until Kyle's face came into focus.

Seeing how his long fingers gripped the bridge of his nose, forced me to say, "I'm so sorry. But you're lucky I didn't karate chop your throat. I live alone, and I never have overnight guests." I craned my neck, scanning his dark room. Who didn't have a clock in their room? "What the hell time is it?"

"It's seven."

I calmed slightly, but not much. "I need to go," I said, hopping out of bed barely caring I was naked… yet again. As I darted around picking up articles of my clothing, Kyle remained laying on his back with both hands behind his head. His sculpted abs were on full display, smooth and utterly lickable. Beneath the pale gray sheet, one of his best assets was also on full display, without being on full display. The fabric lay over his dick, making it so you could see the entire outline and every defined ridge as if he were naked.

A jolt of lust traveled right through me, halting all my thoughts and movements as I gawked at the magnificent specimen not three feet away. His throaty chuckle was what snapped me back to reality.

"What are you laughing at?"

"For a second I thought those gorgeous green eyes were going to pop right out of your skull." With that, he flipped the sheet off his bottom half and gave me a full monty. "Better?"

My mouth watered at the sight of him. I would love nothing more than to hop back on that fine man to really start my morning right.

"Call in sick," he voiced what a tiny cell in my brain chanted, and as that little fucker kept chanting... *Do it...* *Do it...* all the other cells immediately overrode it. They reminded it, and me, that I hated my horrendous job, but I *needed* my horrendous job.

"I can't do that." Irritation caused me to again fiddle with the hook and eyes on my bra as I made a mental note to throw the damn thing out.

"Sure you can. You pick up your phone, call the asshole, and say, 'Mr. Asshole.'" He forced his voice to sound somewhat feminine.

"I don't sound like that."

"You're right." He cleared his throat and added a sexy rasp. "'It's Vanessa Monroe. I'm not feeling well.' And then you hang up."

Aiming a remote that he picked up from his side table, one click had the white pleated shades rising almost ceremonially. "Look what a beautiful day it is. We can have breakfast, fuck, and then you can come make your concoction at the lab." Once the blinds reached the halfway point, he tossed the remote. "Oh, we can also fuck at the lab. I'll pull out my white lab coat for the occasion."

By now I had managed, how I didn't know, to get on my panties, bra, and one leg of my jeans. I hopped around trying to get the other leg in when he bolted out of bed and caught me around my waist. We fell together on the center of the mattress, and I never knew what hit me when a long finger slid my bra down and warm perfect lips latched onto my nipple.

"Kyle! You're trying to get me fired. I can't do this right now."

He lifted his head long enough to ask, "If you get fired, would you be able to collect unemployment?"

"Yeah, but that doesn't pay my bills." No response came because he moved to my other breast, sucking my nipple over the bra.

"I'll make you a deal, eh?"

"No. No more deals. You're a con artist." His head popped up and an electric smile lit his face. Those pale blue eyes sparkled in the morning daylight. "What?"

"Con artist? I like that title." I released a long groan out of frustration. Did this man ever get annoyed, angry, or even insulted? Unfazed, he continued, "If you manage to create something my staff likes, I'll hire you."

"Hire me? Are you insane?"

"Nope. Think about it. I'm offering you a golden ticket out of Asshole-ville."

I shoved him with all my strength, causing him to land beside me with an umph. "You dick!"

"What?" he asked, amused at my outburst. "I told you I'm a man with a plan."

"You're fucking me, Kyle. That's the only reason you're offering me the most demented plan I've ever heard." I huffed my way off the bed to resume getting dressed.

He pulled himself up and stood a foot away in all his naked glory. The space that separated us felt like a magnetic force field. I had to stop myself from catapulting my body onto his and maybe even sliding down him while dragging my lips over every dip and valley until I was on my knees.

This man could flip a switch in me like no other. It felt extremely foreign, and I wasn't sure how to handle it. All I knew at that moment was I couldn't give in to him. No matter how much I wanted to.

A devious expression crossed over his face. "Okay. I'll drive you home."

Narrowing my eyes suspiciously, I asked a stupid question. "Why don't I trust you?" A million other questions raced through my mind. *Should I? Was this his way of having the upper hand? Was I reading too much into our arrangement? Was I passing up an amazing opportunity?*

He raised both hands, palms up, and shrugged. "Honest. No tricks. We'll pick up breakfast on the way to your place."

"But I'm all the way down in SoHo and we're uptown."

"So?"

I heaved a sigh and shook my head. "And then you have to drive all the way back up and over to Queens."

"And?"

There he continued to stand, naked and sexy as fuck, failing to understand my point. It should have been an awkward moment. Kyle's cock sticking straight out, practically winking at me. Me with one pant leg on, one off, one boob in, one out. But when he closed the distance, kissed me, smacked my half denim clad ass, and said, "Be ready in five," it felt normal.

"Miss Monroe!"

"Fuck off," I mumbled while grabbing my notebook and pen.

Kyle managed to get me to work with ten minutes to spare. Having been there only an hour so far, all I kept thinking while typing up his stupid meeting notes was, *I should have called in sick.*

Thank Christ, he was scheduled to leave this Thursday for ten days. But the days leading up to his departure were the absolute worst. Today's errands consisted of going to the dry cleaners and Bloomingdale's for a new navy tie because his old one was a casualty of Russian dressing yesterday. But, the pièce de résistance was going to Duane Reade for a new nose hair trimmer. Granted, as gross as that was it was better than staring at the coarse black strand that hung out of his nostril.

After I finished transcribing his notes, following a few more orders, and fetching another cup of coffee for his lazy ass, I headed out.

As I stood in the drugstore staring at the various types of nasal weed-wackers, Kyle's words telling me to call in sick again played over and over in my head. The man was right; I should have faked the flu. Maybe I should go stand in the cough syrup aisle and have someone share their germs with me.

My phone vibrated and my first thought was to ignore it. For all I knew Mr. Boyd needed me to schedule a waxing appointment for him. With a huff, I plucked my phone from my handbag. Thankfully, it wasn't Mr. Asshole but instead Mr. Flirt.

"Hi, Kyle."

"Hey, gorgeous. How's your day?"

I looked at what was in front of me before answering. "Just fabulous. Do you know much about nose hair trimmers?"

"Um… wouldn't you rather use tweezers?"

"Oh my God! It isn't for me, you jackass."

Kyle let out a laugh. "Whom else would you buy nose hair trimmers for?"

"My boss. Ugh. I told you my job sucked." Not wanting to discuss the grooming habits of my boss, I changed the subject. "How's your day?"

"Much better than yours, except it's unproductive. I'm sitting at my desk and all I can picture is your naked body lying on it." He sniffed. "I can still smell you."

The lower half of my body clenched at the memory. "That is a much better visual than what I've had to endure today."

"See, you should have listened to me. It's not too late, you know. Don't go back to your office."

"What part of *I need my job* don't you understand? Do you think I'd be running bullshit errands all day for *Mr. Boyd-Who-Annoyed* if I didn't need to? There are so many other things I could be doing right now, but those things don't pay me."

"I'd pay you." My nose crinkled, not that he could see

it. When I didn't reply, he said, "Not to fuck me, to work for me. I'm not that big of a prick. Hell, I'm not a prick at all. Don't confuse me with Soren."

I laughed. "Yes, I know. But, working for you while fucking you is a major conflict of interest. Plus, what would your other employees think about you hiring someone without a modicum of the necessary experience or education?"

"As far as my other employees, I'm the boss and won't be questioned. As far as your other concern, I'm not going to stop fucking you, so…"

Before he could continue, my phone dinged. "Hold on, Kyle. I'm getting another call."

"Yes, Mr. Boyd?" What could he possibly need now?

"Miss Monroe, when you go to the pharmacy, please pick up some motion sickness pills and also some diarrhea medication. You know how I always get the runs while I travel."

I may have just thrown up in my mouth. "Yes, sir. It'll be a bit since I just left there." A lie, but it would buy me more time out of the office.

"Fine. Just make it quick." He hung up.

"Asshole."

"What did I do now?" Kyle's voice startled me.

"Oh." I let out a laugh. "I forgot you were on the other line. That was my boss, I need to pick him up medicine so he doesn't get the shits while he's in Paris." This time Kyle was the one who remained silent. "Anyway, I should go."

"Nessa, are you sure you don't want to take the rest of the day off?"

"I can't. Mr. Boyd is going away in a few days, so I'll

get a break then. For now, I'll grin and bear it."

"When do you want to come and play in the lab? I'd love to smell what you would create."

Why he thought I'd make a good chemist or perfumist was beyond me. Did I dare tell him I almost set our lab table on fire in class when I overheated an experiment? *Nah, I'd let that slide.* "Soon. Maybe when my boss is out of town I'll be able to take some time and come over."

"Or, you could come over tonight. I'm getting some new oils in and we can test them out."

My phone beeped again. "Ugh, shithead is calling me again. I'll talk to you later."

Once back at the office, things didn't get any better. I sat at my desk and stared at the picture of my girls and me at Brae's wedding. What a day that was. Thankfully, this picture was taken before my hair was messed up and full of hay. That memory made me smile.

Our dresses were gorgeous, as were the bouquets we were holding. If I thought back, I could still smell the flowers. Maybe Kyle was right and I would have a knack for combining scents. I set the picture down and went back to typing a proposal for my boss.

Kyle began to take residence in my brain. It wasn't something I was comfortable or familiar with. His whole plan of sex with no strings still made me a bit nervous. Especially since the man had no clue how to follow rules. Truth be told, I didn't mind spending the night at his place. His bed was like sleeping on a cloud where mine was like sleeping on this desk.

When I glanced at my phone, it was time to call it a day. Thank, Christ! I shutdown my computer, slung my purse strap on my shoulder, and was just about to leave when I heard, "Miss Monroe!"

Fuck me.

What the hell could the man possibly need now? An enema? I pushed my chair in and walked over to his office. "Yes, sir?"

The jackass grinned at me. "Were you leaving?" He glanced at his gaudy gold watch. "It's not even five yet."

When I looked at my phone, it read 4:58 p.m. *Prick!* "Did you need something?"

"Yes, can you please make me a dinner reservation for tomorrow night at that French restaurant I like? I need to take my lady out to dinner since she'll be missing me."

"Of course." Who in the hell would go out with him? It must be a gold digger. God knows she wasn't dating him for his looks or personality.

"Then you may go afterward."

I almost saluted him, but it would have been with my middle finger. Instead, I smiled and walked away. Kyle was right. I should have called in sick.

Chapter 14

Kyle

I T WAS RARE WHEN MY lab buzzed with social activity. If us scientists were anything, party planners were not it. But every so often, when I signed someone famous to be a spokesperson for one of my colognes or fragrances, Cleary Laboratories became a mecca of caterers, advertisers, and lawyers. That was when all my nerds in lab coats suddenly decided to be social.

Fridays were usually the day everyone crammed to get their work done so they wouldn't have to work over the weekend. But today, no work got done. We were all too busy with the celebrity among us. Lenni Westbrook was probably the hottest female actress in Hollywood at the moment. I managed to nab her for my new perfume, *Risqué*. One of the entertainment networks dubbed her the sexiest woman of the year, which would bode well for sales.

The woman was all legs and boobs. I preferred the real ones, but on her they worked. A curtain of mahogany hair hung to the center of her back, its texture and shine similar to silk.

Frederick practically stumbled up to me. "Boss, she is gorgeous. If you need me to test a fragrance on her pulse points, just let me know. Her body is killer."

I shook my head. "I don't think testing will be necessary, but I'll keep it in mind."

When I looked across the room, Lenni put on a show for the press that our public relations department invited. Her figure was something you'd see out of a Playboy magazine. The tiny red dress didn't cover much. To be honest, I was surprised her tits didn't pop out when she bent over. It must be a Hollywood trick or something.

Every one of my employees was completely starstruck. Once our meeting with the lawyers was over, we walked out into a sea of cell phones all pointed at Lenni.

She played it well, smiling and laughing for her fans. But when almost an hour had passed and no one attempted to get back to work, I made the choice for them.

After a few groans and mumbles, everyone headed back to their workspaces. Except for Frederick who stopped to give her a hug before strutting out of the room.

"Thank you for indulging them. Their workday isn't usually this exciting."

Lenni tossed her hair over her shoulder and placed her hand on my forearm. "I'm sure it is. I've never been to an actual lab. I mean, I've seen one on a movie set. Would you be able to give me a tour?"

"Sure thing, I'd be happy to."

We walked into the lab and now Lenni was the one pie-eyed. "This is so cool." She picked up a test tube filled with water and sniffed it. "I like this, what's it called?"

Doing my best not to laugh, I said, "Solo agua."

"Oooh… is it French? How exotic." Yes, very exotic right out of the pipes. Holy shit, did she have half the world fooled or what? Before I could respond, like a squirrel she was on to the next thing. "Wow, is that your office?"

Without invite, she walked in and planted herself in the chair in front of my desk. What I immediately imagined was Vanessa lying on it.

"This is fantastic."

With my favorite brunette still on my mind, I sat in my chair across from Lenni. "Thank you. The advertising department should have given you any verbiage you will need for the commercial shoot."

"I have everything. Will you be there?" Again she flipped her hair, and if someone had been sitting next to her, they'd get a face full of it.

"I am planning to, yes."

An ear-piercing squeal penetrated the glass walls of my office. "Oh, that's wonderful," she exclaimed, clapping her hands like a happy child. "I just love Paris."

"Well, the shoot should only take a day, so hopefully you'll have time to enjoy the city before you head back to L.A."

She leaned forward in her chair, affording me a nice juicy view of her cleavage. "Maybe we can have dinner… or… whatever."

"Ahem." Both our heads flipped to the door. Frederick stood grinning from ear to ear, and beside him was Vanessa.

Confused to see her there, and even more so to see the scowl on her face, I hesitated ten seconds too long for her liking.

"I'll wait in the lobby," she said, turning on her heel.

Before she could walk away, I bolted out of my chair to stop her. "Wait. What are you doing here?"

Her eyes cut to Lenni, but she responded, "I thought I'd surprise you. I guess I should have called first."

"Why?" Knowing many eyes could be watching us, and not giving a damn, I nuzzled her ear and added, "I love surprises."

Vanessa tilted her head away from my lips. "I'm sure you do, but I think I'll let you continue your meeting."

Lenni stood and walked toward us. The two women stood face to face. "Vanessa, this is Lenni Westbrook. Lenni, this is Vanessa Monroe, she's a good friend of mine."

Vanessa snipped, "I know who she is, Kyle. I don't live under a rock." She held her hand out to Lenni. "It's nice to meet you."

Lenni offered a limp hand to Vanessa, and the two shook. I was ready to be alone with Vanessa to find out the real reason she was there.

"I should get going. I have a dinner meeting with a local director. You know what they say, Hollywood never sleeps." Vanessa rolled her eyes before turning away. "Kyle, call me and we'll discuss the Paris details." She once again placed her hand on my arm. "Walk me out?"

"I'd be happy to walk you out, Ms. Westbrook," Frederick chimed in. I didn't even realize he was still there.

Before they left the lab, Lenni grabbed the water-filled test tube, covered the top with her finger, tipped it, and then ran it between her breasts. Frederick looked as though he was about to come in his pants.

She turned toward Vanessa. "You should try this. It's

divine. Right, Kyle?"

"Yup."

When the coast was clear and it was just the two of us, Vanessa picked up the vial Lenni just held. She put her nose to it and inhaled. "This doesn't smell like anything." She then raised the tube to look at the liquid in the light before taking another whiff. "Is this water?"

The corners of her pretty lips quirked up. When I just nodded, she let out a laugh. "She's not exactly the sharpest tack in the box."

"Why use her then?"

I wanted to say—well, look at her, she has a million followers on Twitter, and she'd probably do anything I asked. All I admitted to was, "She was in our price range."

"Which perfume is she advertising for you?"

I walked over to the glass shelving in the corner where I kept retail samples of all my products. Vanessa was opposite Lenni in so many ways, and I worried she wouldn't approve of the scent.

She raised a brow when she saw the packaging. The hourglass ruby red bottle now seemed ridiculous, obvious. But when I pulled off the cap and held it under her nose, she surprised me with a genuine smile. "It's really pretty. Was this what Lenni had on?"

"Thanks," I said, almost embarrassed. "Yes." It looked like she was about to say something else when she opened her mouth only to close it again. "What?"

"Do you really want to know?"

"Of course."

"I don't think she's right for it." Now it was her turn to look embarrassed. "Sorry. This smelled entirely different on her. It almost smelled cheap and overpowering like a drugstore brand. But what's in this bottle is lovely."

Her comment floored me. "I appreciate the honesty." Strangely, up until that day I was completely comfortable with our decision to hire Lenni. Seeing her true personality, combined with Vanessa's comment, now had me doubting Lenni was the right choice.

"So, dinner?" Vanessa was completely unaware of the way my thoughts were now consumed with fixing this mistake.

"We got absolutely nothing done today. I was planning on hanging here for a few hours."

"Okay. I understand, next time I'll call first," she said, grabbing her bag off the corner of my desk. "You still need to eat. Would you like me to go get you something?" As I shuffled through the papers on my desk searching for the folder containing the contracts, it occurred to me she assumed that I was too busy for dinner.

I took the bag from her hand and placed it back on my desk. "I had another plan in mind. How about we have something delivered, and while I'm working, you can play?"

Her face immediately lit up. "I'd love that, but I wouldn't want to be in the way."

I pulled her into my arms, which might have been a mistake. My eyes cut to my desk and she read my mind. "If you're busy, desk sex wouldn't be the best idea. Plus, your employees are still loitering around."

"You're right, that would be unprofessional. Don't worry, more voyeurism is in your future."

Vanessa arched a brow. "I can't wait."

Well, fuck me.

I pushed a button on my desk phone to alert Frederick that I needed him, but he didn't answer. Just as I was about to text him, he walked into my office. "Boss, I'm going to head out."

"Before you go, can you please set Miss Monroe up in the lab? She's going to be putting some samples together for me."

Frederick looked confused but didn't question me. "Will do, boss."

"Oh, and be sure to get her a lab coat, eh?"

Vanessa's eyes lit up like the Fourth of July. There was no way I'd get any work done tonight. "Kyle, I have no idea what I'm doing."

"That's the fun part."

Vanessa

KYLE MADE THIS LOOK SO easy but it wasn't. Each of the little glass tubes held different scents, ranging from vanilla to some spicy thing. I held a glass beaker in one hand and an eyedropper in the other. In my head, this all made sense. Why wouldn't chamomile and ginger go together as a perfume? They'd make a great tea. But when I mixed the two, it smelled wretched. Shit.

I tapped the tip of my finger to my bottom lip. What could I add? I glanced at the rainbow of liquids sitting in the cascading rack. Hmm… then my eyes landed on a bottle labeled orange blossom. Yes, that should work. One drop turned into five. When I brought it to my nose, my eyes watered.

Frederick had given me a waste bucket to dump bad mixtures in and this was the third one I dumped. With my nose buried in the container of coffee beans, I grabbed a notebook before starting my new concoction. Positioning a clean beaker in front of me, I stared at the array of choices. Something about the one I just dumped challenged me to try again.

I glanced around looking for Kyle who had to bring a file upstairs. Before he left, he gave me a quick rundown of what everything was. He even left me a chart of different notes and measurements, but nothing I tried so far worked. Not sure when he'd be back, I attempted to fix the concoction I created. In deep concentration, I slowly added orange, chamomile, and ginger, but this time in reverse order. Grabbing the glass stir stick, I swirled the liquid around. Said a small prayer, apologized to my nose in advance, and sniffed. It wasn't as bad as my first try, but it wasn't good either.

"What the fuck am I doing wrong?" I slumped on my stool and stared at the beaker, willing it to speak.

"How's it going?" Kyle startled me as he placed his hands on my shoulders. "That looks interesting."

I twisted my head to look back at him. "That's one word for it. Can you and your bloodhound nose smell it, too?"

He released a hearty chuckle. "Yes, but it's not horrible. You just need to adjust the ratio of ginger to chamomile."

"Oh my God. You do have the nose of a bloodhound. But there's one more ingredient in it. Do you know what it is?"

Kyle sat on the stool next to me. "Yes, it's orange. What you need to add is a few millimeters of H_2O." *Water?* When I didn't move, he grabbed a bottle and handed it to me. "Fragrances are made up of different notes. While some are in the same family, they don't necessarily blend well together. They almost fight each other. Sometimes you need to start with distilled water or else the fragrance will be too harsh. A good perfumist can detect what goes into making a scent as well as determine what goes best together." He methodically poured the smallest amount into my beaker.

He handed me the glass stir stick. It clanked against the container as I once again hoped this worked. I leaned over and gently sniffed. "Wow, it's not half bad."

"It's great for your first time, Nessa. It takes practice. Chemistry is all about experimenting. No one can just walk into a lab and create magic. It takes time." I nodded but was still confused. Sensing this, he continued, "Think of a fragrance as a cup of tea. The ingredients need to steep. When making an original, which is what I like to do, there's always one ingredient that is just mine so it can't be duplicated. But, I will tell you, that not many people are able to take into account the chemical makeup of someone's skin and how it reacts to the scent. That's a talent that really can't be taught."

The way Kyle believed in me started to put cracks in the walls around my heart. Maybe he was just blowing smoke up my ass, but he didn't have a reason to. I was his sure thing, so that couldn't be an excuse. Could it be that he truly thought I had a talent?

"What are you thinking?" Kyle spun my stool to face him.

"I'm thinking how jealous I am that you get to come to a place every day and have fun. Whereas, I sit at my desk and watch the clock tick by as if in slow motion. I've been here for over two hours and it feels like minutes." Faint lines appeared on Kyle's forehead. "Now what are *you* thinking?"

He dipped his finger into the scent I just created. I tracked his finger as it disappeared into my cleavage. When he pulled it out, he leaned forward, placing his face close to my breasts. I could feel my nipples harden beneath the lace of my bra. He lifted his head with a devilish grin. "I'm thinking it's time to get out of here."

Chapter 15

Vanessa

WE MADE IT BACK TO my apartment in record time. As soon as we crossed the threshold, Kyle's hands framed my face sending a bolt of heat through my body. "Do you know how bad I wanted to spread you out in my lab today?"

Does he know how badly I wanted him to?

Our mouths met and neither of us could get enough. It was as though we were completely ravenous for each other. With each step forward he took, I took one back. One by one, we lost an article of clothing. Coats, including the lab coat I took, dropped to the floor, his tie followed. He kicked off a shoe and then another. My left pump hit the wall, the other landing between his feet as he shuffled forward.

My hands gripped the hem of Kyle's dress shirt and pulled it out of his pants. Of all the days for him to wear buttons. I thought I'd try the sexy tug like they do in movies and in books. You know the one where the person rips the shirt open and buttons go flying? Well, that didn't work so well because when I tugged I got nothing.

Kyle let out a chuckle before he unbuttoned the top few buttons and pulled it over his head. Jesus Christ. His body looked as though it was carved from stone. Each of his abs beckoned for me to touch them—and I did.

Unlike my weak attempt, he gripped my top and effortlessly yanked it apart. Tiny pearl buttons scattered across my floor. One even hit a picture frame I had on a table. "Hey! Not fair. You made that look so easy." I huffed. "I'm never going to be able to find all of the buttons."

He smirked and dragged his finger down my cleavage just as he did with the perfume. Replacing it with his nose, he inhaled and moaned. "It smells even better with time. I may need to revisit this one on Monday." His thumb then grazed my nipple, causing my head to drop back.

"I'm going to fuck these tits one day." Two large palms cupped my breasts. "Would you like that?" First his lips, then tongue, then his teeth teased and perused my neck. "Answer me, Nessa. Would you? Do you want me to fuck your tits?"

"Yes," came out as a whisper right before his lips crashed onto mine.

Without breaking our connection, Kyle lifted me, forcing my legs to wrap around his lean waist. His hands gripped my ass while mine splayed across his back, relishing in each of his movements.

This man's body was made for sex.

In a flop, he tossed me onto the bed. As if in slow motion, he began to unfasten his belt. My chest rose and fell with each breath, waiting and wanting more of him— all of him. The delectable V, that women lost their minds over, pointed to exactly what I wanted. On its own accord, my tongue ran along my bottom lip.

His pants dropped to the floor, and he stepped out of them. Drilling me with his pale blue gaze, he bent and removed each sock, tossing them to join his pants. Wordlessly, he straightened, paused, and slipped his hand into his boxer briefs. Through the dark navy knit, I could see him working his dick, and all I thought was how much of a bastard move that was. He purposely denied me from seeing something that made every cell below my waist pulse with lust... and from his smirk, I knew he knew what I was thinking.

"Get naked," he commanded from his position of power over me.

"Not until you lose the briefs," I countered. Without hesitation, he slid them off his body and kicked them aside.

"Now what?"

"Resume what you were doing."

"This?" he asked, his right hand taking hold of his erection and picking up where he left off. I nodded slowly and he then said, "Now, you do as I asked."

As I moved off the bed, Kyle's eyes flared. The first thing to go were my slacks. His eyes tracked my fingers slowly pushing the button through the hole, lowering the zipper, and letting go to allow them to fall to my ankles. Just as he had, I stepped out of them before kicking them away. Standing in only my bra and panties, I now held the power over him. That much was obvious in the way he swallowed me whole with his heated gaze, in the way his hand halted on his erection.

I waited, teased him a bit, not moving, not following his orders. He didn't leave me long to wonder if he'd allow a moment to dawdle. "Bra," came out of his mouth, rough and impatient.

A slight tilt of my chin feigned defiance until I reached behind and unclasped my bra. Once it slid down my arms, I again stood and taunted. "The longer you take, the longer I will take to make you come, Nessa," he informed me with an authority that both pissed me the hell off... and turned me the fuck on.

"I can say the same to you, Cleary."

The corners of his perfect lips lifted just a smidgen. "Yes, you can. But you see, I'm a scientist. Patience runs through my veins. You, on the other hand, will not survive for long. Do you know why?" I folded my arms as a response, causing him to chuckle. "Always so headstrong." He stepped closer, pinned his gaze to mine, and with the slightest touch skimmed over the damp satin that covered my pussy. Breathing, labored. Eyesight, blurry. Legs, wobbly—just from that one contact.

The bastard pulled his hand away, stepped back, and grinned. "You think you're funny?"

"Not at all. Just proving a point." He resumed stroking himself. "For the record, seeing you standing there in just your panties is torturing me right now. I could practically taste you on my tongue without having to take a swipe. How it felt when I slid into you for the first time without a condom is engrained in my memory—warm, tight, perfection. But I know how good it will be once I do both those things, and I know the longer I wait the better it will feel."

When I still refused to budge, out of principle and not because I wasn't in pain from arousal, he chuckled again and said, "I'll make you a deal." My eye roll had him laughing harder. "Take off your panties now, and I'll give you a three orgasm head start."

All the saliva in my mouth evaporated. Not that I'd admit it to him, but just watching Kyle's hand moving up and down his shaft was about to cause orgasm number one. Personally, I'd rather my first one come at his hand... or tongue... or cock.

"I know what you're thinking, Nessa. Part of you wants to pull your panties off of your body to submit, but the other part doesn't want to give me the satisfaction of you obeying me. So let's make it easy on your pretty little brain, I'll take them off."

In one stride, he reached me, curled his fingers in the waistband of my panties and yanked them down. His next move was to grip my waist and toss me onto the center of the bed. My panties comically kept my ankles bound together, and I left them there to further taunt him. Lying on my back, with knees together shielding his eyes from what he wanted, didn't stop him from taking it.

The mattress dipped when Kyle climbed onto the bed, yanked off the scrap of lace around my ankles, and threw it over his head. He then braced his hands on my knees and pried them apart. His eyes smoldered while looking at me. I could feel my body clench from anticipation.

With one long drag of his fingers over my opening, I was dangerously close to coming. Kyle knew the effects of his actions and even more so when he put them into his mouth to lick them clean before fingering me. His hand on my belly prevented my hips from thrusting. Not being able to move created a vortex inside of me that I couldn't prevent.

"I need more, Kyle," I said, arching my body as a reaction when he quickened his pumps.

"Look at me, Nessa," he commanded without stopping his movements. Our eyes met, he added another finger and then one more, sending my body into overdrive. I could feel myself tighten around him, and I wouldn't be able to stop myself from coming even if I wanted to.

"Oh my God!" Like a coiled spring, I let go and pulsed around his fingers. It was then he dragged them out of me and slowly ran them between my ass cheeks. When the tip of his finger grazed over the one place no man had ever dared to go, my body involuntarily tensed. He didn't go further, other than applying the slightest bit of pressure. But as quickly as my body wanted to reject that movement, deep down inside I wanted it. The thought of him being the first man to take me there turned me on.

"That's one." He grinned and positioned himself on his stomach between my legs. A warm puff of air hit me right before he said, "Here comes number two."

Kyle

I WAS ABOUT TO EXPLODE in more ways than one. Fuck, if I didn't put my cock in her soon, I couldn't be held responsible for the damage he caused. But, if I was one thing, I was a man of my word. I promised her three orgasms, and number two was on the tip of my tongue… literally.

One quick taste, and then I stopped. I waited for her head to lift and for her eyes to connect with mine. Only then did I run my tongue over her from bottom to top. I felt her thighs pressing against my ears, closing her off to what I wanted to do. I wanted her completely exposed, vulnerable for the taking. For just a few short seconds, I allowed her to adjust to the sensations caused by my mouth. But then with a firm hand on each thigh, I spread her legs until both knees hit the mattress.

My God, she was absolutely stunning. Her beauty, her obvious desire called to me like no woman ever had. Like a kitten with a ball of yarn, it made me want to play. A few little short flicks, a few long laps, a few seconds of staring, touch here, lick there.

Orgasm number two came way too quick for my liking. I barely got started when her warm pussy gripped my fingers as her clit trembled beneath my tongue.

"Kyle," she said, sounding winded. "Please, stop. I need you to stop for a minute."

"Shh." Ignoring the way her eyes pleaded for me to give her time to catch her breath, I dove right back in. It might have been evil of me to do so when she was still so sensitive. There was a fine line between pleasure and pain. In the way her fingers found my hair and pulled, and the way she squirmed in an attempt to close her legs, I knew she was tiptoeing over that line.

I also knew she wanted more. The parts of her body that begged for it, like her breasts heaving with each breath she took. Her folds quivering every time my tongue ran over them. Even the way her mewls strung together like a song, all contradicted her words. It was when she came for a third time, and of the three this one was most violent in her reaction, I knew she was completely and utterly spent.

"You're mean," she accused, throwing her leg around my head to curl up into a fetal position. I laughed at her angry pout and crawled up the bed to spoon her from behind.

"I'll take that insult," I murmured with my lips on the

back of her head. "Ready for a fourth?"

"Go away!"

After a kiss to her bare shoulder, I laughed again and climbed out of bed. "Take a rest, Nessa."

I vaguely heard her call me either a jerk or a prick as I waked out of her bedroom. The clothes we stripped out of when we clamored through her door earlier were like a minefield to navigate in the dark.

The heel of my foot found the spike of her heel, forcing a *fuck* out of my mouth before I found the lights. "Christ," I said, lifting my leg to assess the damage.

"You okay?" she called from the other room.

"No. Your shoes are goddamn weapons." Hunger and thirst overrode the shooting pain from foot to thigh. I searched for wine, beer, something, but came up empty. Except for condiments and frozen meals, not much could be found in either her fridge or freezer.

"Don't you shop?" I yelled, staring at the empty shelves and willing something to appear that I could eat.

"There are chips and pretzels in the cabinet. Oh, and peanut butter."

Bingo.

I found the peanut butter and a large spoon then returned to her room. She had since moved from the fetal position and was now on her belly spread eagle with her face buried in one pillow.

"Did you find them?" she asked, and the words sounded like someone was gagging her. I didn't respond, but instead opened the peanut butter and spread a generous dollop on her ass cheek. "What are you doing?"

"Snacking." I dragged my tongue over her skin, licking up the sticky spread with a moan. "God, I love peanut butter. Normally, I'd have it with maple syrup, but asking for you to have maple syrup in that barren kitchen would be asking too much."

"Eww, that sounds disgusting."

"Don't knock it until you try it. You happen to make peanut butter taste even better, Nessa." I repeated the motion and she giggled.

"Do I have to move?"

"Nope. Not until I'm ready to lick some off your tits."

Without warning, she twisted away and sat up. "Who put you in charge?" She snatched the jar from my hand and dipped her finger into it. My cock literally sprung straight up when she put her finger into her mouth and slowly dragged it out. Her eyes cut down to the obvious excitement rising to the occasion between my legs.

A devious grin spread across her lips. "Oh, look. Who knew peanut butter acted as a fluffer? Now I won't have to work as hard," she said before coating two fingers and smearing it up the underside of my cock.

Just like that, with a jar of peanut butter, Vanessa's wicked mouth, and my cock having reached his limit, she took control of the situation and proceeded to torture me as revenge.

Chapter 16

Vanessa

L ET ME STATE FOR THE record, I usually didn't care to give a man a blow job. But with Kyle, and it had nothing to do with my favorite bread spread flavoring him, I actually got off on it. Inexplicably, my nipples pebbled and my vagina clenched each time I took him to the back of my throat. Every groan from his lips when he bucked into my mouth drove me toward the same goal I drove him toward.

"Nessa, I don't want to come in your mouth. I need to be inside of you."

I wanted to keep going, but my lower half wanted what he did. Still, I needed to torture him just a little bit more. I gently grazed his balls with the tips of my fingers. Kyle tugged on my hair, but I didn't let that deter me.

My cheeks hollowed against him as I slowly released him from my mouth. Not ready to leave my position of power, I puckered my lips, placed a kiss on the tip right before blowing a stream of air from crown to base and back up again.

I trailed kisses along his thighs and that sinful V.

"You're one sexy man."

Kyle gripped the undersides of my arms and hoisted me up until I straddled him. "Ride me."

Without thought, I lifted my hips and slid down on him one slow inch at a time. So much for having control. His hands held my hips as he guided me back and forth, up and down. When his hips bucked up, mine did the opposite. We were in perfect synchrony. At this point, I needed him to come. I wanted him to come.

Doing my best to move faster and end his torture was futile. Kyle flipped us over, pinned my hands above my head, and laced our fingers together. "You're the most beautiful woman, Nessa."

Time suspended. Our eyes locked, he brought his lips to mine, and kissed me sweetly. Kyle didn't attempt to bring his tongue to meet mine, this kiss wasn't passionate by any means... but it still managed to take my breath away. What started out as a frenzy all of a sudden turned intimate. It was opposite of every other kiss we shared, and it freaked me out.

Even when comparing the other times we had sex, it seemed savage in nature, animalistic. I wasn't prepared for this. No... just no!

I unlinked our fingers to grip his jaw and push his face away, ignoring his annoyed expression. Screw sweet and slow. Instead, I increased my speed, thrusted hard against his hips, and chased what I wanted.

Kyle followed my lead, but his silence was enough to speak volumes. We were breaking rules left and right. The one rule I refused to break was falling for him.

His movements quickened, and I grabbed his tight ass. "Don't stop, Kyle."

He lifted his body, the muscles in his arms were taut,

elbows stiff, and he pistoned his hips at a rapid pace. I tightened around him with my fourth orgasm of the night coiling inside me. When I looked up, the cords in his neck strained.

Our sweat slickened bodies moved together. He let out a guttural moan right as my pussy pulsed around his dick. We both reached our peak at the exact same moment. Exhausted, he pulled out, rolled away, and collapsed beside me. Kyle remained silent and still until he slowly left my bed and walked out of my room.

It had been a perfect night up until about five minutes ago. Then in the blink of an eye, things changed, sending our good time spinning off its axis and crashing to earth. The urge to say his name or ask him if he was okay hung heavy on my tongue.

Before I could get up, Kyle was back with a wet cloth in his hand. He sat next to me and gently swiped the cloth between my legs. I couldn't get my brain to work to utter one single word as I watched him get up, step into his boxers, and once again leave my room.

The second time he returned, he resumed his position beside me, but the space between us sent a definite message as to where his frame of mind was. It was the first time since we started our arrangement that I felt uncomfortable in his presence, and something told me he felt the same way.

"Don't feel bad if you want to leave." I internally face-palmed over the most insensitive thing I could say after the silence that loomed like a storm cloud.

He turned his head to look at me. "Who said I wanted to leave? Unless you want me to."

His eyes stayed pinned to mine, forcing me to glance away. "I'm tired."

"Then you should go to sleep."

"Kyle," I sighed, exasperated with the conversation that hadn't happened yet… but I knew it eminent. "We both agreed to the rules we put in place. Since we started this arrangement, we keep breaking them."

The skin between his eyebrows creased. "Fuck the rules, Nessa. This has nothing to do with them and you know it."

"Yes, it does. It has everything to do with them. We weren't supposed to have sleepovers, yet we have. All we were supposed to do was fuck and have fun."

"Excuse me for being confused, but I thought that's what we just did. As far as sleeping over, if you want me to go, then I will."

Kyle started to move, but I grabbed his wrist. "Just stay."

"Are you sure? I wouldn't want to be accused of being a rule breaker." His annoyed tone made me realize that I sounded like a bitch.

"I'm sorry." Without even giving him a peck on the cheek, I smiled weakly, turned over, and tried to ignore the pinching I felt in the center of my chest as I stared at the blank wall in my room.

"Good night, Nessa."

Kyle

SHE HAD BEEN IN MY arms for hours. When I woke to the feeling of her rolling over, I extended my arm as a silent invitation to her. Surprisingly, she nestled her body against mine with her cheek on my chest and her hand resting on my abs.

I didn't want to move a muscle for fear I'd wake her. Maybe she wanted to fight what we had when she was awake, yet in her sleep she wanted what I did. Not that I was sure what that was, but having her in my arms felt right.

After the way we ended things last night, waking up with her in my arms, our bodies intertwined, and a peacefulness on her face wasn't something I wanted to disturb.

Her long dark lashes fluttered on her cheeks before she opened her eyes. "Good morning."

"Good morning. It's much nicer waking up this way rather than you wanting to injure me."

"How did I end up smothering you?" She tried to pull away, but failed when I tightened my hold. "Kyle. You couldn't be comfortable all night."

"I was once you fell asleep at least." Her head twisted so she could look at my face. "What happened last night, Nessa?"

"Nothing. We had amazing sex, or I thought we did."

"We did." I wasn't in the mood for her evasiveness. It was obvious she wanted to avoid the topic, just like she wanted to avoid me last night, which was why I pushed harder. "That's not what I mean, and you know it."

That time when she tried to distance herself, I let her. If getting her to talk meant letting her go, that's what I would do. We'd been at this for long enough, and I could fill a thimble with all I knew about Vanessa Monroe.

"Talk to me," I pushed.

She wrapped her arms around her knees and sighed. "I'm not from the talkers, Kyle. If you need to know something, you need to ask me."

I sat up, mimicking her position. "What happened

that sent you into a tailspin last night? I saw it. It was like a switch had been flipped. One minute you were present, the next you were a million miles away."

Panic passed through her expression before it was replaced with a nervous energy. Self-consciously, she reached for the sheet that rested in a crumpled mess and dragged it closer to cover herself. Again, if that was what she needed to start communicating, I sat back to let it happen. But I wasn't going to make this easier on her regarding my questions. At some point, she needed to be honest with me.

Of course I felt that I misread her, and instead of confusion over what we shared, maybe it was boredom. I thought about it long and hard, and I really didn't know her well enough to distinguish between the two.

"I don't know what you want me to say, Kyle. I like spending time with you, but I worry about the agreement between us…"

"Okay, we need to re-negotiate because it's obvious you're consumed by the rules."

"That's not true," she quipped. "If I was, you wouldn't be here right now."

"Regardless, let's talk about why you don't want me to stay. Why would lying beside each other in a bed after fucking each other's brains out be a deal breaker?" I gripped her chin and turned her head to force her to stare back at me. "Seriously, Nessa, this is ridiculous. I'm not afraid to say I want to know more about you. I have no idea who you are, except that you manage to bring me to my knees more than any other woman ever has. Add to that how much fun we have together, how we can laugh, and have the same sense of humor. You hate your job and envy mine. Your best friend is married to my best friend. That's it. That's all I know."

"That's all you need to know."

"That's bullshit. If we're friends with benefits, when does the friends part kick in?" I got nothing but a blank stare that infuriated me. "I grew up in Canada, no siblings but a ton of cousins. My parents were successful, and I was given a privileged life. I dreamt of playing professional hockey. But as I got older, all I wanted was to get to the states. And when I was accepted to Yale, I practically ran across the border.

"The first two people I met once I arrived were Jude and Luca. It's a miracle one of us, or all three, didn't end up in jail at one point during our friendship. But I'd do anything for those two, as they would for me. They are the brothers I never had, and Brae is now part of my family as well."

The entire time she listened, her eyes shimmered with emotion. "Jude was a huge help when I decided to finance my own company. His expertise enabled me to take my passion and turn it into the business it is today. I love Mexican food, love to travel, and every year I go home for Christmas and actually wear the god-awful sweater that my Aunt Betty knits for me.

"I'm from Canada, but I despise winter. I'm not a fan of the Yankees or the Rangers. Sadly, although I'm a great skater, I wasn't good enough to play my favorite sport, hockey. However, I was a cheerleader at Yale just to meet the girls."

"Get out!"

"Nope. It was a brilliant plan… until I dropped someone and was kicked off the squad two weeks in." She curled her lips between her teeth to stop from laughing. "Go ahead, I had to endure plenty of ball-busting from Soren and Benedetto." At that, she released a string of giggles. "I wasn't always this fit and good looking. When I was younger, this stud was chubby, had braces, and fell victim to acne when puberty hit."

"I find that hard to believe."

"Trust me, I'll show you pictures. So, what else can I tell you?"

"Stop. I get it. But we're different, Kyle. I was never one to open up like you just did. It's just the way I am."

She watched as I nodded, considering her admission. "Okay. I get that. One thing, then. I just need to know one thing, and I'll let you tell me the rest at your own pace."

For a second I thought she was going to tell me no. And then she said, "My parents are divorced and can't stand each other. That makes for an awesome Christmas, birthday, or any other life events that occurs. I have a stepsister who quickly became my father's favorite once he married her mother." Her pause had me thinking she was done. I remained silent, and she continued. "My own mother is bitter, nasty, and hates men. Oh, and I was given a cute puppy on my tenth birthday. It was after they got divorced as a consolation prize. Only a few months later, he was hit by a car. The only thing I did have going for me in high school and college were my looks and sparkling personality, and both made me very popular for the wrong reasons. That pretty much sums things up."

"Did that hurt to admit?"

"No."

"Good. Maybe tomorrow you'll tell me two more things," I teased.

"Kyle, you know more about me than most of my friends do." She jumped out of bed in a panic. "Oh, shit. Speaking of, they're going to kill me."

"Why?"

"I missed yoga. It's because of me they are starting a new studio today." Standing naked at the end of the bed with her phone in her hand, she frowned and shook her head. One thing she wasn't was shy. "Fuck, I missed like ten messages."

"Do you want to go to yoga?"

"Of course not. I hate it."

"Then don't go. Text your friends. You're busy all day, you have the flu, whatever." I reached for her, pulled her back to bed, and held her face. "Thank you."

Her expression softened, and a smile played on her lips. "After I was a complete bitch to you last night, you're thanking me?"

"Not a complete bitch. Shit, woman, I won't be able to think of peanut butter the same way ever again. Speaking of peanut butter, I'm starving. After we fuck, I'll take you out to eat and then we're going grocery shopping."

"How fun." Her eyes rolled up and she added, "What then? Laundry?"

"No, not laundry." Before she could respond, I bent my head and sucked on her bare nipple while gripping her ass. "There's something I've always wanted to do."

"I think I need more time to prepare for that," she said, clenching her butt cheeks beneath my hand.

"Not that… but that's coming. Something crazy and you're just the person I want to do it with." She didn't look scared or worried. Instead, a slow smile spread, and in that moment I knew I had her back. "You're just going to have to trust that I'll blow your mind, eh?"

"Okay, Mr. Cleary. Blow my mind."

Chapter 17

Vanessa

HAVING KYLE IN MY APARTMENT felt foreign. Mainly because men didn't hang out in my apartment. If they did, it was never during daylight hours and never in the morning. Truth be told, in spite of my complaining about him breaking the rules, I liked him there. He moved around my place comfortably, making himself at home.

In some cases, we were exactly the same, and in others we were polar opposites. For example, he easily opened up to me and shared personal information. His admissions rolled right off his tongue, yet when he prompted me to follow, the words felt like shards of glass that could cut my tongue if they were to leave my lips. Oddly enough, I was able to reveal some things I never had, and as I did, speaking them out loud didn't cut me up like I expected them to.

The girls, who I was sure were irritated with me for blowing them off, didn't even know half of what I told Kyle. Hell, Cassie was the only one who even knew about my arrangement with him. Brae and Desiree would most likely be upset with me, but technically it was their fault. If they were at breakfast the day after the Halloween party they'd be privy to this information.

I stood in my kitchen, sipping my coffee, waiting for Kyle to emerge from the bathroom. A slight squeak of the door hinge alerted me that I wasn't going to be alone for long.

"Shit," Kyle murmured. "Fucking button."

When I turned to look at the gorgeous specimen of a man, he held his right foot, which was bare and oddly sexy in his hands while hopping on his left one. I would have laughed if he didn't look so hot. His shirt was open, his pants rested low on his hips, and the way his lats flexed rendered me stupid.

Out of the blue, he asked, "When is your birthday?"

"Why?" I grabbed a cup from the cupboard. "Coffee?"

"Yes, please. Because I have a gift I want to give you." When I narrowed my eyes, he shook his head. "Mine is February twelfth."

Just like last night, he offered his info before I said mine. "You're like Honest Abe." He lowered his brows. "Lincoln?"

"I know who Abe Lincoln is. I'm still waiting for your date."

"August seventeenth."

With a few careful strides he stood in front of me, taking his cup of coffee off the counter. "Well, then I'll get it for you for Christmas." He glanced at my less than neat countertop.

"What is it that you're so eager to give me?"

He lowered the mug from his mouth, his lips twisted into a smirk. "That's a loaded question, Nessa. But what

I'm referring to is the gift of tidiness."

Just as I was about to ask him what the hell that even meant, he bent over and picked up another button off the floor and handed it to me. "Hey, this is your fault. You're the macho man who decided to destroy one of my favorite blouses."

"Am I also the one who had a granola bar yesterday?" He lifted his mug before he nodded his head toward a wrapper I had left on the counter. "And wasn't Halloween a week ago?" I placed my hands on my hips, knowing he referred to the black boots I wore that night that still sat in the corner.

"I've just been busy. Plus, it's just me here. I'm not a complete slob. I happen to know where everything is."

"Of course you do because it's all out in the open."

This subject needed to change. "Please save your money. I'll take care of it. My asshole of a boss is going away, so I can sneak out early and clean."

Kyle set his mug down with a devilish gleam in his eyes, "I know a better place you can sneak off to." He wrapped his arms around my waist and pulled me toward him.

"I think you've had enough ideas. Don't we have things to do today?"

"Yes, why don't you go get ready and then we'll go to my place so I can change before we start our day… and night."

"About that, you do realize we've been together…" I glanced at the digital time on my microwave. "Seventeen hours now."

"Time flies when you're having hot, mind-blowing sex." His eyes flickered with humor, along with his teasing words. "Fine. Point taken. I'll go to my place alone, get ready, and then I'll be back in two hours to pick you up. While I'm gone, do what you need to do, tell whoever you need to tell, we'll be gone about twelve hours."

"Are you kidnapping me? Do I need to pack a bag? Tell my friends I'm with you in case I don't return?"

"Actually, packing a bag would be a good idea. I'll leave it up to you what you tell your friends."

"I was only kidding about the kidnapping."

"I wasn't."

I came to the conclusion Kyle was a wacko. He insisted on the grocery shopping, stocking my fridge and pantry not only with basic supplies, but most of the things he liked to eat as well. I was now the proud owner of a one liter bottle of imported maple syrup. The thing was huge, and I actually had to ask if he planned on bathing with it.

Of course, a tiny fleck of awkwardness over the fact he bought shit that he planned to eat gnawed inside me. But I reminded myself it was just syrup, it wasn't like he took over a drawer or left a toothbrush at my place.

Afterward, he left me at my apartment. And even though I had enough food to now feed my entire building, he insisted on taking me out to dinner. I had two instructions—be ready at seven and wear a short skirt. He poo-pooed my gripes that it was cold out, telling me to wear a long coat.

I could only imagine what he had planned, but referring back to my belief he was a wacko excited me with all the possibilities. The man had no inhibitions whatsoever. Many times during the day, he'd reference places that would be perfect locations to engage in one sexual act or another. It was obvious he was turned on by voyeurism. Since that had always been something I wanted to try myself, I was more than willing to go along with whatever he had planned. Provided he didn't get us arrested.

He picked me up at seven on the nose and stunned me silent when I opened the door. My impromptu coma lasted no more than five seconds, but during I couldn't formulate one thought in my head other than he looked incredible.

The navy sport coat he wore over a sky blue shirt made his eyes look even bluer. Dark denim hugged every sinew of his long lean legs. And his cologne was by far the sexiest scent I'd ever smelled on a man. Woodsy, fresh, clean, all combined into one perfect aphrodisiac.

My long black coat hid my clothing from his perusal, but that didn't stop him from combing over me from head to toe and back. When he leaned in to kiss me, he pulled away and smirked. "No perfume tonight?"

"Nothing appealed to me," I admitted. It was the damn truth. Since meeting him, I'd become much more sensitive to the brands I normally favored. As he confidently stated at Jude and Brae's wedding when he guessed I had on Miss Dior and that it wasn't the right scent for me, I also now felt the same. His adorable boyish smirk when he took my hand as we headed for the stairs meant he was onto me.

We didn't say much to each other as we left my building and walked a short block to where he parked his Tesla. It wasn't an awkward silence, more so a comfortable one. During the ride, he gave me little information on where we were headed except we'd first be having dinner, and then we'd be having *fun*.

Once over the George Washington Bridge, it only

took five minutes to get to our first destination. It was an adorable small colonial house that had been converted into a romantic Italian restaurant. The candlelit tables, linen tablecloths, and mood music softly playing over the speakers made it all seem like a date.

When he took my hand, alarm bells rang reminding me of our rule regarding no lovey dovey-ness. Yet, I held my tongue, not wanting to piss him off by mentioning our "stupid rules" once again. Whenever I did, he countered with an excuse. Since we were there, and the smell inside the foyer as we waited to be seated made my stomach growl, I rolled with it.

Our coats were taken and we were led to a small round table in what would be considered the dining room of the home. There were a few others dining among us, but the tables were spread enough where it didn't feel crowded.

Kyle pulled my chair out and winked when I raised my brows. He read my mind, and clearly he didn't care. His eyes immediately zoned in on the tight knit ivory sweater I wore. I watched him rake his gaze down my body, stopping at my short flowing skirt. It barely covered past my mid-thigh when I sat, which explained why he loitered beside me a bit instead of taking his seat.

When I took the linen napkin off my plate and draped it over my thighs cutting off his peep show, he mumbled, "Cute." Moving to sit across from me, our eyes met and held. The way his pale blue eyes drilled into mine caused me to squirm in my chair. "You look amazing, Nessa. I can't wait to get to the second part of our evening."

A formally dressed waiter appearing with a bread basket stopped a response on my part. "Good evening, and welcome to La Tua Casa. My name is William, and I'll be your server."

"Hi, William," I said cheerfully. He dipped his head

and threw me a stunning smile.

A busboy dressed in the same black slacks, vest, and bow tie filled our water glasses just as handsome William handed us each a small menu.

I took in his sandy brown hair and clean shaven face as he rambled off the specials. The way he spoke directly to me before announcing he would give us a few minutes to decide was very flattering. Had it not been for Kyle sitting across from me, I probably would have flirted back. I had to hide my smile when I saw Kyle follow the man's path into another room with a scowl on his face.

"Do you know him?" I asked innocently.

"Never saw him before. He must be new." His eyes studied the menu for less than a minute before he closed it and placed it beside his plate.

"It smells incredible in here."

Kyle nodded. "I love this place. There isn't a thing I haven't tried."

"How did you find it?"

"One of my clients turned me onto it a few years ago, and I've been coming back ever since."

"It's adorable." I glanced around, taking in the quaint decor. There couldn't have been more than ten tables total in the small rooms that made up the first floor. "What's upstairs?" I asked, remembering the classic staircase that led from the foyer up to a second floor.

"An office and the bathrooms. It's not a big place. In the summer, they do have tables on the outside patio. We'll have to come back; it's cool the way they have it lit up with tiny lights in the evenings."

Come back? I could barely think of my life eight days from now, let alone eight months from now. Again, I held my tongue and smiled before taking a sip of my water. If he noticed that I avoided responding, he didn't let on. Instead, he began telling me what he planned to order for both of us.

"You're assuming I eat everything or don't have allergies?"

"Do you?"

"Yes. No."

"Then we're good." He leaned over the table a bit and lowered his voice. "I kind of assumed you did eat everything. Call it a hunch."

"You know what they say about assuming, Mr. Flirt. And for the record, I don't eat veal. Baby cows are too cute."

The waiter appeared beside us, and his grin meant he heard me. "So, no veal special then?" When his hazel eyes met mine and lingered, I no longer was positive the grin was over the fact I didn't eat veal. "What will you be having instead, Miss?" He waited with a poised pen on his pad, his gaze still steadily holding mine.

"To start," Kyle responded firmly, catching his attention. Once he had it, he leveled him with a glare before saying, "We'll each have a bowl of your minestrone soup. She'll have the linguini arrabiata, and I'll have the pollo parmesan. Also, please bring a special order of focaccia with the soup, and a bottle of your Brunello di Montalcino." Kyle held his menu up for the gentleman to take and waited for him to retreat back to the kitchen before he murmured, "Prick."

Three things occurred at that moment. First, Kyle speaking Italian—even if it was just food—was super sexy. Second, Kyle showing a jealous side was even sexier. Third, I liked points one and two far more than I should have.

Chapter 18

Kyle

"ICE SKATING?" HER EYES WERE lit with excitement as we pulled into the lot. We were in Paramus, New Jersey. The rink was in its usual crazy crowded state for adult night. Knowing what I had planned for us had me equally excited, but it wasn't my eyes that were lit up. "What is this place?"

"I found it years ago when I moved to New York City. The rinks in Manhattan are all overcrowded. I came here during off hours to get in a workout and keep my skating skills sharp." I offered her my hand and walked into the building. Bass from the loud music vibrated around us. "The second Saturday of the month there's always a theme. Based on Rick Springfield singing *Jessie's Girl*, I'm guessing it's 80s night."

"I love 80s music."

I smiled at her adorable reaction to my plan. "Then tonight's your lucky night."

It took a few minutes to pay our admission and check our coats. I led her to the skate rental, and she traded her sexy ankle boots for a pair of white blades. "You're lucky

I wore socks tonight."

"If you didn't, they sell socks here. Come." The bar set up for the twenty-one and older crowd was three deep. "Do you want a drink now or later?" I said directly into her ear, competing with Bon Jovi's rock scream.

She leaned toward me and shouted back, "Later. I'm still buzzing from the wine."

Taking her hand, I tilted my head toward the rink and she nodded. Many of the female skaters dressed for the occasion, sporting anything from Madonna inspired outfits to Joan Jett. Vanessa fit in perfectly with her tight fitted, boob enhancing, sweater and short flowy skirt. Her toned legs looked amazing, and the skates on her feet were their own turn-on.

Surprisingly, she had great balance and admitted to having had skated a time or two in her high school days. Hand in hand, we took a few laps with the other adults looking to capture their youth.

We weren't necessarily there for that reason. What I hoped to capture tonight was a side of Vanessa that could lead to so many possibilities. The rink was oblong in shape. The entrance on one end was flanked with skate rental and refreshments in each corner. Restrooms and a lounge area were found in the far right corner. The far left corner was just that, a corner. A railing surrounded the rink, and a narrow walkway allowed you to exit any of four locations.

The strobe lights slowed, darkening the rink. Tiny circles of light danced on the ice as the music changed to *Crazy For You* by Madonna. Single skaters exited the ice, but the couples continued to hold hands. Not wanting to be the same as the others, and maybe to show off my skills, I pivoted my body until I skated backward. Vanessa smiled, which I was sure was because of my suave move.

With her hands on my shoulders, and mine on her waist, we glided around the ice as if we were on a ballroom floor.

At one point in the song, Vanessa closed her eyes allowing me to take control. That alone assured me this was the best idea I could have had for our night out— and we weren't even at the best part yet.

When the song ended, it morphed into *Push-It* by Salt-n-Pepa. The ice once again filled with skaters, but this song encompassed what I wanted to do.

Vanessa threw her hands in the air, "I love this song!"

Shit.

I spun back around, taking her hand with me and started around the rink until we made it to the small break in the railing. With a tilt of my head and a small tug, she knew I wanted off the ice.

Rubber mats greeted the blades of our skates. As if we were marching rather than walking, we carefully made our way to the dimly lit corner of the rink. The small corner was the perfect place for what I had planned.

"What are we doing back here? I could go for that drink now." She started toward the opposite end where the bar was located.

"Stay." Her eyes glanced up at me. I lowered my mouth to her ear. "Turn and face the rink." Vanessa's brows furrowed, but she did as I asked. "Put your hands on the railing, and don't move until I tell you to."

Her head craned back. "Okay, but why?"

The strobe lights were back in full force. I pressed my body against her back and kissed the curve of her neck. "I'm going to fuck you." Even in the dimly lit rink, I could see her white-knuckled grip on the railing. "Do you remember when Jude and Brae almost walked in on us fucking in the barn? Do you remember what you said?"

"Something about getting caught was hot?"

"Yes. You said the thought of getting caught in public was a complete turn-on. When you said that, the thought of fucking you in public made my dick stone hard. I know I'm turned on right now... are you, Nessa?"

"Very."

"Good. Ready?" A short quick nod and her ass shifting backward into my crotch could be compared to the effects of a green flag for a Formula One race car.

I lowered my zipper and pulled out my rock-hard cock. Careful to keep my hand shielded, I skimmed my fingers from her knee beneath the back of her skirt to her pussy. Vanessa's body shifted, but rather than block my movements, she spread her feet apart.

"Good girl."

I hooked my finger in the now damp tiny scrap of material between her legs and tugged it to the side. With the same finger, I made sure she was ready for me. Based on the change in her breathing, the dampness of her thong, and the way she continued to push her ass back, I was sure she was, but selfishly I needed to touch her.

Wet heat coated my middle finger. "You're nice and wet for me. Are you turned on, Nessa?" I whispered in her ear right before I slid the same finger against the tight pucker between her ass cheeks.

She silently nodded. I took my cock in my hand and eased into her pussy one slow inch at a time. Once my dick was fully seated in her, I braced my hands next to hers on the railing.

"Kyle," she said, tilting her face toward mine. I kissed her as if we were the only people there. In my mind, we were. Even with over a hundred people skating around the rink, she was my sole focus.

I moved my left arm to circle around her waist, holding her in place as my hips moved back and forth. Fuck, she felt good. I both needed to be quick and wanted it to last all night.

Her one hand continued to clutch the railing, and her left moved to my forearm and squeezed. With each thrust, her fingertips dug deeper into my flesh.

The loud pumping music continued, melding into the next song without pause. Screams erupted when a song I never heard in my life started playing. Everyone in the rink began singing along, screaming the lyrics and circling the ice in tune to the beat.

"Are you close?" I said into her ear. There was no need to whisper or to worry about my voice carrying.

"Yes. Don't stop, Kyle."

"No worries, baby." From the unsuspecting eye, it looked like we were dancing in place along with the other nutjobs losing their shit over the music playing. While still holding her, I tucked my right hand beneath her skirt from behind and skimmed her goose pebbled flesh toward her clit. By just applying pressure with the pad of my middle finger, as I drove into her, caused her to come around my cock moments later.

Once she relaxed, I moved my hand away to squeeze the base of my dick. That was all it took for me to release inside her with a guttural groan directly into her ear. "Fuck, Nessa. Don't move," I ordered, forcing her to swallow every tremor that occurred as my orgasm went on.

No one had a clue what just happened in our dirty little corner. Not one of those speeding by us had any suspicion that I just had one of the hottest sexual encounters of my life. This woman was my match in so many ways, the reality of how compatible we were practically knocked me on my ass.

A few long moments passed before either of us moved. I slowly pulled out and tucked myself back into my boxers while still wet from our fuck.

"Stay still." Again she followed my orders, turning her head to look into my eyes. In the way her brows lifted, I knew she had no idea why I asked her to stay still. With my gaze pinned to hers, I removed a handkerchief from my pocket, and from behind I wiped her pussy clean before moving her underwear back into place.

She turned in my arm just as I folded the cloth in half and shoved it into my pocket. "That was unreal, Kyle. It was so erotic with you in me while strangers passed us by over and over."

"I know, baby, and I can't wait to do it again."

A slow smile spread over her gorgeous lips. "Me, too."

Perfection.

The woman was absolutely perfect. Spurred by what, I had no idea, I held her face and kissed her long and hard. She opened for my tongue, and in comparison to what we just did, our passionate kiss seemed too sweet of a way to end our raw and primal act. Yet, it continued… and the longer it went on the more I knew I wanted it to.

Vanessa

AFTER OUR ADVENTURE, WE WENT back to his apartment. I was so relaxed, so wrapped around this man in every way. What we did tonight made me crave so much more. I reasoned it was the thrill, the sex, the excitement I craved... not more than that.

When I looked at him lying next to me, I couldn't help but smile. "What's that look for? Or do I need to ask?"

I rolled to my side to face him, resting my head on my bent arm. "I'm just surprisingly happy."

His brows lowered. "Surprisingly? Wow, you're such a sweet talker."

I swatted his bare chest with my hand. "You're such an ass. What I meant was, tonight was more fun than I thought it would be."

"Thank you... I think?"

"No, you don't understand." I strummed my fingertips up and down his abs as if they were a guitar. "My week was horrible—as usual." He nodded because he knew all of this. "Then we went to your lab and I had a great time. And then tonight, was just... wow." I wanted to say so much more, but refrained from doing so.

Kyle smiled wide as he propped his head on his hand, mirroring my position on the bed. "There's something I want to talk to you about." He tucked my hair behind my ear, sending a shiver to run through my body. My heart halted, and he picked up on the shift in my expression. "What?"

"It sounds serious." I held my breath waiting for him to continue. If he went down the, *I have feelings for you,* road, there would be no way I could handle that. We were having such a great time together, and opening that door would ruin everything.

"Well, it is, sort of. But it's also your fault based on what you said in the lab yesterday. So technically you shouldn't deny my next request."

Relieved it wasn't what I suspected, I let out a laugh. "This should be good. Okay, what did I say?"

"Remember Lenni?" I rolled my eyes. "Great, you do. Well, I fired her."

In an instant, my curiosity piqued. "Why? She's been trending on social media because of her upcoming movie. That could do wonders for your business."

"Or just the opposite could happen, and she could harm my business. When you were at my lab, you told me she wasn't the right person for the job. The more I thought about it, the more I knew you were right."

"I was?" Holy shit. He fired one of Hollywood's most popular people because of me? "What are you going to do now?"

"Well, that's where you come in."

"Oh, no. Nuh uh. I'm not a spokesperson. No one even knows me. Oh my God, Kyle."

His eyes went wide then he grinned. "Actually, I hadn't thought about using you for my spokesperson, but now that you mention it..."

"Then what are you talking about?"

"Well, if you shut-up for a second, I'll tell you." My lips twisted into a snarl, but I kept them sealed. "Come to California with me to help find a replacement. Your insight means a lot to me. I need to interview candidates when I'm there. I leave on Monday."

"As in tomorrow Monday?" At first thought, I wanted to go to my place and pack my bags, but then there was the reality that I just couldn't up and go away. But, California. I'd always wanted to go there. I didn't even care which part. Just to see the west coast was a dream of mine. "That sounds wonderful, but I have a job."

Saying those words made my stomach roll. Going

with Kyle would be so much better than enduring the bullshit at work. Then I remembered my boss was away. A little voice inside my head told me to go. I waited for the other voice—you know my common sense good conscience voice to say the opposite, but it didn't. "How long are you going for?"

"If you come, then for the week. We can see the sights. If not, I'll be back Wednesday."

Fuck, a week? I'd have to lie, fake a deathbed illness. The thought of being stuck at that hell all week, knowing Kyle was having fun in California would be torture.

"What are you thinking?" Kyle cupped my cheek with his hand. Then he placed his thumb on my temple, running it in small circles. "I can see your wheels spinning again."

"I'm thinking, yes. I'd love to go with you." This was a huge risk on my part. Mr. Boyd didn't need to know I was gone. No one in the office would know anything other than I wasn't there. I'd continue to check my phone for emails and lie my ass off.

"Really? That's fantastic." He pulled me in for a chaste kiss. "We'll be in Los Angeles, but if there's someplace you'd like to see then we can work it into our schedule."

Everything. That's what I wanted to see. "I'll leave that up to you."

He arched a brow. "Challenge accepted. I'll have to find a place in L.A. that beats ice skating."

Kyle

THE AWE WRITTEN ALL OVER her face was truly a thing of beauty. The one thing Vanessa wasn't—giddy. But from the moment her fine ass sat in her plush first class seat, I witnessed a side of her that I'd never seen before.

We departed from JFK on time. Between the conversations we had, being served our gourmet lunch, and watching the inflight movie, time went by fairly quickly. For the last fifteen minutes, Vanessa's nose had been plastered to the small oval window as the landscape beneath us got closer and closer during our descent into LAX.

Her big green eyes cut to mine when I chuckled because of her enthusiasm. Turning back to watch our landing, she pouted, "Stop making fun of my first time on an airplane. You're ruining it."

"I wouldn't dream of it." I leaned closer to share her view and placed my lips on her ear. "Next flight you need to wear a skirt. Those jeans aren't ideal for fooling around on a plane. It wasn't easy finger-fucking you underneath that blanket."

My request caused the fire in her green eyes to ignite. She glanced over her shoulder, meeting my own heated gaze. "You managed to navigate that obstacle nicely, Mr. Flirt. But no worries, on our way back to New York, I'll be sure to wear a skirt."

"Good girl." The captain requested all flight attendants take their seats in preparation of landing. I glanced around first class, debating if I had time to repeat what I'd done to her at thirty-thousand feet.

She immediately read my mind, kiboshing my plan. "No. I want to watch our landing," she scolded with a rigid finger in my face.

"Fine. I'll have to wait until the limo ride." With her face pointed toward the window, she reached behind her and caressed my cock over my jeans. He'd been at half-mast most of the flight but with that one simple touch, she was about to raise him the rest of the way.

"Not now, Nessa." I gripped her wrist and moved it away. "The last thing I want is to navigate the throngs of people in the airport while sporting a hard-on." The older gentleman sitting behind us cleared his throat.

"Fine. I'll have to wait until the limo ride," she said, repeating my words back to me. Undeterred with our eavesdropper, she then added, "I never gave a man a blow job in a limo. Another first, Mr. Cleary."

"Fuck." She giggled at my response. The man behind us mumbled something, and I turned in time to see through the crack in between our leather seats, him adjusting himself with a scowl.

Again, Vanessa seemed unfazed. She pointed out the window to the Pacific Ocean in the horizon. "Look, Kyle. The water is so blue."

Yeah, as blue as my balls.

Chapter 19

Vanessa

WHAT A DIFFERENCE IT WAS waking up in Los Angeles in November compared to New York. I fell in love with California immediately. Even our hotel room boasted west coast beauty. I had so many things I wanted to do once our plane's wheels hit the tarmac. But not once had he warned me how exhausting traveling was.

Although we arrived at the hotel at five p.m. Pacific time, my body's east coast clock betrayed me. Combined with the adrenaline of flying, the extra-curricular activity in first class at his hand, and not having a good night's sleep because I was so excited all caused my energy to crash. Barely making it through dinner, courtesy of room service, he tucked me in with a chuckle and a chaste kiss on the forehead.

The upside, I woke refreshed, ready, and anxious to conquer California. After consuming the breakfast Kyle had delivered to our suite, we worked off the calories in that great big California King.

While Kyle showered, I admired the scenic pictures

on the wall of our bedroom. The Hollywood sign, Rodeo Drive, the Santa Monica Pier, and the Walk of Fame, were all places I wanted to visit. Maybe not all on this trip, but one day.

I smelled him before I felt him. Kyle wrapped his arms around my waist, resting his chin on my shoulder. "Do you see something you like?" His warm breath caressed my ear, eliciting goose bumps to form all over my skin.

When I spun in his arms to face him, our eyes locked. "Yes, as a matter of fact I do."

A genuine smile spread across his face. "I'm glad to hear it, but I meant the pictures. How about after our meetings we start checking off a few of these sights you're dying to see?"

I clapped like a child and beamed. "Oh, yes, please! Can we also do Mann's Chinese Theater? And Jimmy Kimmel's show is up the street. Wouldn't it be great if we got tickets?" I dragged in a breath and remembered something else. "Wait, Madam Tussaud's, we have to do that. And we absolutely must find Marilyn Monroe's star on the Walk of Fame, but I'll have to lay on her name because… well, how often does one get to see their last name on a star?"

"Are you done?" His eyes crinkled in the corners, the mirth on his face obvious. My head bobbing caused him to laugh before kissing my lips. "We will see everything and more. The limo is at our disposal for our entire stay."

At the mention of the limo, all I could think of was that poor limo driver having to endure our antics from LAX to the hotel yesterday. Regardless that the privacy glass was up, I was sure he felt the rocking of the car. What started out as a blow job ended with me riding Kyle like a world-class jockey ready to win the blue ribbon.

Once we were both dressed and presentable, I grabbed my bag and dragged him by the hand out of our suite. "Let's go, Mr. Flirt. We have things to see."

When we walked out of the hotel, I popped on my sunglasses. The same limo driver greeted us with a smirk... *yeah, he knew we defiled the back seat of his car yesterday.*

I gave him a quick wave before sliding into the car. Kyle told him where we were headed before he settled on the seat next to me. This car could seat eight, yet we treated it as if it was a small coupe.

"Who are we meeting with first?" This process excited me, but I couldn't help but feel pressured. Kyle was so sure I had instincts when it came to selecting the right person for the job, it started to make me nervous.

He opened the calendar app on his phone. "We're meeting with Roxanne DuMont at ten and then Bailey Hughes at eleven." He tucked the phone back into his pocket. "After that, we'll grab a bite to eat and hit everything on your list."

"Did you say Roxanne DuMont? As in *the* Roxanne DuMont, one of the highest paid swimsuit models? Wasn't she also in the latest centerfold where she had nothing on but her smile?"

Kyle chuckled. "Yes, the swimsuit model. I have no idea about the other magazine you're referring to."

"Liar."

He held up three fingers. "Scout's honor."

"Were you a scout?"

"No."

We both laughed at his nonsensical comment. "Well, she's stunning. Let's hope her skin has a good chemical makeup."

He smiled brightly. "Listen to you and your scientific lingo." Kyle pulled my hand to his lips to kiss the back of it. "Thank you for coming with me." Again our eyes locked, and the static between us replicated a bug zapper taking victim after victim. If we had been in a romance novel, the moment would have been perfect for a long meaningful kiss. Those so-called moments had been happening more frequently. Somewhere between the Atlantic and the Pacific, along with the carnal hunger to want to devour each other, there was this new spark I couldn't understand.

The car came to a stop in front of an office building, giving me the opportunity to douse the flame. "Where are we?"

Kyle dipped his head to look out the window beside me. "Soren's office. He keeps a small team in L.A. to cater to his west coast clients. When I told him I planned to come out here, he arranged for me to use a conference room."

"That was nice of him." The driver opened my door, and when we got out I realized Kyle didn't have any samples with him. "Did you forget the fragrance samples in the hotel?"

He shut the door and took my hand. "I had them shipped here. Bringing liquids on a plane is a pain in my ass."

Once inside, I pulled out of his grasp. "What?"

"I work for you for the next few hours. It's unprofessional." On the ding of the elevator, I walked past him with a smirk.

No sooner had the doors closed when he pushed me up against the back wall. "No one in here to witness my unprofessionalism, Miss Monroe." For the duration it took to climb the eleven floors, Kyle's mouth was fused to mine. On the twelfth floor, he pulled away. "You may want to fix your lips, Miss Monroe." He swiped his thumb across his lips and presented it to me as evidence.

"Sexual harassment on the first day," I quipped. Gazing at my reflection in the closed elevator doors, I quickly repaired the damage he did to my lipstick while he chuckled beside me.

Jude's staff was all very welcoming as they gave a quick tour of the fourteenth floor that housed Soren Enterprises. A few minutes later, we settled into the conference room waiting for Roxanne to arrive. I must have organized the small bottles on the rectangular table a dozen times.

"Nessa, relax."

"Okay." I sat in the chair next to Kyle, who was at the head of the table, and calmly folded my hands on the legal pad I brought with me.

A slight knock on the door frame caught both of our attention, and we both stood. Pictures of this woman were nothing like the real thing. Photoshop was not needed when it came to Roxanne DuMont. Her platinum blonde hair cascaded over her bare shoulders and down to her size D breasts. There was no doubt in my mind she could be the next Baywatch babe.

The corners of her naturally plump lips curled up when she saw Kyle. I, on the other hand, had become a ghost. That was until Kyle asked, "Would you like something to drink?"

"Can your secretary grab me a green tea?" Roxanne then brought her attention to me. "Thanks, love."

What the fuck did she just call me?

When I didn't budge, Kyle picked up the phone and

asked the receptionist if she could please bring in some beverages... including the prima donna's tea.

Once again right off the bat, I didn't like one of Kyle's selections. A pang of worry hit me square in the chest. What if I didn't like anyone? This would be so much easier if it was for a man's cologne and a lot more fun.

Kyle stood next to me. "Roxanne, I'd like to introduce you to Vanessa, my vice president in charge of special projects."

Rather than appear shocked at the title he gave me, I stretched my arm across the table to shake her hand. "It's nice to meet you." *There, that was nice.*

Her long boney fingers wrapped limply around my hand, and a fake smile made me wonder if maybe I was wrong and her lips were filled with Botox.

"Let's all have a seat." Kyle pulled out my chair and while he did the same for Roxanne, I scribbled a note down on my pad.

He took his seat beside me, his eyes cut to the message, and he turned to Roxanne. "Thank you for coming in today. As you know the reason you're here is to determine if you're a good match for a new fragrance I created, *Risqué*."

Her voice came out like a porn star's. "I love that name."

Of course she does.

"*Risqué* is part of our Destination line. Each fragrance is intended to transport the wearer to a romantic location." Kyle spritzed the inside of her wrist. When she rubbed it together with her other one, he cringed. I wasn't sure why her action ignited such a response from him. Roxanne brought one of her wrists to her nose and inhaled. "It's okay. But don't worry, I'm a good actress, too. People will think that I love it."

"Picking the right perfume is a personal thing." He took my hand in his, flipped it over, and sprayed a touch of *Risqué* on my wrist. I brought my nose closer to my arm and inhaled. This woman was clueless. This scent had me instantly sitting on an island sipping a piña colada.

Kyle gave my hand a squeeze, looked at Roxanne, and said, "Thank you for coming in today. We will let your agent know our decision."

At first she looked stunned until she realized he dismissed her. Then she wordlessly stalked out of the room, and when the door closed behind her tight ass, I let out a breath. Kyle called reception and cancelled her tea.

"For what it's worth, I do love *Risqué*. For me, I imagined sitting in the sand staring at turquoise blue water."

He smiled, lifted my hand to his nose, and inhaled. "It smells so much better on you. I knew there was a reason I wanted you here—you're a natural. A beach is exactly where you should have pictured yourself."

Pride caused genuine happiness which was obvious by the look on my face. No one had ever paid me such a warm compliment. "Thank you. I do have a question, though. Why did you make that face when she rubbed her wrists together?"

"Because when someone rubs their wrists together immediately after the fragrance is applied, it inhibits the release of the top note. Imagine sex without foreplay." His voice deepened. "You won't get the entire experience."

Staring into his gorgeous eyes, and hearing his explanation, made me want to prove his theory right there on the conference room table. And since he dismissed Roxanne, we had the time. Kyle was super sexy on a normal day, but dammit, scientist Kyle did me in.

When he said, "Bailey is the opposite of Roxanne," I was reminded why we were there.

Once again that damn pang hit me. "Kyle, what if I don't like Bailey? Then what? Do we need to start all over again?"

"No. If Bailey doesn't work out, I'm adding spokesmodel to your title."

Kyle

OVERALL, OUR TRIP TO L.A. was a complete success. Bailey turned out to be a perfect spokesmodel for *Risqué*. As quickly as our interview with Roxanne had gone, the one with Bailey went on for hours. The girls immediately hit it off, and I witnessed a side of Vanessa I'd never seen before. She was just as much of a perfectionist as I was. No detail was too small to overlook.

After we left Jude's office, we grabbed a quick bite, and hit as many landmarks as we could. That started a trend for the entire week. Each night while in bed, I promised her the next day would be even better. My promise to top the skating rink experience was fulfilled on Wednesday night when I took her to Griffith Park. It wasn't easy by any means, and our hearts pounded from fear more than passion. But while staring at the Hollywood sign, as she announced her orgasm, made it all worth it.

Another G-rated highlight was Disneyland. Before my

very eyes she morphed into a little girl thrilled with everything her gorgeous green eyes witnessed. Today was our last day, and we spent it in Santa Monica enjoying the beach, the pier, and each other.

I wanted to bring in room service again and spend our last night naked in our suite, but there was one more thing I wanted to show her. Fortunately, it would make a perfect backdrop to things I planned on saying.

The tiny inn I found was a forty minute drive from L.A. Known for their ambiance, as well as their locally grown organic menu, I thought it'd make a nice way to end our perfect week. It took a bit of begging on my part to even get us in on such a short notice, but never underestimate a man with a plan… if we ever got there.

"Nessa, we need to go," I called through the closed bathroom door.

"Coming."

I sauntered over to the mirror and adjusted my tie. Through the reflection, the door behind me opened just as she hesitantly stepped through it. In a knee-jerk reaction, I spun to be sure my eyes weren't deceiving me. There she stood in a fitted, strapless black dress that hugged every curve she had from her breasts to her knees.

"Too much?" The uncertainty in her voice surprised me. How could she even doubt what she chose to wear was anything less than perfection?

Only when she began fiddling with the hem had I realized I hadn't moved or spoken. In three short strides, I came toe to toe, gripped her face, and crushed my lips against hers. She stumbled a bit, holding my wrists to steady herself. When I pulled away to allow her to breathe, her eyes remained closed for a moment before sliding open to stare into mine.

"I take it you like it?"

"So much so, I regret making this reservation." I couldn't help but give her another hard long kiss. "Vanessa, you are breathtaking."

"Uh oh. You called me Vanessa." She smiled demurely. "You only do that when you're serious."

"I'm dead serious." I stepped back, taking her hand in mine and spreading her arms wide so I could get a close-up look at her. "You're perfection."

"Thank you." Her eyes raked over my black suit as she flexed her fingers. I released her hands and watched as she straightened my tie before smoothing it down under her palm. "You don't look too bad yourself. This tie does wonders for your eyes."

The feel of her hands on me, even with my shirt and tie as a barrier, caused my skin to sizzle with need. "We better go... now. Or we'll never get out of here."

Romance oozed from every corner of the inn. On purpose, tables were small and intimate, accommodating two diners. Vanessa scanned our surroundings with a small smile, but otherwise said nothing.

In fact, since arriving she became very quiet. I attributed it to sadness over our time in California coming to an end. After we ordered our entrees, I asked, "Are you okay?"

She looked up and smiled. "I am. Thank you for an amazing week, Kyle. You cannot begin to understand how much this means to me. Showing me all that you did, making each and every day more fun and more exciting than the one before. I don't deserve all this attention."

"What a silly thing to say, of course you do." I took her hand in between both of mine. "Nessa, you're very special to me. Before you came along, the only way I knew how to connect with a woman was through my master flirting skills. In these weeks we've been together, I learned two things."

Her eyes widened as she waited for me to continue. I stared down at her hand in mine, tracing a pattern over the top of hers. The first thing was easy to admit as I said, "I almost feel like you tamed the flirt in me. But oddly enough, it seems like he needed to be tamed by someone like you. When I'm around you, I'm different."

"Different how?"

That was a loaded question. Different in the way I couldn't imagine my life without her in it, but admitting that much to her now would no doubt send her running in fear. If there was one thing I learned about her, it was baby steps were required to get her to accept the changes between us. For instance, her ridiculous rule stating no sleepovers was now long forgotten. No romance was another thing I broke her of.

"Different in how I see women now," I finally admitted.

She laughed and shook her head. "I'm afraid to ask how you see them."

"Not at all." The smile fell off her face. I lifted her hand and placed a kiss on the inside of her palm. "The thing is… now… I only see you."

Chapter 20

Kyle

IMAGINE IF I HAD ADMITTED what I really wanted to?

Imagine if I came right out and said I was falling for her?

Because, by just saying that she was the only woman I saw, based on her expression, you would've thought that I admitted to fucking every female in Los Angeles.

She sat across from me shaking her head in denial. "What, Nessa?"

"Kyle. Let's not ruin our time."

I released her hand and replaced it with my wine, drinking half it of it in one large gulp. Before I could even formulate any response other than, "are you fucking kidding me right now, Nessa?"—our meals appeared. That ended the conversation, that ended my confession of sorts, that ended anything to do with feelings.

The rest of our dinner went by benignly, filled with idle chitchat of the things we saw during our stay and nothing else. She even stayed away from the topic of all the amazing sex we had. Like somehow it meant more than just sex, which of course to me it did.

Clearly, I was way off the mark.

It wasn't until we were back in our suite and getting undressed when she said, "I'm sorry."

Stopping on the fourth button of my shirt, I stared at her before asking, "For?" I knew damn well what she was sorry for, but the prick in me needed to hear her say it.

"You paid me an amazing compliment, Kyle. I'm sorry I freaked out over it." In spite of her words, she still had the same bewildered look on her face as she had earlier.

Unable to speak, I walked around the bed to where she stood and pulled her into my arms. This complicated woman was out of her element. Baby steps, I reminded myself. It had to have taken a lot for her to even offer an apology. If small doses were the way to turn her around, then my scientific background prepared me to have the patience I needed.

"Forgive me?" she asked, her face resting against my partially opened shirt.

I pulled away with a devious smile. "Well, you'll have to make it up to me somehow. I'm not that easy of a pushover."

"I beg to differ, but okay. If payment of some form is required, then I'm game." Her fingers resumed unbuttoning my shirt where I had left off. "Of course, you owe me an apology as well."

"Is that so?" I reached behind her and found the zipper of her dress. Her fingers paused at my waistband when I slowly slid it down its entire length. "What do I need to be sorry about?" I continued, just as I pushed her dress down her body to allow it to pool at her feet. Offering her my hand, I took one pace backward. She placed her hand in mine, moving toward me after she stepped out of the dress.

"The romantic dinner." A perfectly sculpted brow lifted in challenge. "Did you think I didn't realize you chose the most romantic restaurant in Los Angeles tonight?"

"Was it?" My hands roamed over her smooth skin, and I followed with my lips. Starting at the silky spot under her ear, I sucked and nipped before adding, "I really didn't notice. The food was good though." I paused long enough to place a few more kisses on her. "Not as delicious as you are. On that note…" I lifted and placed her in the center of the bed. In just her black strapless bra and panties, my cock struggled against the fabric that confined him. Our eyes locked while I removed my shirt and remained that way when I unbuttoned and unzipped my pants.

She sat up and reached behind her back. "No," I said with a firm shake of my head. "Don't move." On my command, she reclined back, leaning on her elbows, and remained perfectly still.

Gorgeous green eyes remained focused on me as I removed my pants and then each sock. Like a lion with his prey, she licked her lips when I lost my boxers. The way she looked at my naked body propelled my excitement within seconds. I hadn't even touched her yet, or she me, yet I was hard as stone because of the look in her eyes. I could see right through to her soul. And whether she'd admit it or not, based on that look, I knew she felt the same.

At that moment, I needed her more than I ever had. Maybe to negate her behavior at dinner, or maybe validation of how great we were together was what I was searching for. In either case, the desperation to feel every inch of her surrounding me became more important than my next breath.

I climbed on the bed beside her. I couldn't stand waiting any longer. Digging one hand into her hair and sliding the other between her panties and her ass, I pulled her body over mine. In slow motion, I initiated a kiss like no other we shared.

Kissing really wasn't our thing. We did it often, but never for a purpose. With this kiss it was important that she felt her universe shift ever so slightly. This kiss needed to become a force in its own right, and not just foreplay.

The warm skin of her belly pressed up against my abs. Our legs entwined, our hands didn't know where to touch first. Yet throughout, as our bodies tried to fuse, the kiss never faltered... until I pulled away.

Her eyes were wild for more. And I would resume soon. After I got her naked. My hands smoothly released the back clasp of her bra. I pulled the fabric around to her front and dropped it to cup a breast in each hand. Goose bumps riddled her flesh when I sucked on her neck while rubbing her nipples with the palms of my hands.

For the first time since being with Vanessa, I wouldn't rely on anything other than our connection to blow her mind.

I rolled us into the missionary position, and the next to go were her panties. As I dragged them over the curve of her ass and down her magnificent legs, I followed their path with my mouth. She lay before me naked in every sense of the word. There wasn't dirty talk, suggestive innuendos, or even promises of things to come.

Reversing back up her body, once face to face I

resumed our kiss. With our lips communicating in a profound way, I slid into her and stilled. She held my head firmly as we devoured each other's mouths. I felt her inner thighs gripping my hips, her heels pressing into my ass. She even went as far as whimpering to get me to move faster.

I pulled away far enough to stare into her eyes, and with our gazes tethered, I made love to Vanessa. For a few moments, I felt her responding in the way I needed her to. Long minutes passed, the magnetic energy between us doubled in intensity. Until she broke the connection.

Looking over my shoulder, she drifted off, suddenly feeling a million miles away. I needed her to come back to our moment. With my hand, I gently held her cheek waiting for her eyes to meet mine. But when they did, the look we shared just minutes ago was different.

Words I needed to say lodged in my throat, and I found it almost impossible to breathe. No words were spoken. Instead, in the silence so much had been said. Combined with the glistening in her beautiful eyes, it felt like a good-bye.

The day felt a lifetime long. By the time we dragged ourselves into her apartment, the seed of tension that sprouted the night before had become a dense forest.

Every, *are you okay* was met with, I'm fine.

Every, *what's wrong* was met with, *nothing.*

I couldn't compete with whatever consumed her, especially if she wasn't going to open up and tell me what it was. Nor could I force her to do so. I could, however, do my part to help her understand where I was coming from. And maybe, it would be enough to break down the wall she carefully built around her heart.

My eyes tracked her moving around her place busying herself with nonsense. It wasn't ten minutes before I finally cracked. "Can we talk?"

She looked up from the pile of mail she had been flipping through. "Sure."

Stepping to where she stood, I removed an envelope from her hands. "Nessa, the time we spent together in California was the best time I've ever had in my life. Going in, we had clear expectations on what we wanted this arrangement to be. But somewhere along the line, and I can't even say it was in California, things changed for me. There were moments here and there that made me want more of them. There were times when apart that made me want you by my side. So many times I'd laugh over something and make a mental note to tell you about it. And when I would, you'd find it just as funny as I did. All those tiny flecks of feelings somehow converged and overruled my original motives for wanting to be with you." I took her face in my hands, the words I'd been dying to say for days now no longer clogged in my throat. "Vanessa Monroe, I think I'm falling in love with you."

"No." She shook her head vehemently, breaking away from my hold. "You can't be falling for me, Kyle. That's not what I agreed to."

"You can't tell me how to feel, Vanessa." Her eyes widened, watered, and then narrowed. "You need to let this happen." My heart felt as though it was ready to burst through my ribcage.

She stepped away, turning her back to me. "You need to go."

Vanessa

"**N**ESSA." WHEN I DIDN'T TURN around, he forced me to. "Why are you fighting this?" His crystal blue eyes scanned my face, waiting for me to answer.

What did he expect me to say? Why? Because this wasn't part of the agreement. Since day one I'd been the gatekeeper to this unorthodox arrangement we had between us. And there was a reason for it. What he was forcing me to feel, to admit, to accept was *the reason* I fought it.

Every single thing I tried to avoid came to fruition. This person I sort of morphed into since meeting Kyle was not the happy-go-lucky Vanessa I worked so hard perfecting for years. Normally nothing fazed me, nothing ruffled my feathers.

And then *he* came along.

Kyle made me feel things I had no business feeling, and I couldn't allow that.

He was fucking with my mind. I shouldn't have him and only him on my mind. The last time that happened, my world imploded around me. I absolutely couldn't handle that kind of heartbreak again.

"Jesus, Nessa. What the hell?" My silence caused him to lose his patience with me. "I can't keep up with your moods." He advanced, forcing me to step back until my lower back hit the countertop behind me. With his face an inch from mine, he trapped me between his arms as he gripped the edge of the Formica.

"Let me ask you a question." I needed to drive this conversation to prove my ambivalence. "Do you believe in soul mates?"

"I didn't, until now." Through his gorgeous blue eyes, I could see the honesty behind his statement.

"Giving your entire heart to one person is a huge risk." And one I didn't want to ever take again. His eyes remained pinned to mine, forcing me to add, "What if we all get just one chance at it, and for whatever reason it doesn't work out?"

He rubbed his jaw with his hand. "One chance at finding your soul mate?"

"Yeah, just one," I said, sounding desperate. "Once you find the right formula, the one that works better than all others you've tried, and you wake up one day and it's gone, then what?"

"You try again." His head tilted a bit to the side. "You mean to tell me you wouldn't? So, if I created a perfume that I thought was perfect, I shouldn't try again because I thought I had it right the first time?" I offered a shrug. "That's ridiculous, Nessa. On the flip side, if you don't find perfection the first time, you keep trying. You can't give up because it didn't work out the way you wanted it to. Hell, if I did that I wouldn't even have a business."

His words hit me with a dull ache in my heart. There wouldn't be a next time for me. No one could or would convince me otherwise. Insisting to get my point across, I shook my head in disagreement. "What I'm saying is, once you find the right formula that you think is best, that should be it."

"You're wrong. Life is about chances and in order to live it, you need to learn to take them. Did you find the perfect formula for yourself, Nessa? Is this…" He gestured between us with a long pause. "This works for you?" Kyle's eyes penetrated mine as if they were searching for a clue or a hint of what I felt. "Please communicate." When I didn't offer any guidance, he tucked his hands in the pockets of his pants and sighed. "What is it that you want, Vanessa?" Again he waited patiently for me to continue.

"Space," I blurted out. I finally found the nerve to say what I wanted to. In a much softer tone, I did even more damage by adding, "You're suffocating me. I need space, Kyle."

"Suffocating?" All emotion drained from his face. Instantly, I regretted my choice of words. It wasn't him who was suffocating me, more so the emotions he forced me to feel. But the words were out there, and I couldn't take them back. Based on the tension in his jaw, the damage was done. He stood glaring, not making it easy on me. "I'm suffocating you?"

"Yes."

We once again locked gazes in a battle of wills. He blinked his eyes, nodded his head once, and turned to leave. Every fiber of my being wanted to grab his arm and explain more, but I had nothing left. As it was, I felt like open book. Instead, I watched him walk away. He draped his jacket over his arm and grabbed the handle of his suitcase with his free hand. Right before he pulled my door open he turned to look at me. "If space is what you want, it's yours. I'll see you around."

The gentle click of my door sounded like a loud slam. I wanted him to go… no, I needed him to go. Yet, it felt as though he took a piece of my heart with him when he left.

For the longest time, I just stood staring at that door. I was the one responsible for the change in atmosphere. Drama wasn't my thing, ever. Yet, I couldn't help but feel I overreacted whenever he crossed that invisible line I drew in the sand.

Chapter 21

Vanessa

AFTER A SLEEPLESS NIGHT, I spent most of my day cleaning my apartment. The entire time I thought of him. Hours later, I flopped down on my couch and took in my handiwork.

My place hadn't looked this neat and tidy in ages. It even smelled better. Involuntarily, I tilted my head back and took in a generous whiff. The can said it was lemon scented, but I smelled something else. With my eyes closed, I concentrated on what that might be.

Channeling Kyle's lab, I gave myself a moment and declared it was lemon with a hint of orange. In order to prove myself right or wrong, I grabbed the polish off the table and read the ingredients on the back of the can. Some of them I couldn't pronounce, but what I did see were the two ingredients I had guessed. Maybe Kyle was right and I did know a thing or two about fragrances.

I hadn't heard from him. So many times I picked up my phone to be sure it hadn't died, or I hadn't missed a call or text. No such luck.

At that moment my phone pinged with a text

message, causing my heart rate to spike… until I saw Cassie's name on the screen.

> **Cassie:** Welcome back! Don't forget Dispatch at 8. You better be there! By the way, this morning's yogi was a hot dude… in spandex.

She made sure I got her point with the eggplant emoji that she attached.

> **Me:** That figures. Okay, I'll see you tonight.

Dispatch was hopping. Couples and singles alike lined the bar and filled the tables. Dressed in a pair of dark skinny jeans, a red V-neck top, matching stilettos, and my favorite cropped leather jacket, I caught the attention of some male customers. Weaving my way through, I received a few winks and heard a couple of, "Hey babes," until I found Cassie and Desiree sitting at a table toward the back of the bar.

"Hi." I sat next to Cassie and across from Des. Instantly, they bombarded me with their *welcome backs,* and *we need all the details* flying from their lips. "Soon. I need a drink first. What's everyone having?" I asked as we all sat back down.

Des raised her glass. "Pomegranate Martinis, and they are fantastic. They're also on special tonight."

"Sounds good to me." I raised my hand in the air catching the attention of a passing waiter, pointed to Desiree's glass, and with a nod he headed toward the bar. "So, what's new?"

Cassie started detailing the yoga instructor. "You should have seen him, V. Honestly, I have no idea how he did the tree pose with the package he sported. A few of the women in the class nearly fell over. Including this one." She tipped her glass toward Des before laughing.

Des's mouth dropped open. "Don't go acting like Miss Innocent. I wasn't the one who asked for his teaching schedule." She batted her eyes and doing her best Cassie impersonation said, "Excuse me." Des flipped her hair over her shoulder causing both of us to laugh. "This class was the best I've been to. When will you be teaching again?" Des batted her lashes in an over-exaggerated manner.

I turned my head toward Cassie who just shrugged. "So, sue me. He was sexy as fuck. Even Mrs. Sun-sets-and-rises-on-Jude-Soren thought so."

"This is true," Des confirmed with a firm nod. "Okay, tell us. How was Cali?"

The waiter was back with my cocktail. "Good."

Des's eyes narrowed at my one word response. "Just good? Nope, not buying it. One minute you are both friends who had sex in a barn, the next you're traveling with him? Spill."

I looked at Cassie, who read my mind. "I didn't tell her."

My time was up on my secret affair. Once the counselor suspected something, she wouldn't stop until we fessed up. With a resigned sigh, I said, "Fine. But, you need to promise me on Cassie's life that you won't tell a soul."

"Hey! Why my life?"

I flapped my hand back and forth at her. "Kyle and I have an arrangement of sorts."

"What kind of arrangement?"

"A sex buddies arrangement," Cassie blurted out before draining her glass.

"So much for keeping it to yourself, Cass." Unfazed, she shrugged.

Des looked between the two of us. "Wait, you mean to tell me that you have been sleeping with Kyle for weeks, and I'm just hearing about this now? Who else knows besides this one?" She pointed to Cassie. "Does Brae?"

"No! And please don't tell her. She's in love-land right now and will want the same for me and Kyle, and we don't want that." *I don't want that.* He broke the rules.

Des innocently asked, "What do you want?"

"I don't know. I thought I did, but now I don't. We sort of had a disagreement yesterday."

"A disagreement? About what? Positions?" Cassie let out another giggle. *How many drinks has she had?* My eyes cut to Desiree's, and that "attorney" expression she mastered had her lips pursed and her brows drawn inward.

Just as I was about to tell her to spit it out, a deep baritone voice rang out. "Ciao, bella donna!" When we looked confused he clarified, "Hello, beautiful ladies!"

Luca gave us all a kiss on the cheek before sitting next to Des and setting his beer down in front of him. I guess he was joining us.

"I'm so glad you came!" Cassie leaned over and whispered, "I invited him. I hope you don't mind."

As nonchalantly as I could, I glanced around looking for his sidekick, but Kyle was nowhere in sight. A pang of disappointment hit me.

Des asked what I wondered. "Is Kyle here, too?"

"No, he isn't. I called him, but he said the trip was exhausting and was staying in tonight. Which, if I know my friend, is code for he's fucking someone." He looked at me and shrugged. "To be honest, I figured he was with you, but I guess not."

What was I supposed to say to that? *Yeah, well it's me he should be fucking.* When I looked at Des, her jaw was slack and sympathy was etched in her eyes. Of course Luca was oblivious as to why we all remained silent.

Suddenly, the air felt stifling around me. Heat rose up my neck. My head began to spin, and I wasn't sure if it was the alcohol or jealousy that consumed me. Before I could think it through, I blurted out, "I think I'm going to head home." The two sets of eyes that belonged to my best friends focused on my face. And the way they stared, you'd think I sprung antlers from my forehead. "What?"

"It's like nine." Again, Des sported her interrogation face.

"I know. I'm beat and this drink went right to my head. Maybe I'm still jet-lagged." Fine, I just blatantly lied to my friends, but if I sat there any longer I was sure to have a panic attack.

Luca had no idea of the conversation that occurred between the three of us without words. Through Desiree's all-knowing look, and Cassie's pitiful one, I knew come tomorrow I'd get a lecture.

As if reading my mind, Des said, "I'll call you in the morning." It wasn't a question or a request.

"Yes, Mom."

Quick good-byes led to me rushing out of Dispatch while digging in my bag for my cell. And as I walked away punching out a text, between the table and the front door aliens descended and abducted the body of Vanessa Monroe.

Kyle

AFTER A SLEEPLESS NIGHT, I showered, changed, and hopped in my Tesla hoping that a long drive would clear my mind. But, it did just the opposite. Every time I drove past someone with long dark hair, I thought of her. Then I'd start to wonder what she was doing.

Did she regret her words?

Did she enjoy her space today?

Did she want more?

Vanessa didn't need to be sitting in the passenger seat beside me, because she was there in every other way.

I added a few hundred miles to my odometer and felt no better when I finally dragged my ass home. It didn't help that as soon as I walked in the door, Luca called to invite me to join him and the girls at Dispatch. When I declined, he asked me a plethora of questions as to why I wouldn't go.

My curiosity piqued, and I wanted to go to see how she'd react to me being there. But, I tamped that down not wanting to see other men hit on her… thus, I declined the invite. Maybe I was wrong and no one flirted with her or bought her drinks. No, that was a lame thought. The woman was drop-dead gorgeous. Everywhere we went while on our trip, male eyes followed her. Men would have to be blind, dead, or gay not to hit on her. That was how it all started with us. I saw her, I flirted, she flirted back, and I was fucked—literally.

"Just come out for one drink. Then you can take your lame ass home."

"Sorry, man. Maybe next week."

"You're starting to sound like Jude. Don't force me to find another wingman, Cleary. You know I'll do it."

I let out a chuckle. "You know that no one would ever be able to take my place in that category."

"Yeah, whatever. It's fine. Stay home. More women for me." I heard the sound of a horn. "I need to go, my car is here."

Since Jude met Brae, Luca and I had been left to ourselves on the weekends. And now since the wedding, Vanessa and I had been spending significant time together, and Luca had been on his own. The man wasn't dumb; he knew my time had been occupied with a woman or women. What he didn't know was that it wasn't women, plural. It was just one woman—Vanessa. He should have guessed as much. Nessa and I didn't exactly hide our shenanigans at the wedding, but Luca wasn't the type to pry. Unless I came right out and said I was fucking Vanessa, it was conveniently ignored that I could possibly be fucking Vanessa. Admitting so didn't feel right. It might have had to do with our arrangement; in any case, I kept it all to myself. He didn't even know she was with me in California. And now, I wish I had told him everything so he could talk some sense into my dumb ass.

Between jet lag, lack of sleep, and the crap mottling my thoughts, I should have been exhausted. Sleep was the last thing on my mind. Last night while lying in bed, I desperately wanted her beside me. And it had little to do with sex. We spent several overnights together, and it was enough to cause an addiction. Like a drug, after only a few hits I was now hooked on Vanessa Monroe.

I sat on my couch, beer in hand and flicked through the channels trying to find something to watch. Maybe mindless television would do the trick. I chuckled when I came across some bizarre love connection type show remembering how Jude and Brae got together. But after about ten minutes it reminded me of Vanessa, and I continued to surf the channels.

It was official, every part of today sucked.

My day had been utter shit. To think just yesterday I woke up beside her, taking her one last time before our flight, and continuing the pattern in first class. Like a fool, I assumed our trip was a pivotal moment in our relationship. Like a fucking moron, I finally spoke my mind and said things I'd never said to a woman before. I stupidly had expectations of what our relationship would be like once we got back to New York.

What an idiot I was.

I clicked the off button on the remote and tossed it to the side. My mind kept replaying Vanessa's words over and over again. Well, two specifically—space and suffocating. And after an entire day of obsessing over our conversation, the last thing I wanted, or wanted to give her, was space. The more I thought about it, the angrier I got.

Fuck.

My phone vibrated next to me. I was surprised to see Vanessa's name on a text message, yet seeing it further annoyed me. It was a Saturday night, I was home brooding, and texting games was not something I was in the mood for. Regardless, with a slide to the right, I opened it.

> **Vanessa:** I saw Luca tonight. He said you were home because you had an exhausting trip. I hope I wasn't the cause of it.
>
> **Me:** Nope.

Vanessa: Okay, I'm glad to hear that. What are you doing?

Me: Just hanging out at home.

Vanessa: Why didn't you come out tonight?

Me: Giving you space, just like you asked.

Vanessa: When I said that, I didn't mean for you not to go out with your friend.

What the hell was I supposed to say to that? I started to text back, to tell her I was in no mood to socialize, but stopped. Then I thought I'd tell her it was because of her, but deleted that text as soon as I typed it.

Maybe I should've admitted that all I had been doing since I left her place was think of her. Or ask if she'd been thinking of the multiple times we had sex in L.A. like I was? Or come right out and ask her if our last night in L.A., I hadn't imagined her pulling away and saying good-bye?

Instead, I changed the subject and typed a reply.

Me: Luca told me he and Cassie had been talking.

Vanessa: Does Luca know we've been hanging out?

What the fuck did that matter? Again, I began typing furiously, only to backspace over the incriminating evidence that I was fucking pissed at her. Rather than send another stupid text, I pushed the little phone icon so I could talk to her like an adult.

"Hi, Kyle."

"Hi. Just so we're clear, I didn't tell Luca anything. He doesn't even know you were with me this week. Was I supposed to? Are we telling people about this fucked up arrangement we have going?"

"This fucked up arrangement, as you called it, was your idea. Tell me this, Kyle, is the arrangement part still intact?" Her sharp tone was full of annoyance, and her question confused me.

"What does that mean? Still intact?" What the fuck? This morning she wanted space and now had the nerve to ask if the arrangement was still on?

"Did you break another rule tonight?"

I dropped my feet from the coffee table in front of me, pushed myself off my sofa, and began to pace the length of my living room. "Which rule are you referring to now? According to you, I've been breaking them left and right."

"Your pal seemed to think you were fucking someone else tonight."

"And you believed him?"

"I don't know, that's why I'm asking. If we're going to continue this, we're supposed to let each other know if we're fucking or want to fuck someone else."

"Wow. I know the rules, how could I not? You bring them up every chance you get. And let's be honest here, is that the type of guy you think I am?" The more I thought about this conversation the more annoyed I became. "One minute you're kicking me out of your place and the next you're wondering if I'm breaking rules and fucking someone else tonight? I get it, you don't want me for anything other than to get you off—you made that perfectly clear."

Silence. She didn't even have the decency to admit I was right. "For the record, *Nessa*, no. I didn't fuck someone else. But when I do, I'll be sure you're the first to know."

"Thanks. I appreciate that," she said tightly.

"No problem. Was that it?" I didn't let her answer because I didn't want to know. "Have a good night, Vanessa." I ended the call, turned my phone off, and went to bed.

Fuck this entire day.

Chapter 22

Vanessa

HAVE A GOOD NIGHT, VANESSA.

Not Nessa… *Vanessa*.

He rarely used my full name, so it wasn't an accident he did so now.

My first reaction was anger. He was the one changing what we agreed on. I knew after that first suggestion of a sleepover it was only a matter of time before he'd screw around with the rest of our terms. But as the night went on, with every turn in my empty bed, anger turned to something else… regret.

I started to feel bad for giving him a hard time and thinking the worst… or that I wasn't capable of moving past all my issues when it came to relationships. It was just the way I was wired, and maybe agreeing to this with Kyle was stupid on my part. Going in I knew one of us would get hurt. Call me selfish, but I wouldn't survive it if the "one of us" turned out to be me. And based on the way I couldn't stop thinking about him, he had the power to destroy me if things progressed between us.

Yet, I felt like crap, seeing his handsome face every

time my eyes slid shut and remembering every moment we had spent together thus far. So, who was I really hurting?

The scent of his cologne still lingered in my apartment, and on my sheets from the night before we left for L.A. Even after cleaning, I could still catch a faint smell of him in my space.

I was a weekend sleeper, meaning if I didn't have to be somewhere I could stay in bed until early afternoon without issue. That should have been the case today. Besides being tired from traveling, the thought of having to go back to work the next day would have guaranteed I slept in. But there I was up and bored by seven a.m.

I should have paid attention to the yoga moves Brae shoved down our throats. It seemed like the perfect time to know how to center myself and meditate. I knew I wanted to keep my thing with Kyle from her, but she would know what to do. And if not, she had a knack for putting things into perspective. That was what I needed, someone able to think clearly for me. Because my vagina controlled my body, but my heart had no idea how to control my mind. I couldn't fault it. The thing had one experience in my lifetime, and it barely survived. So, how could I expect it to know what to do now?

I waited for a respectable hour, which was torture, and reluctantly dialed her cell. "Hey, V. What's wrong, why are you up so early?"

"Nothing's wrong. I ended up in bed fairly early last night. Flying is exhausting."

"Yeah, about that. I loved finding out via a text from you that you were in California with Kyle to help him find a spokesmodel. Is there something going on between you guys that you aren't telling me? Are you two seeing each other?"

"It's not like that, Brae. We've had sex a few times, but that's it," I lied and hated that I did. "California was impulsive and dumb. I helped him at work, and he seems to think I have an intuition for his business. Stupid if you ask me, but at least I got to see parts of California."

She must have detected a hidden tone in my few words when she changed the subject. "How are you? I miss you." My friend, always so cheerful now that she found love. A teeny, tiny part of me was jealous. "You sound stressed, and you need to destress. Yoga would do wonders for that, V. You should have been there yesterday. It was probably the best class we ever took."

"Yes, I heard. Did it have anything to do with the fact that the yogi was well hung?"

"No comment." She lowered her voice and added, "That's our secret or the next yoga class we get kicked out of is at Jude's hand and not yours. Got it?"

"Holy hell. So, it's true, my love-sick friend was ogling the yogi. Shit, I regret skipping it."

"V. He's hot! Plus, I'm married, not dead." Brae's giggle started to make me feel better. "Um... so, yeah, Cass stumbled all over herself. It was adorable to watch. Hold on, V." I wondered why she spoke in code until I realized she put her hand over the microphone on her cell. Although their voices were muffled, I could still hear her husband making suggestive comments mixed with the unmistakable sound of kissing. "Sorry. Jude is heading out to meet the guys at the gym." After a short pause, she then said, "That was close. I had no idea he was behind me. So, what are you up to today?"

At the mention of the guys, I desperately wanted to blurt out everything that went on with Kyle. Instead, I said, "Not much."

"Seriously, are you okay, V? I'm worried about you."

Now is your chance. Just ask her already, spit it out, and get her opinion!

But again, instead of opening up I clammed up and said, "I'm okay. Being in California reminded me how much I hate my job, that's all. I just called to say hello. Love you, Brae. Say hi to Mr. Right." I hung up before my friend could force me to open up... which was the point of my phone call before I chickened out.

I hugged my knees, occupying a single couch cushion, as I stared blankly at the television. Three consecutive knocks on my door brought me out of my haze.

"Coming." Truth be told, my heart rate increased thinking maybe it was Kyle. But when I pulled the door open, my three best friends stood in front of me with big smiles, coffees, and a bag.

"Hi, I hope we're not intruding." Brae kissed me on the cheek as she walked into my living room.

Des and Cassie followed and before I knew it, my small table was covered in bagels and spreads, plus of course, fresh fruit courtesy of Brae.

"What's all this?" Cass and I sat on my couch while Brae and Des each sat in a chair at the opposite ends.

Cassie handed me a cup of coffee and glanced at my two other friends who were waiting for someone to say something.

Brae's eyes darted between the three of us. "Fine, I'll say it. It's an intervention." Her eyes cut to me. "You're in a funk. We're here to help. First thing is getting you a new job." She pulled her iPad out of her bag and fired up a career site. "We'll plug in your qualifications and apply for some jobs. Before you know it, you'll be out from under your asshole boss."

"Can we not do this? I'd rather work for a dickhead I know than take a chance on someone worse. Who knows what I could get myself into."

"Maybe you should tell her it's not your job... this time," Des quipped.

Brae stopped punching at the screen on her lap. "Then I'm confused. When you called me this morning it sounded as though you had something to tell me. I assumed it was your typical *Sunday-bad-mood* because you need to go to work the next day. But, if it isn't work then what is it? Did something happen in California? Did Kyle hurt you? Oh my God, I'll kill him."

Great. How did I admit that he did hurt me, but not in the traditional way they would assume. More in the way he was so wonderful he broke all my rules.

Cassie and Des shared an all-knowing look while Brae's eyes darted between the three of us. "Okay, someone care to tell me what the hell is going on? And don't tell me nothing, because I know something is up." With an intake of air, her hand went to her chest. "You're not sick are you?"

"No, of course not!"

She let out a tense breath. "Thank God. Then what is it?"

Doing my best to avoid the interrogational stares my other two friends shot my way, I angled my body toward Brae's. "First, promise me you won't get mad at any of us."

Her eyebrows furrowed. "Why would I get mad?"

Rather than think too long, I blurted it out. "Truth is, I've been sleeping with Kyle. It wasn't just a few times.

Actually, we're in an arrangement of sorts." When Brae just stared at me, I continued. "After the wedding, we kind of agreed we're good at having sex and wanted to keep doing so. For lack of a better term, we're fuck buddies and have been since Halloween. Cass was the only one who knew because she was the only one who made it to brunch the next morning. If you both were there, I would have told you as well."

"Wait," she raised her hand, "do you mean to say, you have been sleeping together since my wedding? That wasn't a one-time roll in the hay, pun intended?" When I shook my head, she added the question I didn't want to deal with. "Do you have feelings for him?"

I sipped my coffee, refusing to answer her questions.

Brae leaned closer to put her hand on mine. "I'll take that as a yes?"

"No, you can't take it as anything. It's not like that between us."

All the while, Cassie sat back sipping her coffee and eating a bagel to avoid ratting me out.

"Then you need to explain this to me. I understand what fuck buddies are so please spare me those details. But, does this mean you two are exclusive?"

"It means we have rules and he keeps breaking them… and it's messing with my head."

"What rules?" Brae looked at the attorney in the room for clarification.

"Hey, don't look at me. I don't know any more than you do," Des sounded off.

I drank more of my coffee, giving myself a moment as the hot liquid caffeine slid down my throat. "It doesn't matter anyway because I think we're done."

"He didn't!" Cassie snipped. "Was Luca right?"

"Wait, Luca knows?" Brae continued to try and put the pieces together.

I shook my head. "No, no one but Cassie knew." After I explained to Brae what happened between me and Kyle in L.A. and after, in addition to what Luca said last night about Kyle fucking someone else, our rules, and last night's phone call, she just shook her head. "What? Why the head shaking?"

"First, I can't believe the two of you went this route. Jude and I knew this was inevitable. Then at the wedding, well, we all know what transpired in my family's barn." I blushed at the memory. That was a great night. "Second, I've gotten to know Kyle since I've been with Jude and he's a really great guy, V. Yes, he can be a clown, but he's genuine. It didn't matter that they constantly tried to one-up each other's pranks, those guys would do anything for one another. They're like us—but with dicks." Brae smiled and winked at me. "So, if you think that he might be someone special, then you should trust in that."

My hand went up, palm facing outward. "Whoa... hold on. I never said he was someone special. I said we were having sex and had a disagreement."

"Really?" Brae tilted her head. "Then why were you upset when you thought he was with someone else?"

"Because..." Damn, her. She raised a perfectly sculpted brow and waited. "Stop looking at me like that. As I said, we had an arrangement. If either of us wanted to have sex with someone else, we needed to say so—no hard feelings. Kyle has been breaking rules since we started and now it's beginning to feel less like an arrangement and more like a relationship."

"And that's a problem, why?" Brae's expression softened to match her voice. "If something wonderful develops out of this fucked up arrangement, why would that be so bad?"

"Because, true love only comes around once." The words tumbled out of me without warning. They all looked at me as if I had three heads. "I had my chance," I whispered. I needed to get it out once and for all. I needed to put on my big girl panties and brace myself for the pain that came when I went down this road. I dragged in a deep breath and released it through pursed lips. "His name was Robert, we fell in love, and someone else stole him from me."

The girls were stunned silent. This was the first time I ever mentioned him to anyone since he died nine years ago.

Desiree asked, "You mean to tell me because this guy cheated you're giving up on love?"

I slowly shook my head as the tears welled. My chest constricted, the memory of the day he was killed slamming into my heart. Years of suppressed agony came to the surface, and the pain I felt back then returned full force.

"He didn't cheat," I croaked out. "Robert was a wonderful guy, my prince. We met our freshman year in college. It didn't take long to know we were soul mates." I smiled at the memory through my tears. "He told me the day we met that we were going to be married one day. Of course, I laughed at him but somehow deep down I knew he was right. We spent every free moment with each other. We even scheduled our classes to make sure we could see one another as much as possible."

My voice hitched through a sob. "Then my world fell apart. It was right before final exams sophomore year. We were supposed to meet in the library, but he never showed. When I went to his dorm, police officers were there, and I knew." The ache in my chest intensified.

"One of Robert's roommates looked at me with red-rimmed eyes and gave me the news that Robert was killed in a car accident. Someone ran a red light and hit the driver's side of Robert's car. According to the police report, he died on impact."

Tears were now freely flowing down all of our faces. "When I went to the funeral, I never thought it could get worse until I saw his poor mother. She fell to her knees in front of his casket and wailed. I'd never experienced such raw pain in my entire life. Until I woke up the next morning and realized it wasn't a nightmare but reality.

"Each day that I walked around campus I would look for him, refusing to believe that he was gone. From then on, so was my heart. That's why I can't have feelings for someone. I'll never survive that type of agony again."

The four of us sat in silence for several minutes. My friends cried for me, and I cried for Robert and what could have been.

"So, now you know why. I'm not the commitment-phobe I had you all believe, and it's not that I want to be alone... but all I can offer and accept are casual relationships. What I had going with Kyle was perfect until he started plaguing my thoughts when we weren't together. And then we had such a great time in California, until he tried to force me to feel our connection, by saying things he shouldn't have."

"Does he love you?" Cassie, our hopeless romantic, asked.

"It doesn't matter. No one knows better than I do that you can lose everything at a drop of a dime. All the dreams I shared with Robert, the places we wanted to travel to, marriage, kids, vanished the day he died. And I can't even get my life together to do all those things to honor our plans. I'm stuck in every way a person can be."

Brae came over and sat on my other side. "V, maybe Kyle is meant to be the one to finally push you along. Don't you think Robert would want this for you?"

I couldn't speak as I continued to cry. Brae's arms came around me, and before I knew it Cassie and Des were doing the same. Our group hug was filled with tears that substituted so many of my unspoken words.

Chapter 23

Kyle

WHEN LUCA CALLED AND SAID to meet him and Jude at the gym, I jumped at the opportunity for a distraction. It'd been a while since the three of us hung out. Funny thing with guys, it didn't matter how long since we saw each other, we always fell right back in sync.

After almost an hour, the ball-busting between Jude and Luca, the sound of cast iron hitting against the weight stack on various machines, and the burning in my muscles did nothing to clear my head. Normally, going to the gym would settle my mind. But today with each rep, I'd see Vanessa's face and hear that damn word, "space."

All night long I thought about our phone call. I knew women were confusing creatures, but Vanessa took the cake in that department. How everything got so fucked up in a short amount of time was beyond me. The woman I met several months ago wasn't the same woman who I spoke to last night.

It was all so messed up and most definitely validated the argument that love truly did suck.

Jude and I switched places, putting me behind the weight bench to spot him. The man was the happiest he'd ever been, and I was jealous. He and Brae made it look so damn easy. I knew it wasn't, especially when they had just met. Jude admitted Brae could barely stand being in the same room with him, never mind sharing the same bed when they were forced to live as a couple. That thought gave me hope Vanessa and I were ahead of the game—A, we weren't forced to be together, and B, we couldn't keep our hands off each other. That had to mean something, right?

The positive vanished once I remembered being accused of suffocating her, and all my hope flew out the window with it.

Then there was my friend, Luca, who I was equally jealous of. He seemed perfectly content with his life, lifting his free weights without a care in the world. No woman to drive him nuts, like my woman. Pfft, my woman. *What the fuck?*

I knew enough about the opposite sex to know her behavior wasn't normal. The irony that she needed *space* was most definitely something I could relate to. I'd been there.

"So, the little woman let you out today?" Luca said with a smirk. "Where's your leash, Soren, in your locker?"

"Fuck you, asshole." Luca let out a grunt-filled laugh as Jude nodded with a shit-eating grin on his face. "You're just jealous of my life."

"You're onto me, Soren." The look of complete sincerity on Luca's face lasted about three seconds before he cracked up.

"Fuck you," Jude repeated. After a few more sets, with the bar still lying across his chest, he announced, "Okay,

I'm done."

"Done? It's been barely an hour. When was the last time you worked out?"

While lying on his back, Jude twisted his head to look at Luca. "With my wife this morning. And I'd still be *working out* with her, and not you two idiots, if she didn't have to run to Vanessa's for some kind of pow-wow."

No doubt discussing me.

"Not true. I asked you here before Brae and the girls decided to go to Vanessa's."

Jude sat up after I helped him set the bar back on the rack. "How the fuck do you know that?"

"Cassie told me." Luca shrugged and continued his reps.

"Cassie? Are you and Cass…"

"No!" Luca immediately ended Jude's sentence. "We're friends. She's cool and easy to talk to. We talk about you guys all the time, especially Cleary."

I barely listened when they both focused on me. "No snide comment? Are you okay, man?"

"Yeah, why?"

"You're not your sarcastic self."

"I just have a lot on my mind."

"Was California not what you hoped it'd be?" Jude stared me down while wiping his neck with a hand towel. "Did my office staff accommodate you to your liking?"

"Yeah, they were great. I hired Bailey, so success all around." Part of me was just about to blurt out every other damn detail of my trip. Instead, I paused, debating if I should go down that road. Then I considered what he had going with Brae, and that pang of envy again hit me square in the chest.

In spite of Jude's manwhore history, he had to be doing something right. In fact, if someone like him could go from zero to sixty in the relationship department, maybe he could share the knowledge? So—I went for it. "Can I ask you a question?"

"Depends on the question," Jude said with a shrug. "I don't kiss and tell." When I sat on an adjacent bench with a heavy sigh, he frowned. "Jesus. Again, no comeback?"

Luca froze mid-lift, picking up on Jude's vibe. "What's wrong, Cleary? Did you knock someone up?"

"No, I didn't *knock someone up*." Although the thought did opposite what it should have. I turned my attention back to Jude. "With Brae, did you just... know?"

"Know? What, that I couldn't live without her?"

"Yeah."

"Fuck, no. She hated me, and because of it I enjoyed busting her chops. Our relationship was a slow build." He looked at me like I had three heads. "Wait, why?"

"This is gonna be good." Luca dropped his weights into their holders, and then sat on the floor between us. The ass looked like all he needed was popcorn for this drama.

"Okay, there's something I haven't told you guys. Vanessa and I have been..."

"Fucking," they both blurted out at the same time.

"Tell us something we don't know," Jude added. "You must think we're idiots."

"We're not just fucking, not anymore at least. She was with me in California. We had a great time until the last day. Once we got home we fought."

Luca raised a finger and announced, "Ah. That explains your mood on Saturday night, and hers. What did you fight about?"

"Um… we kind of started this whole thing as nothing more than just fuck buddies. But I…" The words stuck in my throat like a glob of peanut butter. Fuck, why was this so hard? Maybe because by saying it out loud it made it more real, more official. I didn't care what these clowns thought of me. But admitting it to them, and then having to admit that we were already through before we started, wasn't appealing.

"Dude, you look like you're about to be sick." My eyes cut to Luca's again. "Spit it out."

"I think I fell in love with her." Instantly, their eyes widened at my admission.

"Fuck. Seriously? Does she know?" Luca couldn't hide the shock in his voice.

"She does now." Two guys came by yapping about the ass on some woman using the elliptical. Once they were out of earshot, I continued. "She didn't take it so well." At their confused expressions, I added, "She wants space. Do I give it to her? If I cared, which I do, shouldn't I walk away? I just want her to be happy. I'd like it to be with me, but if not, then so be it."

Truth was, my heart wasn't on board with the second part of my statement. That's how I knew this wasn't just lust, sex, or a passionate affair. My heart never piped in its opinion before now, and it was hard to tell it to shut up.

When I glanced at Luca, it was obvious he was clearly out of his element. "Don't look at me." He raised a palm and motioned to Jude. "He's the one that found love."

"It's not like panhandling for gold, Benedetto." Jude sighed impatiently. If I didn't feel like shit, I'd laugh over the fact that suddenly the man, who wanted nothing to do with finding love, was now the guru among us regarding soul mates. "There's no warning. And once it hits you, there's no turning back. If you think you've fallen, you already have. Love is black and white, you are or you're not. I learned that the hard way. And if you believe you *have* fallen for her, then dude, you fight for her. It's as simple as that."

"It really isn't as simple as that. The woman is anti-relationships. I have no idea why, and when we started this fucked up arrangement I was no different. Who had time for that? As it turns out, I was right. I haven't been able to think of a damn thing other than her since getting home."

"Been there," Jude again offered his two cents. "Regardless, if she is someone you can't imagine living without, you chase her—end of story."

Being out of the lab for a week meant my Monday was crazy busy. Now that we hired Bailey, we fired on all cylinders to get paperwork signed, photoshoots rescheduled, Paris plans confirmed, and lawyers brought up to speed.

It wasn't until two p.m. when I had five minutes to breathe. I walked into my office to shove a sandwich down my throat, and without warning I pictured Vanessa spread across my desk. Surprisingly, I hadn't thought about her all day, but now that I had there was no turning the visuals off. One by one they popped into my head— how I took her in the barn, my office, on her bed, at the ice skating rink, and even in California—over and over I remembered every damn time we were together and ached for her.

After working out with the guys the day before, I

spent a good part of my evening trying to analyze why she had such a hold on me. Sure, she was gorgeous... so what? I had plenty of beautiful women before her. Her personality was definitely part of the attraction, but there was something else that pulled me in. It felt like I had a fishhook firmly stuck in my chest and she controlled the reel.

I hadn't spoken to her since Saturday, not that I expected to. Today would be her first day in the office after being off last week, and if I remembered correctly her boss was back tomorrow.

Arguing I wanted to be sure she was okay, I picked up my cell and held it in my hand. I meant it when I admitted to Jude I just wanted her to be happy, and if that meant respecting her wishes then that's what I'd have to do. On that same note, I knew how miserable she was at work. I had the ability to change that.

Having her working for me could be, by far, the stupidest thing I'd ever do. Every day, being near her, while not being with her, was asking for a fuck-ton of trouble. Before I could change my mind, I opened my contacts and tapped her name. Apparently, I was a glutton for punishment.

She picked up on the third ring. "Hi," she said hesitantly.

"Hi. How's your day?"

"Awful."

"I figured as much. The asshole comes back tomorrow?"

"Yeah. I feel sick." In those few words I could hear her anguish. "It was so nice having him gone, and being out of here last week is just making me feel worse." She only allowed a moment to pass before she quickly added,

"That came out wrong. I meant, it was such a great trip, it's hard to be back to reality."

"I know what you meant." It was time for me to pause, but mine was a hell of a lot longer than hers. "Um… listen. My offer to come work for me still stands, Nessa. I wanted to let you know that. Being that we're no longer… well, the conflict of interest is gone. If you didn't feel comfortable reporting to me, you can work for Frederick. He's been bothering me for an apprentice for months now to lessen his workload. The position would be a great way for you to get your footing." The silence over the phone was so deafening, I pulled it away to be sure the call hadn't failed. "You still there?" I asked, even knowing she was.

"Yes. Kyle, that's an amazing offer. And a few months ago I would have jumped on it, but now I think it would be too weird. I know I'll regret that decision someday."

"Just take time to think about it. You may change your mind." When she didn't respond, I prompted, "Okay?"

"Okay." The ringing of a phone caused her to say, "Sorry. I have to go. Take care."

"Yeah, you, too."

A solid knock on the glass door of my office caught my attention. Frederick stood holding a box full of samples. "Sorry to interrupt your lunch, but you're needed on five."

"I'll be right there." I balled up the wax paper containing three quarters of my sandwich and dumped it into the trash. Snatching my phone, I halted from shoving it into my pocket and instead punched out a quick text.

Me: Please think about it.

No reply came, but I really didn't expect one either.

Chapter 24

Vanessa

I SHOULDN'T HAVE BEEN SURPRISED that the last few days had been pure hell. Whenever my asshole boss came back from a trip, he was the devil incarnate. Add to the mix the fact I lied about having the flu last week while in California, and his behavior made Lucifer seem like a saint.

For a good part of his first morning back, he berated me on all the things he expected done that weren't. In my defense, even if I hadn't gone to California, there would be no way I could have made a dent in his to-do list.

The part that had surprised me these past few days was my constant state of depression. It lingered after I left the office, and through the night, until I started the pattern all over again the next day. A few months ago, as miserable as I'd been at work, I could always count on leaving it all in the office the minute I walked out. Sure, I'd joke, bitch, and moan to my friends over and over how much I hated my job. But being out with them was an instant elixir for my ire. Even if I just hung out in my apartment, no matter what I did after work it never failed to lighten my mood.

My methods were no longer working. I suspected it had to do with a sexy Canadian.

The girls were sure to check in on me frequently. By Wednesday, it became obvious they must have concocted some sort of schedule. The morning call came from Brae as she made her way to work. Cassie always checked in during her recess period. And Des had the honors in the evening as she finally dragged her ass home from work.

I really couldn't blame them for their concern, having dropped such an emotional bomb on them as I had. Although I appreciated their support, the whole thing exhausted me. My mind wouldn't shut down between all the memories with Robert fighting for space with the ones I had shared with Kyle. Remembering how we started the weekend of Brae and Jude's wedding brought a smile to my face. The ache of wanting to go back to that time, when it had been so easy and carefree between us, overrode the joy.

Every night I stayed up later than I should have. In my subconscious, I stretched out the inevitable. Going to bed to do it all over again the next day forced a dread to consume me.

Normally, on a Wednesday night, I'd be celebrating Hump Day at happy hour. Comically, while in my pajamas at seven p.m., I settled in to begin watching a *Friends* marathon that would go on for hours, and during which I couldn't promise I'd remember what episodes aired.

When my cell rang, I was so engrossed in my own thoughts, I startled from the sound. "Hey, Brae. What's up? It's not your scheduled time to check in on the wacko once known as Vanessa Monroe. Des's obligatory call is due next."

A short pause led to a giggle. "Okay, so you're on to us. We're just worried about you, V."

"I know. I'm teasing, and I love that you guys worry about me. I'm fine, though. Really. I'll find another job soon." Even as I said the words, I knew, and I knew she knew, my mood wasn't all about my job.

"You're lying," she responded predictably. "Really nothing has changed at work. Let's not kid ourselves, V. It's okay to admit you miss him. What's not okay is sitting at home day after day denying that you do. You haven't been out all week."

"Neither have you," I interrupted.

"My reasons are way different than yours." This was true. Her hot Swede liked her home as much as she'd allow. The fact that Brae actually obeyed meant she was equally addicted to Jude as he was to her. "So, here's the deal. Friday night, Jude is getting the boot. It's time for one of our all-night-girls-only-get-togethers. The works."

"We haven't had one of those since..." I actually couldn't remember the last time the four of us pulled a Sex and the City kind of night.

"Exactly. You can't remember either," she quipped. "Even Des couldn't remember when we last had one, and the woman's memory is like an elephant's. I know it's all my fault, but that changes Friday. Be here at seven."

I thought of Jude's place and the luxury. That alone made me eager to accept. None of our apartments came close to what he had going on in his high-rise haven. A visual of me in his Jacuzzi sealed the deal.

"I'll be there. Just one condition, there will be no discussing my pathetic life."

"We can't promise that. It *is* the reason we need this."
I was about to argue when she said, "How's this? We
have one hour to say what we want to say, and then no
more mentioning your job, or Kyle, or anything that
involves the two. Deal?"

"One hour? I can handle that. Deal."

I'd only been there a few times, yet the doorman at
Jude's place no longer stopped me. Kyle wasn't the only
one to corner the flirting market. I gave a half-hearted
wave and headed for the elevators. Preparing for my cell
to ring any minute asking where the hell I was, I rapidly
pushed the floor indicator circle a few times as if that
would shave twenty minutes off my arrival time.

The minute Jude answered the door with his
trademark smirk, I knew something was up. *Girls' night,
my ass.* There was no doubt they were staging another
intervention.

"What the hell are you doing here?" I asked, my tone
much harsher than was necessary.

"I live here." He quirked a brow and winked. "Come
on in. She's been pacing."

"When I get through with her, she'll be running."

"Over my dead body. Leave my wife alone," he said,
moving aside to allow me access.

Ignoring him, I yelled, "Brae!" I barged into the living
room like a bat out of hell.

Brae was nowhere in sight, but Kyle looked like he
was expecting me. Our eyes connected, and I had to
force my legs to lock otherwise I would have run to him
like the woman in the condom commercials on T.V.

"Oh, hey, V." Before I even had my coat off, Brae

appeared and handed me a glass of white wine with a grin on her face. "You're late," she had the nerve to add.

"Seriously? What the hell, Brae? You lied."

"A lie to help a friend is forgiven."

"Says who?"

"Me… and Des and Cass. We're all in agreement." She waggled a finger between me and Kyle. "You two need to talk, and there was no other way to get you to."

Jude appeared with her coat and bag. After he helped her into it, she leaned up and kissed his mouth. "Thanks, baby." The intimacy between them made me want to spit nails for so many reasons.

Still holding my wine, I fisted my hip. "Where do you think you're going?"

"To go grab dinner," she said as if it were obvious. "Your dinner is on the kitchen island, so help yourselves. Have fun, kids."

The lovebirds walked out of their own apartment, and all I could do was stand there and gawk. Something between fury and disbelief caused the fist on my hip to clench. As if having a mind of its own, my other hand lifted to my mouth, enabling it to take a large gulp of the wine.

"Don't be mad at her. She's just trying to help." My eyes cut to where he was now standing instead of sitting.

"You knew about this?" His curt nod spoke volumes. He looked so dejected, my heart hurt.

"Yes. I tried to tell her to let you be, but she wouldn't listen." He still wore his white dress shirt from work, opened at the collar with both sleeves rolled up to reveal those arms that I loved so much. His black slacks fit him perfectly from waist to feet. The way they creased over his black leather loafers was weirdly sexy as hell. When he lifted his right hand and dragged it through his hair, I remembered how that hand felt when he finger-fucked me.

I couldn't start breaking down all the parts of him I missed or this night would take a dangerous turn. "Kyle…"

"Look," he cut me off, "I know you don't want to be here. And I'm not going to force anything to happen, it's not how I roll. For some reason, Brae seems to think we have unspoken business between us. She wouldn't divulge what it was, claiming it wasn't her story to tell. But if that's what it'll take to get some closure, then I think we should indulge her. I also think you owe me that."

It wasn't fair to push him away without explaining myself. Resigned that he was right, and so was Brae, I said, "Fine. Let's talk."

He watched as I placed the wine down and removed my coat, tossing it on one of the club chairs in the corner. With a wave of his hand, he motioned for me to sit on the couch beside him. Instead of sitting, I stared at the space. It was too close for comfort, and there were at least ten other places to sit in the room. At my hesitation, he sat first, leaving a long stretch of couch for me to choose from.

Slowly, I moved toward him and sat a few feet away. The black leather separating us seemed ridiculous. I'd done all sorts of lewd things with this man and chastised myself for appearing like a bitch. The fact was, I wasn't a bitch. I was a woman tormented between my past experience with love and a new one that was now knocking at my door… a door I had dead-bolted shut years ago.

It didn't matter what my justifications were for my

behavior. If he wasn't told otherwise, the label of bitch was deserved.

He bridged the gap moving closer and laid his arm along the back of the couch. I hoped he didn't touch me because I couldn't guarantee that wouldn't cause me to catapult into his arms. "Have you been okay this week?"

I remained sitting with both legs pressed together. I could feel his gaze on my profile at the same time as a lump formed in my throat. Swallowing past it, I shook my head. "No, not really."

"I know he probably gave you hell for taking off last week. I'm sorry, Nessa. I feel responsible for that." Guilt added to the mix of emotional bullshit that swirled within me. This wasn't his fault as much as it was Robert's fault to die. "But to cut off your friends and sulk every night in your apartment is not the answer." I should have been pissed at my traitorous friends, but the anger wouldn't surface.

Brae's comment that my behavior had little to do with my job rang true in my mind. She was right in that nothing had really changed at work. It was time to come clean and let Kyle in on my atypical behavior. "Kyle, this isn't about my job." I turned, mimicking his posture, bringing our knees a few inches apart. "It's about you."

My words caused genuine confusion to alter his features. "Me?"

"Yeah."

"Nessa, you asked for space, and I gave it to you."

"You have, physically at least." I could tell his wheels were turning with tons of questions, but he remained silent. Reluctantly, I pulled in a huge breath and released it like a professional yogi would. "Kyle, I wasn't prepared for you to crash into my life as you have. And I'm sure you're thinking I'm just a cold-hearted bitch who is afraid of commitment." This time his silence caused me to laugh. "*I don't think you're a cold-hearted bitch, Nessa*," I said in a deep masculine voice with a stern expression on my face.

It was his turn to laugh. "I don't think that... not the cold-hearted part at least. I believe you have a kind heart."

"Um... gee thanks?" Again, he chuckled and shrugged. "Well, I apologize for making you think I was a *kind-hearted bitch,* but really that wasn't my intention. The truth is, I have no clue how to navigate the feelings you managed to dig out of the concrete that formed around my heart. Nor do I have any idea what to do with these feelings now that you brought them to the surface."

"What kind of feelings?"

"You know damn well what kind, Kyle." Regardless of my accusation, he didn't budge in helping me out at all. Annoyingly, he continued to sit and stare. "Look, I'm not conceding that I'm okay with feeling them. I do apologize for how I handled things when you opened up to me. That was really shitty, and I'm sorry. But, I can't go down this road again. Nor can I believe I'd somehow survive a second round of heartbreak."

He moved closer and took my hand. "Vanessa, I'd never hurt you. I don't know who did, and if you aren't ready to tell me now, then I hope someday you can. But I'd never intentionally break your heart."

"I know that, Kyle. That's exactly the problem."

"I'm not going to pretend I have any idea what you mean," he said, frustration lacing every word out of his mouth, every expression on his face.

Lifting my free hand, I gripped my forehead, trying to

lessen the pounding that began between my temples. When I dropped my hand and looked into his eyes, their sky blue depths forced me to choke back a sob. "My heart wasn't broken because someone intentionally hurt me. It was broken because my boyfriend, Robert, died. Without warning, in the prime of his life, he just left me to live without him while trying to glue together the fragments of my shattered heart."

Kyle's mouth gaped open in shock. With that one statement, all the pieces of the puzzle in Kyle's mind merged to reveal the whole picture. The tears surfaced as they always did when I spoke of Robert. Kyle used his other hand to gently wipe one away. Apparently, that contact wasn't enough for him when he suddenly gripped my upper arms and pulled me onto his lap.

The way he soothed me as I cried made it worse. This man killed me with his affections, and his love, *almost* as much as losing Robert had.

"Baby, I'm so sorry for your loss and that you had to go through that heartbreak. I wish I could undo what you've been through. But the selfish prick in me would have to admit you wouldn't be in my life if you hadn't had to endure that horrific event." He moved back enough to grip my chin and lift my head. Once he had my attention, he softened his voice. "Things happen for a reason, Vanessa. I'm not suggesting Robert had to die for you to find happiness. What I'm saying is, maybe this is the universe telling you it's time to be happy again?"

I couldn't speak, not one word could find its way out of the sobs racking my body. It all felt cathartic in a heart-wrenching way. He gently placed his lips on mine, just once. When he pulled away, he palmed my face. "Before you, I didn't believe in soul mates. The day Jude married Brae, even seeing them so in love and so wrapped around each other, I was still skeptical. I couldn't relate, but now I get it. I know I was meant to meet you and feel I was destined to be with you. I love you, Vanessa. Let me."

The way he stared into my eyes combined with his no bullshit declaration was hard to combat against. The fight, the need to push him away, left me like a spirit leaving a body. In that moment, I knew I lost my self-imposed battle. All I had feared for all those years, experiencing the crushing pain deep in my heart, seemed insignificant now.

It should have all terrified me because if I were to lose him, my sorrow would no doubt end me a second time around. Yet, as much as I never wanted to go through such heartbreak again, having this man beside me, confessing his love for me, made me realize something. Not having Kyle Cleary in my life from that day on would be worse than what I had already endured. I needed him, and in that moment I knew I couldn't live without him.

"You know what else, Vanessa?" He caught the tears that silently rolled down my face. With a warm smile that lit up those beautiful eyes, he nodded and said, "I believe you love me, too."

I couldn't argue with that. He was absolutely right.

Chapter 25

Kyle

SHE DIDN'T EVEN LOOK SURPRISED at my suspicion. I knew deep down, just like she did, that she did love me. Getting her to say the words was a different story. "Talk to me, Nessa, please." The fact that this poor woman had been through hell—a hell I couldn't even bring myself to imagine, pained me.

Her red-rimmed eyes met mine. "When Robert died, not only did I lose him, I lost a part of myself. Getting through a loss like that was something I promised my heart I'd never force it to do again. The only way I could ensure that was not to fall in love." She sniffed. "Then you came along. Your charm, wit, and the ability to make me forget. That's what you did. When we were in California, I was so happy. Not just because I was able to see things I had always wanted to, but because I was seeing them with you."

That last comment triggered something inside of me. "Did you feel guilty because you were experiencing things Robert never would?" When she shrugged, I knew she did. "Baby, don't you think he'd want you to love again? Maybe Robert was the *first note* in your life. The one that taught you how to love and to be loved. But, you need to allow the rest of the notes to breathe—you need to allow yourself to love again."

"I know that now. I've been so scared, Kyle. When I thought about how great it would be to fall in love again, fear hit and I pushed back…"

"And you asked for space?"

"Yes."

"Do you still want it?"

She tucked her hair behind her ear and shook her head from side to side. "No, I don't think I do. It was futile anyway." A half chuckle/half sniff escaped her. "All I did with my *space* was think about you." I quirked a brow and smirked. "You know, for the most part."

"Are you saying you love me?" As soon as that question flew from my mouth, I stopped her. "Wait, don't answer that yet." I shifted my body and gently slid out from under her.

When Jude called to tell me about Brae's plan to get us together tonight, I made sure to bring what I made for her. I worked on it before we left for California, but it needed something. Then when we got back, I perfected it.

I walked to my blazer that was draped over a dining room chair and pulled the gift I had for her out of the inside pocket. It wasn't wrapped in any fancy paper, just a no-frills blue box.

She looked at it curiously when I handed it to her. "What is it?"

"Open it."

When she flipped the top up and pulled out the green tinted elongated bottle, her tear-stained face brightened.

"Nessa?"

I took the bottle from her, untwisted the top, and put a bit of it on my finger. When I looked to her, she licked her lips. Of course, my first instinct was to drag it between her breasts, and taking it upon myself to assume she had thought the same, I merely said, "Later."

With a coy smile, she extended her right arm. I dabbed it on the inside of her elbow before sliding my finger down to her wrist.

She brought her nose to her wrist and sighed. "Wow, it's beautiful." *Just like you*, I thought but kept my comment to myself. Her swallow was audible. "You made this for me?"

I knew that question was redundant because she was the only Nessa I knew. But, I humored her anyway. "Yes."

Vanessa sat back on the couch, staring at the bottle in her grasp. The seductive scent lingered in the air which started to feel thick. I snapped my fingers to break the tension. "I know what I forgot to put in it." When I went to snag the bottle from her, she jerked her arm back.

"What?"

"Phenylethylamine."

"What-a-what-a-mean?"

"It's a chemical that is supposed to help people fall in love. It releases…"

She stopped my words with a raised hand. "I don't need the explanation any more than you needed to add it to this perfume."

"Vanessa Monroe, are you saying that you *are* in love with me?" I asked with a smug smirk.

Her eyes narrowed. "You're going to make me say the

words, aren't you?"

"Damn straight I am."

"Fine, Lyle Cleary, I love you."

"It's Kyle. Ky… with a K… Kyle."

"Whatever."

We both laughed at her dumbass Lyle joke, which was the name she had mistakenly called me the first time we all hung out as a group.

"Nope, still not satisfied." I took the bottle and placed it on the table. Without warning, I then flipped our bodies until she was flat on her back and I hovered over hers on the couch. "Say it again."

All humor from her expression evaporated. "I love you, Kyle."

"I know," I said with a smirk. "And I love you, too, Nessa."

Our mouths fused together in a not-so-gentle kiss. It was evident how much we missed each other's touch and taste. "I want to make love to you, Kyle."

I could have easily taken her right here on the Sorens' couch. But not only did the thought of them coming home make me rethink that decision, so did the fact that I wanted to wake up with her in my arms.

"Come home with me."

Vanessa

ALL OF THIS WAS SO different to me. Even saying those three words, which I had said before, had new meaning now. When we walked into Kyle's apartment, a warm feeling settled in my heart. It may have been nerves or the fact that we were a couple now… I suspected it was happiness.

I thought we'd burst through his door in a frenzy, but it wasn't like that. Of course, we'd have to be sure that passion we shared since day one didn't fizzle out. And knowing Kyle, that would never happen. We'd have plenty of time for the raunch. This moment, however, needed to be special.

"Can I please use your bathroom?"

Kyle lowered his brow and laughed. "Sweetheart, you don't need to ask. You can use the one in my room. I'll wait for you on my bed… naked."

I needed to buy some time to put my plan into action. "Can you please pour me a glass of wine? And since we never ate all that food Brae had for us, do you mind if we order something?"

My stomach rumbled at the mere thought of eating. "Of course. Anything in particular?" He walked into the kitchen and pulled out an array of menus, fanning them like a deck of cards.

"How about Mexican? I remember you telling me it's your favorite."

Kyle nodded with an electric smile. I rolled up on my toes, circled my arms around his neck, and pulled him toward me. Our kiss was slow, gentle, and if I didn't release him, my plan would be for naught and we'd never have dinner.

When I walked into his bedroom, every one of my senses were assaulted. I loved his room and the tranquility of the space. His bed was perfectly made, there wasn't an article of clothing to be found—unlike my room where last night's clothing was still on my bed. But my favorite thing was the way his cologne permeated the air and forced me to take a deep breath. I'd say he should bottle it, but he already had.

Sliding open his closet door, I pulled out one of his many white dress shirts. Once I was in his bathroom, I clicked the door closed and took off my clothes, leaving just my mint green lace bra and matching thong. I knew he'd love it since it complemented the color of my eyes.

When I looked at the heap on the floor guilt flooded me, so I folded them and placed them neatly on his vanity. I couldn't help but chuckle as I did so.

Snagging my purse, I slicked some gloss over my lips and applied a touch more of "Nessa" between my breasts and behind my ear. I slid on his shirt, buttoning it up to my cleavage. I stared into the mirror and smiled. If someone would have told me, that I would have fallen in love again, I wouldn't have believed them. Even less believable was who I ended up falling in love with. We were so much alike, not wanting anything serious, yet there we were. Looking back, the transformation that we made, now seemed so obvious.

Three gentle knocks made my heart race. "Nessa, dinner is on the way up," came through the door.

"Okay, I'll be out in just a minute."

"Are you okay? Do you need anything?"

"I'm fine. I'll meet you in the living room. Don't forget my wine."

"Okay, your wine is poured." Silence followed so I thought he was gone but then he spoke once more, "Hey, Nessa?"

"Yes?"

"I love you. Don't make me wait much longer or I'm coming in there."

My heart flipped, hearing him blurt that out, and not

in a bad way. I had no idea why the universe gifted me with two amazing men, but this time around I wasn't going to take one moment with Kyle for granted.

Not wasting anymore time, I cracked the door open to make sure I was alone. Confirming it was just me in the room, I tiptoed across his floor and slid on my pumps.

I heard voices coming from the other room and smelled our dinner. Once the door closed, I moved to stand in front of the dining room table.

Kyle walked closer, smiled wide, and inhaled. "I love that you're wearing your perfume." He wrapped his arms around my waist. "My shirt has never looked so good."

"I beg to differ, but if you say so." When I looked up at his handsome face, I saw the man who now owned my heart. "So, should we eat dinner?"

"As much as I want you right now, you look a bit thinner since last I saw you." His hands trailed up my back until they rested on the sides of my face. "Let's eat and then go to bed. We have all night."

"Maybe I should have put something more appropriate on to eat in. I can go change."

"Don't you even think about it."

We sat at the table with an array of Mexican dishes in front of us. Kyle served us a little bit of everything from the white plastic takeout containers. "While you were changing, I sent a text to Soren, letting him know we left together and Brae's plan wasn't in vain."

"Can you even believe those two?" I dug in, savoring the delicious spicy enchilada. "I swear if you would have asked me the night they met that they'd be blissfully married I would have laughed at you."

"If memory serves, you were hooting and hollering

when she picked Jude." Kyle took a few bites, smirking as he chewed.

I smiled at the memory. "You saw me?"

"Of course I did. You were the most gorgeous woman in the room... and the loudest," he quipped with a raised brow.

"Oh, come on, how could I not? He was the best out of all of them. That's who *I* would have picked." His eyebrows shot up to his hairline. "Not that he's my type, but he clearly didn't want anything to do with a relationship. And not that Brae knew this at the time, but even you have to admit that the man is gorgeous."

"I have to do no such thing."

"Fine, but I call bullshit that you didn't think Brae was gorgeous."

"Not denying that. I once told Jude I thought she was hot as fuck, but he didn't take too kindly to that."

I couldn't help but laugh. "I can only imagine."

Kyle shrugged. "What did you think of me when you first laid eyes on all of this?" He swept his hand over his body from neck to waist.

"I thought you were, handsome, and sexy. And I was a little bummed you were seeing Brae's friend, Shelly. I would have totally done you that night we danced at José Ponchos."

"First of all, I wasn't seeing anyone when I met you. I had dated Shelly for a bit, but it was nothing."

"What about me, Kyle? What did you think of me?"

"I already told you I thought you were the most gorgeous woman in the room." He took a moment, then linked his fingers with mine across the table. "I thought you were feisty and sexy as fuck. Also, you have a perfect ass. Did you know that?"

"Yoga." How I kept a straight face when I said that was a miracle.

"Well, it does a body good because yours is perfect. But, even if it wasn't, you're perfect on the inside, too. Your heart is genuine, and I'm so happy that you decided to share it with me."

My eyes began to prickle with tears, and crying was the last thing I wanted to do. All I wanted was to be in his arms, to lie next to him in his bed, and love him like I never had before.

"Kyle, finishing dinner can wait. I want you—every part of you... now."

I stood up, unbuttoned my shirt, and watched it fall to the floor. I allowed him to admire my bra and thong before they also landed at my feet. There I was naked in his kitchen in just a pair of high heels. When I started to reach for my left shoe, he stopped me.

"No, the shoes stay."

In a matter of seconds, I was in Kyle's arms en route to his bedroom. He set me down on his plush bed, and my eyes watched him strip naked. When the mattress dipped next to me, he pulled me to my side until we faced each other. "I'm going to love you now."

"I was sort of hoping you would."

For the first time since we started this crazy arrangement, I was okay with Kyle making love to me. Every loving touch, expression, and word from his lips was no longer dreaded. In turn, my mind was free of trying to block feelings, my body was free in a way it had never been, and my heart was finally free to accept the fact that I was with my soul mate.

"Kyle?"

He tucked an errant strand of my hair behind my ear. "Yeah, babe?"

"I just wanted to let you know that even if our friends hadn't intervened tonight, I would have eventually come around."

A brilliant smile graced his handsome face. "Yeah?"

I nodded. "I don't want to be without you. You make me laugh when no one else can. You make me relax when I'm tense... thank you, Kyle."

"For what?"

"For teaching me how to love again."

Chapter 26

Kyle

I T HAD BEEN ONE WEEK since Vanessa and I ended our arrangement and became a real couple. We hadn't spent one night alone. She was either at my place or me hers, but as long as I woke up with her by my side, I didn't care whose bed we were in.

Yesterday was her Thanksgiving. Being from Canada, it wasn't a holiday I'd usually celebrate. Over the years, I'd been to a few friends' homes, and to be honest I had no idea what all the hoopla was about. Jude and Luca, being immigrants themselves, felt the same. Now that he was married to Brae, the poor bastard was stuck with the in-laws eating a turkey Brae's dad killed himself with pride.

Vanessa had no emotional ties to the holiday. With a father who was all about his new family and a mother who was off frolicking in Florida somewhere with her bitter divorce club, my girl admitted her last Thanksgiving involved bad takeout and a *Sons of Anarchy* binge… she had a serious Charlie Hunnam crush.

So, that was basically what we did. For most of the

episodes, I voiced I didn't see the draw. But then I got into it and couldn't wait to finish the series to find out how it ended.

Tonight would be the first time we would be hanging out with our friends as a couple. "Nessa, are you ready to go?"

I stood in her living room waiting for her to get changed out of her work clothes. Once again, she had a shitty week at work and was delayed because her boss needed her to drop off his dry cleaning or something equally ridiculous.

When she appeared, she had on dark denim skinny jeans, a blue top that made her tits look amazing, and a pair of come-fuck-me heels that made me want to stay home.

"How do I look?" She pivoted on the balls of her feet, slowing down to give me the perfect view of her ass. Ever since I told her I thought she had a great one, she was sure to emphasize it as much as she could. "Stunning. If we weren't meeting our friends, I'd opt to stay home with you looking like you do. But, they'd probably come here and fuck up my plans anyway. So, let's go. Just know that when I get you home, that ass is mine."

She leisurely picked up her purse off the chair. "Promises, promises."

Before I could give her a witty retort, or bend her over the side of the couch, she patted my chest and walked out of her apartment. A tightening behind my zipper caused me to look down at my jeans with a sigh. Silently, I promised my dick that I'd make it up to him.

The journey from her place to Dispatch was comical. We each kept our hands and lips to ourselves, knowing one slip-up would have us back in her apartment and forgetting our friends.

We walked into the bustling bar. Cassie had texted Vanessa to tell her they had a large table in the back. I'd be lying if I didn't say my heartbeat accelerated, because it had. This was it, our coming out. After tonight, there would be no hiding, sneaking around, or pretending we were something other than what we were—two people in love and not afraid to show it to the world.

Before we made it to our friends, I noticed various men checking out my girl. Not that I blamed them, but in a caveman-esque move, I released her hand and tossed my arm around her shoulder.

She glanced at me with a quirked brow. "Everything okay?"

"Yes, just making sure these hornballs know you're taken. Is that okay with you?"

"Yup, it's more than okay. Besides, the only hornball my eyes see is you."

"As I should be," I said with a nod and a firm kiss to her full lips.

When we finally made it to where our friends were, I released my hold on her. Desiree sat next to Jude and Brae. His arm was draped over his wife's shoulder, and the way he held her left hand, putting her sparkling diamond on full display, left no doubt who she belonged to. Then there were Luca and Cassie sitting across from them.

Desiree's face lit up when she saw us. "Hi, you guys!" Two chairs were left, one next to Cassie and the other at the end of the table. Well, that wasn't going to cut it. Luca met my narrowed glare with a snarky grin.

"Move, Benedetto."

"Say please," he ball-busted as he shifted to the empty

seat. Cassie then moved down, allowing Vanessa and I to sit next to each other.

As soon as our asses hit the seats, and we shrugged off our coats, the waiter was at our table. "What can I get you?"

I turned to Vanessa and said, "Babe?" Luca let out some sort of stifled chuckle—probably because of my term of endearment. "What?"

He shook his head and raised his palm. "Nothing. Proceed."

Unfazed, Vanessa said, "I'll have a margarita, no salt." Then she turned to me, laying it on thick for our friends' viewing pleasure. "Sweetie?"

I gave her a quick wink. "I'll have a Labatt's Blue, bottle not draft."

"So." Brae smiled at both of us. "What's new? Did everyone have a nice Thanksgiving? Vanessa, did you spend it with Charlie? Did anyone else join you?"

If she wasn't so damn cute I would have laughed. I knew she wanted us to come right out with some sort of formal announcement that we were officially a couple. Brae and Jude were the only two who knew of our epiphany. Brae had been relentless this past week with her impatience. Tonight was a compromise of sorts. We had told her we'd let the gang know soon if she stopped bothering us.

The whole thing was ridiculous since everyone sitting at the table most definitely knew, making me wonder which Soren cracked. My money was on Mrs. Soren.

"Yeah, I joined her." Deciding to indulge Brae, I threw my arm around Vanessa and said, "Well, everyone, we'd like you all to know that the two of us are now off the market."

"Who's the lucky guy, Vanessa?" Luca asked with a grin on his face.

Rather than answer, Vanessa fisted my shirt and pulled me toward her until our mouths fused together. Getting lost in the moment, I speared my fingers into her hair. Our tongues moved in unison, and when she moaned in my mouth, I wanted nothing more than to go back home.

Jude cleared his throat as the waiter appeared with our drinks. "Why do they get to do that?" he asked Brae, who ignored him.

Vanessa swiped under her bottom lip with her finger before taking a sip of her margarita. She then smiled at Luca. "Any more questions?"

"Nope." He lifted his bottle of beer in the air as a silent toast. "Tanti auguri," he said in his native tongue.

"Thanks, Benedetto." I lifted my beer toward Brae and winked before adding, "I have no doubt you're next on her radar, eh?"

His eyes cut toward Brae, and he held his free hand up in mock defense. "I can get my own woman, thank you."

"I'll give you six months before I interfere, Luca," she said with authority.

"Great. I'll mark my calendar." He followed his eye roll with a smile.

"Cleary, thanks to my wife I no longer have to be indebted to you for meeting Brae. You're welcome," Jude quipped.

I considered his admission. "Fine. We're even now. You don't have to name your first born Kyle, unless you want to make him a lucky bastard."

"Yeah, no." Jude lifted his beer and tipped it my way.

"But the name Luca sounds like a good fit for Soren, though."

Asshole.

"Well, I'm very happy for you both." Cassie beamed, as did Brae. The woman couldn't contain her excitement, and if I were Luca I'd take her threat very seriously. Jude was right, and it was really thanks to Mrs. Soren's meddling ways that we were together sooner rather than later.

We all fell into comfortable conversation. Every once in a while, I'd steal a kiss, just like Jude had done so many times with Brae. Now, I understood why. Before I fell in love, I thought he was just a sap. But now I knew he just wanted a taste of her every chance he got.

"So, V, how was work this week, any better?" As soon as Des asked that question, I knew Vanessa's mood was going to shift and not in a great direction.

She gave a one shoulder shrug, "It sucked as usual. I honestly don't understand how he's even successful. He's not nice to anyone including some of his clients."

"Just say the word and you can quit on Monday and come work for me," Jude said casually, but I knew he meant it.

I knew my pal wanted to help, but the way Vanessa looked as though she was contemplating his offer didn't sit well with me. I needed to put a stop to it. I didn't want to put her on the spot or anything, but she belonged at my company.

"Did you all know that when Vanessa and I were in California she was instrumental in finding the right spokesperson for my company?" Jude smirked at my obvious rebuttal. When no one said anything, I continued. "Well, she was. So much so, that I offered her a job. She's a natural in the perfume industry. She even created her own scent in my lab, right, babe?"

Vanessa slowly nodded her head.

"Oh, is that the perfume you're wearing? What's it called? I'd love to buy one if it's for sale." Cassie leaned over and gave her a sniff. "It's so pretty on you."

A blush creeped up Vanessa's cheeks. "No, I only wish I was this good. Kyle made this for me, it's called *Nessa*."

"Wait, you have a perfume named after you?" Brae let out a sigh. "That's so romantic and such a cute nickname. I'd flip if someone did that for me."

"I'd be happy to create a scent for you." Jude cleared his throat, and I ignored his glare. "But, if Vanessa comes to work for me, she can do it for you. Wouldn't you, Nessa?" I tossed in her name for added effect, just wanting her to be happy.

"Well, I don't think I'm at the point of creating a perfume for Brae yet, but I do need a change." She looked at Jude. "Thank you for the offer, but I'm going to decline. I'd hate it if I took a job at Soren Enterprises and it not working out. I couldn't bear the thought of it coming between me and Brae, so I'll work for Kyle."

What did she just say?

Luca started laughing, clearly hearing the same thing I did. "Did she just imply that she wouldn't care if a job came between you and her, Cleary?"

"That's not what I meant," she explained.

Wait… she's going to work for me? "Vanessa, are you saying you're coming to work for me?"

"That's what I'm saying."

I pulled her into my arms. "I'm so glad. I can't wait to

have you on my team."

Cassie clapped her hands with vigor, "See V! I knew you'd find the job of your dreams."

The waiter came by and I ordered another round for everyone on me.

Vanessa

FOR THE FIRST TIME SINCE I started working for this asshole, I didn't dread dragging my ass into the office on a Monday morning. In fact, I practically skipped my way from the lobby to my desk.

"Miss Monroe!" he bellowed the moment he heard me pull open a drawer to deposit my handbag.

I snatched my notebook off my desk and stalked into his office while still wearing my coat. "Good morning, Mr. Boyd. Did you have a nice weekend?"

His head snapped up as his beady little eyes narrowed. "It was fine."

"That's wonderful." I sat, smiling the entire time he glared at me. "Before we get started, I'd like to say a few things if you don't mind."

"We have a lot to cover, and since you're so behind I think it's best we don't waste time."

I feigned a pout. "Oh, I understand. But, you see, I'm quitting. As of right now, without giving you two weeks, without warning." I crossed my leg over my knee and smiled pleasantly. "You're a nasty man, and I wish you the best of luck trying to replace me." I stood and tossed my notebook on the center of his desk. "You can pass this onto your new slave. I don't mind her seeing every truthful thing I wrote about you."

His face turned bright red with fury. "Sit down, Miss Monroe. You aren't going anywhere."

Ignoring him, I walked to the door and folded my arms. "Or?" I prompted. "You'll fire me? Oops, too late."

"You will never work in this city again. You can forget a recommendation. You work here for the next two weeks or I will be sure your next employer knows what an unprofessional employee you are."

A natural, care-free laugh escaped at his threat. "Good luck with that…" *You asshole.* "I will not be sitting back down, but I can bend over before I leave so you can kiss my ass."

I didn't bother to look back at him. With purpose, I strode over to my desk, grabbed my one picture, my handbag, and my—'There's a chance this is wine' coffee mug. With a wave to my now former coworkers, I smiled wide and said, "See ya,'" before hightailing it out of the hell I was forced to endure for too many damn years of my life.

Kyle knew I planned to quit today, but he didn't know I'd be walking out, too. That decision was made in my shower this morning.

I hailed a cab and recited Kyle's lab address to the cabbie. I hadn't felt this excited over my future in a very long time, and knowing Kyle, he'd want to be part of this unprecedented emotion I was feeling.

The city streets were clogged with commuters running late, combined with bridge traffic, it took far longer than I hoped to get to Cleary Laboratories. By the time I made my way into his building, my knees were knocking from a combination of nerves, anxiety, and adrenaline.

I announced myself to the first floor receptionist, and

she looked up with a knowing smile. "You're Vanessa?"

"Um... yes," I replied, wondering how she knew me.

"Mr. Cleary is on the fifth floor. Would you like me to call him?"

Showing up during his workday could cause a disruption that I didn't want. I couldn't assume he wasn't busy or in an important meeting. Internally, I had decided while here I was indeed his employee, and the only way this would work is if we kept those lines of professionalism intact during the work day. "Um... no, thank you. Would you mind calling Frederick instead?"

"Not at all." She did as I asked and then motioned toward the posh seating area facing her desk. "Make yourself comfortable. He'll be down in a few minutes."

Frederick appeared through the elevator doors as they slid open. "Vanessa. He hadn't mentioned you would be coming today. I assumed you'd be joining us in two weeks."

Impressed that Kyle had filled Frederick in, I stood and smiled shyly. "He doesn't know. I'm here to let you know, as your new apprentice, I'm ready to begin now. I no longer have any obligations with my former employer, and I'm all yours."

A genuine smile lit up his handsome face. "That's awesome... and I could definitely use the help. Let's get you set up and started. Welcome to Cleary Laboratories."

Chapter 27

Kyle

"THANKS, GUYS." I STOOD AND stretched as my men's aftershave team filed out of the conference room. I'd been spending so much time on my women's line of products, I felt I was neglecting the men's side of the business.

My concern was unwarranted as my team made it obvious they had it all covered and the division moved along like clockwork. With a new launch coming in the next few weeks, I listened to their detailed itinerary knowing they could handle what was needed to accomplish a successful campaign.

When I glanced at my phone for the fifth time this hour, Vanessa still hadn't sent me a text or tried calling me. All I could picture was her dickhead of a boss giving her a hard time or working her to the bone because she gave her notice. The only reason I didn't try to contact her was for fear it would interrupt while she quit—that would only make things worse.

Just as I stepped off the elevator, I swore I heard her voice. When I turned the corner, I saw her sitting at one of the tables in a white lab coat, her hair pulled back into a ponytail, and intently watching Frederick as he combined liquids into a beaker. She diligently took notes after each step he made.

I could stare at her all day. I had no idea she'd be there, let alone starting her new job as Frederick's apprentice. Something must have happened at her office for her to be here already.

Thoughts of that prick kicking her out caused my blood to simmer. That was until I pulled open the glass door and she turned in my direction and knocked the wind from my lungs with her beauty. Damn, being with her every day would be both amazing and a huge challenge. As it was, I already had visuals dancing in my head over all the places we could have fun in my lab.

An electric smile lit up her face. "I see we have a new employee."

Frederick glanced over her head. "Hey, Boss. Let me introduce you to Miss Vanessa Monroe," he teased.

Per our agreement, I kept it professional. "Welcome to Cleary *Laboratories, Miss Monroe." I extended my hand which she took in hers. After a quick shake, I released it. "Is everything all set with Human Resources?"

Vanessa nodded. "Yes, all of my paperwork has been filled out. My coffee mug and picture frame already have a place of honor on my new desk, and I even got a tour of the employee lounge. This place is really something, you should be very proud."

I was proud of what I had accomplished, but hearing it from her made it mean more to me. My business was my baby. It was something I dreamt of as soon as I won that award for my first scent made with my at-home chemistry kit. Granted, telling my manly friends I wanted to make perfume garnered a few questioning looks. But when I tossed in I'd have to work with a lot of women to get the formulas just right, their tune changed and suddenly I was a genius.

"Thank you, I am proud. Everyone who works here is responsible for its success. My name might be on the door, but my team is very good at what they do. I have high standards and as long as they're met, then I'm happy."

I glanced at Frederick who intently stared at us. Giving him a silent message via a nod, he got the hint. "I need to check my emails, I'll be back."

When he walked away, I took his seat. "What happened with your boss? Did that prick throw you out?"

"Just the opposite," she boasted. "It was so great, Kyle. I walked in, told him what I thought of him, quit, and walked out. I could finally breathe. That man was like a two-hundred and fifty pound weight on my chest."

"I've been worried about you. But, I will say, I'm glad you're here—surprised, but glad." All I wanted to do was take her into my arms and hug her. Knowing that wouldn't be the best idea because I'd end up sending the rest of my staff home and we had work to do, I shoved my hands in my pockets instead.

"Thank you, Mr. Cleary. I'm happy to be here." Her tone was soft and seductive. *Fuck.*

I leaned in toward her, taking in a whiff of her new perfume. "I want you to call me that later when I'm fucking you on my desk, understand?" She shimmied her ass on the stool. Good, she was turned on as much as I was.

"About that. During the work day no funny business,

Mr. Cleary. I was serious when I said I worried what your staff would think. The chick spreading her legs for the boss is not the way I want them to know me by."

I lifted my hand to rub my chin to contemplate her words. Torture was what came to mind, but she was right. It wouldn't be fair to put her in that awkward position with my staff. "You're right, but come end of day, all bets are off." Being the consummate professional, I stood and said, "If you need anything, I'll be in my bathroom." And when she watched me nonchalantly adjust myself, she grinned knowing why that was where I was headed.

The lack of ringing phones and the silence of office chatter was one way to know we were probably alone in the building. Looking up and seeing her standing in my doorway was another. She had kept her distance all day, and fuck if that wasn't a torment. At one point when we passed each other in the hall, I swear if my cock had arms he'd bust through on his own and reach for her.

"Busy?" she asked, taking a few steps in but stopping way too far away for my liking.

"Not at all. I was just wasting time waiting for this day to finally end. Did Frederick leave?"

"Just now. He said to tell you to have a good night. The smirk on his face as he said that was a bit embarrassing, though."

"No one knows here, except him." I stood and closed the distance between us, pulling her into my arms. "And no one needs to, Nessa. Whatever you're comfortable with is fine with me. I purposely didn't pull everyone together today until I spoke to you first on how you wanted to be introduced."

"As Frederick's new apprentice, please. But I'm sure they're going to know the only reason you hired the inexperienced, non-degree-holding chemist was because you're fucking her."

Her words lit a spark of anger within me. "First of all, I'm not just fucking you, so knock it off with that. Secondly…" I released her to cup her face, forcing her to hold my gaze. "There are quite a few of my employees who started here with nothing more than an interest in the business. We pride ourselves in giving young professionals a head start in a rewarding career. Once they learn the basics, my tuition program enables them to continue their education and earn the degree they need to advance within."

"Is this something I can do, too?" she asked, intrigue written in her gorgeous green eyes.

"Of course. You're part of the Cleary team now, which means you will also receive any and all benefits my company offers." I pulled her firmly into my body, leaving no doubt why. "Plus, you get fringe benefits, which include fucking the boss, as you so eloquently pointed out. Win-win, if you ask me."

She skimmed her thumb across my bottom lip. "Definite win-win. Can I admit that so many times during the day I questioned why I wanted to keep our relationship secret?"

"Well, no need to now. The workday has ended, and you're off the clock." I crushed my lips against hers no longer being able to hold back all the desire I felt since seeing her this morning. The kiss exploded into an all-encompassing green light, of sorts. It very clearly told our bodies, our minds, and our hearts all systems were a go.

When I pulled away first, it took a few seconds for her to open her eyes. "Don't move. I'll be right back."

A slow wordless nod meant she heard me. I closed the blinds and retreated quickly into my bathroom, not wanting to waste even another minute without being physically connected to her in some way.

I stripped naked before grabbing my lab coat that hung on the hook behind the door. In its pocket, I pulled out my glasses and slid them on my head.

When I opened the door, I found my girl sitting on my desk in a red bra and black panties. She looked up salaciously, swinging her one leg where it crossed over her other knee. The sight of her ruby tinted toenails and all that smooth skin had me forgetting my name.

"Ta-da," I said with my arms spread. "Your fantasy has arrived."

She curled her lips between her teeth to stifle a laugh. Her reaction to seeing me wasn't what I expected. It was then when I looked down to see my hard-on comically sticking straight out between the front panels of my coat. Like an over-zealous entertainer, he poked his head between the curtains to assess the audience who waited for him.

I shrugged, taking another step toward her. "I can't help it if he's anxious."

She giggled. "He's so cute. It looks like he's winking at me."

"I can assure you he's not cute, but angry. Poor guy has been held captive all day long."

Vanessa kissed the tip of her index finger before placing it on the tip of my dick. "Poor baby, don't worry. You'll be a happy camper soon."

In a slow methodical move, she swung her legs around my desk, dodging any accessories I had until she was flat on her back with her head dangling over the edge. She licked her lips and reached over her head to grip my lab coat pulling me close to her.

"Fuck my mouth, Mr. Cleary," she said before opening her mouth to me.

Between her words and the position of her lips an inch away from the tip of my dick, I had to stop myself from thrusting into her in one fell swoop. Instead, I pushed the red lace fabric of her bra to release her breasts and said, "Tits first." On my request, she released my lab coat and positioned her hands to hold herself in preparation for me. Without delay, my cock sat at the edge of her cleavage, and once I slid down she squeezed them together, creating a soft, warm cocoon of perfect flesh.

The more I moved, the harder I grew. Taking it upon herself, she slid far enough away to capture the tip of my cock with her puckered lips. I then slowly slipped into her mouth, feeling her tongue caress the underside of my cock before it hit the back of her throat.

"Fuck," I muttered when a new kind of warmth engulfed me. I cradled her head with my hands as I moved my hips back and forth. In this position, I could see the outline of my dick move in and out of her throat. There was no way I'd ever get this visual out of my head. Thoughts of moving her desk into my office as soon as tomorrow would not bode well for my job productivity, but the upside outweighed not making my monthly quota.

"Jesus Christ, Nessa." The vibration when she moaned almost caused me to come. She fisted the base of my cock with one hand while cupping my balls with her other. This woman was sure to be the death of me, and I wouldn't want to die any other way.

I continued to piston my hips in search of the ultimate release. The way she held me captive with her mouth as she was spread out on my desk pushed me over the edge. "I'm coming."

At my announcement, she tightened her grip and hollowed her cheeks to suck me in deeper. After one more thrust, I came spectacularly down her throat with a grunt. "Fuck." I continued jerking my hips forward, watching her swallow every drop I released.

Still supporting her head, I reluctantly dragged my dick out of her warm wet mouth. The way she used her tongue to constrict my cock during my exit made me want to go for round two, but it was her turn now.

"Come here, gorgeous." I helped her swing her body into a sitting position until her legs were dangling off the edge.

She held her head and laughed. "Give me a minute. I just got a head rush."

I couldn't help but laugh as well. "Babe, that was the best fucking blow job. I don't even want to know where you acquired that talent."

"Good, because a lady never tells."

"Get naked, Nessa. It's my turn." Her pretty pink tongue peeked out to swipe her lips. First her bra hit the floor, then her panties. "Put your feet on the edge of the desk." Following my orders, she did as I asked.

But when I told her to spread her legs she came back with, "Whatever you say, Mr. Cleary. You're the boss."

Damn straight I am. In a nanosecond, I was on my knees and between her legs. Her pussy glistened, beckoning me to taste it, which of course I did. How could I not? It practically begged for it. When I blew a gentle puff of air on her, I watched the soft skin around her opening tighten in anticipation right before I lapped her juices.

Stopping long enough to ask, "Did sucking me off

turn you on?" She hooked her legs over my shoulders, and I finger fucked her while sucking on her clit.

"It did." Her breaths came in pants. "I almost came myself." She shifted her hips up and down to ride my face. "Ahh, fuck, that's so good, right there, Kyle."

And that's where I stayed, stroking her sensitive flesh with my tongue, bringing her closer and closer. I could feel every tremble that coursed through her as the back of her knees lay heavily against my shoulders. I could hear her climb higher with every sound out of her mouth.

When I felt her hands gripping my head, I replaced my fingers with my tongue and plunged deep inside of her. My thumb massaged her hardened clit until she screamed something incoherent, bucked her body forward, and came against my mouth. I loved that she didn't warn me just as much as I loved the taste of her.

"Fuck me, Nessa. I need you again. You're like a hit of the right kind of ecstasy. But if we don't get out of here now, my staff will be walking in tomorrow morning to see us looking thoroughly fucked and wearing the same clothes... and then there will be no doubt what our relationship is."

Based on the way she laid across my desk, limp and unresponsive, I couldn't guarantee she heard me.

Chapter 28

Vanessa

YOU HAVE **GOT** TO BE *kidding me.* One thing about staying over at Kyle's on a work night was his damn cell phone alarm sounding off at five a.m. Yes, I loved the Canadian National Anthem; it had always been my favorite when I watched the Olympics, but having it play in my head over and over was a bit much.

I nudged Kyle with my elbow—okay, I gave him a little jab to the ribs but the man slept like a log. "Kyle." No movement. I tried once more a bit louder this time, "Kyle!" Again, nothing. Rather than hit him harder, I crawled over his half-naked body to reach his phone on the nightstand.

As soon as my T-shirt covered chest hit his bare one, his arms embraced me. His sexy morning voice greeted me. "Mmm, my plan worked."

He pulled my head to his, fusing our mouths together. My lips stayed closed in protest. When I pulled away and turned off his phone, I uttered, "Morning breath."

Knowing he wasn't going to win that argument, he smacked my ass. "Then get off me and go brush your teeth. I need my morning kiss."

"You're awfully feisty this morning," I said as I rolled off the bed. Then I took a peek out his window and gasped. "Everything is white! Kyle, I can't even see the building next to yours."

Rather than get out of bed, he flipped on the television to the local news channel. A litany of school and business closings scrolled across the bottom of the screen along with some mass transit issues. It was then he decided to join me at the window. When he saw the flurry of snow, he roped his arms around my waist.

"Looks like the meteorologist was right this time around. Aren't you glad you listened to me and brought your winter clothes over with you yesterday? I need to send an email out to my employees telling them I'm closing the lab. It appears you're stuck with me today."

I craned my head back to look at him. "What will we do with the time?"

"I'm sure we'll figure it out. Now go do what you need to so I can get a proper good morning kiss while I notify the staff."

After we had breakfast, a culinary treat consisting of peanut butter and maple syrup sandwiches, we sat on opposite ends of the couch facing each other and drinking our coffee. He tossed a blanket over our legs. It felt very domestic but not overbearing. The snow continued to fall, and from what I could tell, another six inches had accumulated since the last time I looked. Although the snow was pretty, I wasn't a fan of it.

"I remember you telling me you hate winter. Isn't that against the law if you're from Canada?"

Kyle let out a laugh. "When I was younger, we didn't

have many snow days since getting dumped with a few feet was a common occurrence. If everything shut down like it does here, nothing would ever be opened. Life went on, we just rolled with it or we'd go skiing."

"Oh, do you ski?" It was then I realized we really didn't know too much about each other.

"I do… and what's that look on your face? Can I take it you don't?" He sipped his coffee and waited for my reply.

"No, I don't see the joy in strapping sticks to my feet and careening down a mountain at a rapid speed." My fingers traced the rim of my mug, around and around as I realized there was so much about him I didn't know.

"Nessa, what is it?" he asked, picking up on my pensiveness.

I gave him a half-hearted shrug. "I really don't know too much about you, and I know it's my fault for not wanting to share a lot when we got together, but is it weird that we barely know each other, yet we're in love?"

"Nope. People who fall in love at first sight don't know anything about the other person. Not saying that's us, but it's not that uncommon. We can rectify that right now. Ask me something."

There was a glimmer in his eyes as he peeked at me over the top of his mug. He wanted to have this conversation a while back, but I wouldn't open up. Now, there I was, wanting the same thing.

"What's your middle name?"

"Steven. What's yours?"

"Lee. What was your childhood like? Were you a good student or were you a wild child?"

His bare foot met mine under the blanket. "Not really, I went to an all-boys school from kindergarten until I graduated. There was an all-girls sister school on the same campus, but for the most part it was all dudes."

"So, not a lot of girlfriends?"

"Nope, you're the first one." My jaw went slack at his admission. "Well, except for little Maggie who lived next door. Hers were the first tits I touched… I was eleven… she was thirteen. I thought for sure she was the one." A combination snort-laugh flew out of my mouth. "Sure, laugh it up, but I thought we had something special."

I feigned a sad pout. "I'm sorry."

"I got over her eventually," he admitted with a smirk. "Then I went to Yale and met Jude and Luca. As you're aware, I was a bit of a trouble maker, knew the Dean by his first name, and had lots of fun with my pals who relied on me to get them out of certain situations. But they weren't saints. Believe me, they screwed around as much as I did. Soren was smart and started investing other students' money in the market. One could argue that he started his business back then. He even recruited me and Luca as salespeople for him."

"How did that work out for you?"

"Not so great, but I got laid a lot. After grad, I started my own company with my life long savings account, fell in love with a sexy woman, and the rest of my story is still waiting to be written."

Everything sounded so much different than my life which was boring in comparison. He took my mug, walked into the kitchen, and came back with fresh cups of coffee for both of us.

Once he settled back under the blanket, he nudged me with his leg. "You're turn. Tell me the tales of young Vanessa Monroe."

"There really isn't much to tell that you don't already

know. My life was the complete opposite of yours—except for screwing around in college."

"Where did you go to school?" he interrupted.

"SUNY Albany." I smiled. "After graduation, I ended up doing a few odd jobs until I was hired by the asshole. Since then, I started working for this extremely handsome guy who loves his country's anthem."

"Yes, he's lucky to have you. And speaking of Canada. As you know, I go home for Christmas and I'd like you to come with me."

I shook my head. "No way, I'd be too nervous. Plus, what if they don't like me?"

"They will love you. Please come with me. I'll take you to Niagara Falls before we get to my hometown just outside of Toronto."

I had never been to the Falls or outside of the United States for that matter, but I did have my passport just in case I needed to jet off to Europe on holiday... in my dreams. "If you're sure I wouldn't be an imposition, then I'd love to go with you."

"Good, because I already told my family you'd be joining us," he informed me while grinning. "I'm sure Aunt Betty is knitting you a sweater as we speak."

"I can't wait to see it—if I get one, that is."

"Well, I'm sure if you don't get one this year, you will next."

I set my mug down on the table and straddled his lap. "Next year, huh? You're being a tad presumptuous. By then I could be sick of you."

"Or I could be sick of you." His lips twisted into a snark-filled grin.

"Nah, that won't happen. How could you get tired of

me? I'm a ray of sunshine."

"This is true." He leaned in and kissed my lips long and hard. "So, next year then?"

"Yeah, next year sounds great."

Kyle

WE HAD BREAKFAST, TALKED, AND watched the last three episodes of *Sons of Anarchy*. Hearing her swoon over Charlie Hunnam was getting old. We made love in the shower and were finally going outside to enjoy our snow day.

I waited in my living room and watched the snow continue to fall outside my window while Vanessa got ready. It was a good thing I didn't put my heavy jacket on yet or I'd be sweating.

"Nessa! Let's go."

When she came out of my bedroom, I just about died and went to ski bunny heaven. There she stood in black tight-fitting snow pants that looked more like leggings, a red turtleneck sweater, a black and white form fitting ski jacket, the cutest red, white and black striped hat with a pompom on the top, and black boots.

"I thought you said you didn't ski?"

She glanced down at herself. "I don't. That doesn't mean I want to look frumpy when it's cold outside."

I shook my head. "Grab your gloves and let's get out of here."

The two of us trudged through the snow-covered sidewalks. Some New Yorkers braved the weather and were out, but for the most part the city was quiet. It took longer than normal before we finally made it to Central Park.

Vanessa's cheeks were tinged red from the cold. Snowflakes clung to her eyelashes, making her look even more adorable than she already was.

"So, what now?" She glanced around the mostly deserted park. Some families took advantage and were building snowmen or making snow angels.

"Have you ever built a snowman?"

"Nope."

"No?" Was she kidding? My question was meant to be rhetorical.

"I told you, I was never a fan of the snow or being cold, so why would I go outside on purpose?"

"Well, I hate to break it to you, beautiful, but that changes today."

Vanessa could say she hated the snow as much as she wanted, but it was all a lie. My girl was a champion at making snowmen, or snow people, since she thought it was chauvinistic for all of them to be men. I will say, watching her gloved hands form the perfect set of breasts out of snow was a bit of a turn on. Of course, a few of the moms in the park looked at our snow people as if they were nude paintings. That just spurred her on. In my opinion, the moms were lucky she didn't start making the men anatomically correct.

The white flakes finally stopped falling from the sky, leaving the park and its surroundings looking like a winter postcard. Everything from trees to park benches were white; it was the cleanest the city had looked all year.

Taking her hand in mine, we strolled through the park admiring the beauty the storm had left behind since tomorrow it could all look different.

"Want to see if there's somewhere to grab a bite to eat? We never had lunch since you were too engrossed in Charlie Hunnam."

"Haha, very funny. Food sounds great. I could even go for a slice of pizza."

"Then I know the perfect place."

We were both thankful the cabs were running since we were cold, wet, and tired. After a short car ride, we arrived at a small Italian restaurant. It was one of my favorites in the city.

Vanessa inhaled deep as soon as we walked in the door. "It smells amazing in here."

Before I could agree, Pasquale, Luca's uncle and owner, approached us. "Ah… Kyle eets-a so good to see you. Eets-a been-a long time, no?" He kissed both of my cheeks.

"Hi, Zio Pasquale. Yes, it's been too long." I took Vanessa's hand in mine. "This is my girlfriend, Vanessa. Vanessa, this is Pasquale Benedetto, the owner and the best Italian cook in the five boroughs. He's also Luca's uncle. Vanessa knows your nephew, too."

Her face lit up. "It's a pleasure to meet you, Pasquale. It smells so good in here. Your restaurant is lovely."

Pasquale's olive complexion took on a reddish hue. Leave it to my girl to make him blush. "You are-a so pretty. Why you with this clown?" We all shared a laugh before he took her free hand and kissed the back of it. "Come, I bring you to the table."

Once we sat down, Pasquale went to the kitchen and a younger man filled our water glasses and left us menus.

"Looks like the snow kept people away."

Vanessa glanced around at the empty tables surrounding ours. "That's okay. More food for us." She shrugged off her jacket and turned to hang it on the back of her chair. "Luca's uncle is so cute. I love his accent. He sounds just like Luca. Well, Luca's English is a lot better, but still adorable."

"You think Luca is adorable?"

She opened her menu. "Of course I do. All three of you are gorgeous specimens. Toss in your accents and it's a no-brainer. We all thought so the night Brae met Jude."

"Wait, I don't have an accent."

Vanessa grinned. "I know." When I didn't push further, she let out a laugh. "I'm just kidding, Kyle. Out of the three of you, you would be my first choice."

"Okay, enough of the small talk." Little did she know I had texted Luca to have him join us—something I now regretted.

We ordered a bottle of Chianti and suddenly the room was filled with boisterous voices. You would have thought twenty people walked in, but it was just Luca introducing Cassie to his uncle.

Vanessa turned her head and beamed, standing as they came to our table. They hung their coats up on the rack against the wall, and the girls hugged as though it had been months since they last saw each other.

I took it upon myself to fill everyone's glass and ordered another bottle. Cassie shivered. "How about this weather and it's only December? It's so cold outside, I can't stand it."

"Um… hello? Why are you together?" Vanessa asked, wiggling a finger from Cassie to Luca and back.

"I was on the phone with Luca when Kyle texted, and he asked me to come." Cassie rolled her eyes. "Lose that look, V. We're just friends. Besides, why were you two out in this mess?"

"We were at the park today and Kyle brought me here to have dinner. It was nice having a day to just play in the snow. With the holidays coming up, we all get busy. Plus, we will be leaving for Canada... and..."

"You are?" Cassie looked at us in shock. Luca had an *I told you so* look on his face.

"Yes." Vanessa smiled at me. "I can't wait to see Kyle's home."

Cassie reached across the table and placed her hand on Vanessa's. "This is so great. You're happy, right, V?"

When I turned my head to look at my girl, she nodded at Cassie before turning to me. "Yes, I've never been happier."

I cupped her cheek with my hand and placed a soft kiss on her lips before whispering in her ear, "I love you."

She looked into my eyes. "I love you, too, Lyle."

"It's Kyle. Ky... with a K... Kyle."

"Whatever."

Chapter 29

Vanessa

I'D NEVER BEEN ONE FOR Christmas shopping. The only people I ever thought to buy a gift for were my girls. Since this year Kyle was taking me to meet his family, my list was much longer. Well, Kyle's was. He was an only child, but he bought presents for everyone invited to be there.

Kyle admitted he generally gave gift cards, but because we had decided to drive to Canada rather than fly, this year he went all out. To alleviate the pressure caused by the city's traffic, he hired a car service to follow us around. Only after a few stops, the trunk had started to fill up. After the driver closed the hatch, Kyle told him we were headed to Rockefeller Center, and he'd text when we were ready to be picked up.

Hand in hand, we braved the throngs of people clogging the sidewalks. Every once in a while, we'd stop to gaze at the awesome holiday window displays. "It's so pretty, Kyle. I've never taken the time to appreciate Manhattan during the holidays." I let out a sarcastic huff. "Truth be told, I've never really taken the time to sightsee in my own city. Aside from visiting Ground Zero, I haven't been many places—unless I walked by it of course."

He pulled me into a recessed area of an office building. "Wait, what? You've never been to the top of the Empire State Building, Statue of Liberty, Yankee Stadium, or a Broadway show?"

"No to all of the above."

"How about ice skating at Rockefeller Center?"

"Nope, but I do love ice skating… now." I winked.

"We'll need to rectify this." He pulled off his gloves before cupping my cold face with his warm hands. "I'm confused though, how is it that you want to travel and see the world, yet you've neglected this magnificent city?"

Great question. I took time searching for any answer that would make sense and not make me sound like the ultimate New York loser. It was when our eyes locked that I knew why. "Because I didn't have anyone to share it with."

I looked away, but Kyle's touch forced me to look at him. "Talk to me, Nessa."

"All of what you said were things that Robert and I talked about experiencing together. I guess when he passed away, I felt guilty."

Kyle's soft lips met mine. "When you're ready, I'd love to show you all those things and more. But, I don't want to rush you."

"I'm ready to finally live… and I want to do it with you, Kyle."

Based on the way he stared right into my soul, my words were profound. He bent and slowly placed one single kiss to my forehead. "I love you." He then wrapped his gloveless hand around my mittened one.

"Let's do this. Next stop, seeing the prettiest Christmas tree in our city with the most gorgeous girl in New York."

"New York?" I pulled my hand away and placed my mittens on my down-covered hips. "Just New York?"

He pulled me back into his arms and nuzzled his nose beneath my ear. "No, the world, baby. I meant the world."

"Uh huh. Good recovery, Mr. Flirt."

"You can't call me that anymore… you tamed me. You better come up with a new nickname."

"Ok, Lyle."

"You're ridiculous."

I reached up, grabbed the back of his head, and pulled him down for a quick kiss. "Fine, Mr. All Mine."

"Now that's a name I can live with."

By the time we reached the spectacular pine, I was exhausted. After about fifteen minutes of staring at multi-colored lights, I reached my limit. I couldn't prevent myself from yawning and leaning into his body as he held me from behind.

"You ready to go?"

I nodded my head against his chest. "Yes. I've never walked or shopped so much in one day before. I'm going to need time to recover."

Kyle sent a text to our driver to pick us up. "Come," he said, leading me away from the tree and toward Fifth Avenue. Relief flooded me when I saw the black SUV heading in our direction. Even my feet were thankful to see him.

We settled in the backseat and exhaled. Just as I was ready to close my eyes, that damn Groupme app simultaneously dinged on our phones. Brae forced us all to download it before her wedding so we could all stay connected. None of us used it, except for her.

> **Brae:** Hi! Sorry for the group text but we're having a holiday party next Saturday. It's a white elephant party so just bring one unisex gift. Don't put anyone's name on it. Fifty bucks max... be creative. ;-)

We both uttered, "What the fuck is a white elephant party?"

Ding.

> **Des:** Fun! I'll be there.

Ding.

> **Cassie:** Is there a minimum limit?

Ding.

> **Brae:** Nope! :)

Ding.

> **Cassie:** Great!

Ding.

> **Kyle:** So a pack of gum is okay?

Ding.

> **Jude:** She said creative, not cheap.

Chime.

A message appeared:

> Luca left group.

Ding.

> **Kyle:** Why does he get to leave?

Ding.

    Brae: :(

Ding.

    Jude: We'll make sure Luca gets the gum.

Ding.

    Brae: That's not how a white elephant works.

Ding.

    Vanessa: We have no idea what you're talking about.

Chime.

A message appeared:

    Kyle added Luca to the group.

Ding.

    Luca: Asshole

Ding.

    Des: Can you boys grow up?

Ding.

    Cassie: I'll bring Christmas cookies.

Ding.

    Brae: Yummy!

Ding.

    Luca: I'll bring a gun.

Ding.

    Kyle: Leave the gun... bring the cannoli.

Ding.

Jude: Hahaha

Ding.

Cassie: Ugh... The Godfather.

Ding.

Vanessa: I still don't know what a white elephant is.

Ding.

Luca: Google it.

Ding.

Kyle: Watch your tone, Benedetto.

Chime:

A message appeared:

Luca left the group.

Ding.

Brae: You can buy him gum.

Kyle turned to me. "This will go on all night."
Ding.

Kyle: Nessa and I will be there. Bye.

He took my phone from my hand and shoved them both in the pocket of his jacket. Just as he did that, from the lining of his coat we heard—ding... ding... ding... ding... ding.

Kyle

WHEN WE WALKED INTO THE Sorens' apartment, Brae had it decorated to the hilt. Their dining room table was adorned with a red and green plaid tablecloth and a poinsettia centerpiece with a gold candle protruding from the center and random gifts surrounding it.

Frank Sinatra crooned, "Jingle Bells," through the Bluetooth speaker.

"Hey, you two," Jude greeted us at the door. He kissed Vanessa on the cheek. "I'm glad you could make it."

Like we would have a choice. Vanessa reached into her bag and pulled out her gift. At the sight of it again, I snorted.

"What the hell is that?" Brae asked when she approached us.

"If you have to ask, Jude is lacking," I said when the dildo was placed on the table.

"Vanessa, really? You didn't even wrap it." Brae's nose crinkled in disgust. "A huge dick is sitting on my dining room table."

"Wouldn't be the first time," Jude said with a grin, turning his wife's face the same shade as the poinsettia.

"Nice one, Jude-alicious." Vanessa high-fived Jude. "Brae, you said to be creative, and this is the gift that keeps on giving."

Luca joined us. "Hey, Benedetto." I shook hands with him before he pulled Vanessa into a hug.

He glanced at the dildo and shook his head. "Well, I know which gift I'm staying away from."

Desiree and Cassie laughed, but Brae took this all very seriously and scolded Luca. "It doesn't work that way, Luca."

Vanessa chimed in, "About this white elephant shit, it's way too confusing. I vote for a grab bag."

When everyone started agreeing with my girl, Brae

conceded. "Fine."

A pretty waitress appeared and asked what we wanted to drink, while another one, just as attractive, walked around with a tray of appetizers. The old Kyle would have been flirting up a storm, but I already had the prettiest girl in the room. Luca, however, took the opportunity as being the only single man there. That's when I noticed they both had wedding rings on, so he was out of luck.

The Sorens didn't spare any expense—not that Jude ever had. The man went all out with everything he did, a party with just the seven of us didn't deter him. When Brae walked into the kitchen, Jude rushed over, dipped her as if they were in a dance, and planted a kiss on her mouth.

"Babe, that mistletoe is my favorite decoration." Jude smiled as he looked up at the greenery hanging from the archway.

Once we all had a drink in hand and food in our stomachs, Vanessa and the ladies walked over to the table. Desiree picked up a box and gave it a small shake. "Are we going to pick gifts now?"

Brae clapped her hands. "Okay, who wants to go first?" She motioned toward the pile of gifts. Without hesitation, Cassie, Des, and Luca all reached in and grabbed one. Brae and Jude shrugged and took the last two remaining gifts leaving Vanessa's and mine as the only ones left standing.

I snatched up the phallic gift. "Gotta love a good dildo. Looks like I'm the lucky one." My eyes cut to Vanessa, and I added, "Or you are. There's nothing hotter than watching a woman using a dildo."

Vanessa took my contribution and unwrapped it.

"Oh, look! Custom lube made by Cleary Laboratories. See! The gift that keeps on giving."

No one else made any motion to open their gifts and really how could anything follow such a hard act? Brae came to the rescue and said, "Maybe this would be a good time to sing *Happy Birthday* to Jude."

All eyes cut to her husband just as he rolled his. "Baby, you promised."

"There was no way I wasn't acknowledging your birthday. You should know me by now." She smiled at one of the waitresses and seconds later, the other appeared with a huge cake lit with the appropriate amount of candles.

Cake led to everyone sitting casually in the living room sharing stories. Most of them revolved around Jude, Luca, and my college days. The girls piped in with some of their own tales. I wasn't a mushy, emotional kind of guy. That was obvious in the way I chose a non-mushy, emotional kind of girl. But sitting there among our best friends, having her by my side, warmed me like nothing ever had in my life.

I had a lot to be thankful for, and I had no intention of taking any of it for granted. My girl had already lost so much in such a short amount of time. It was my goal to add only great memories, love in spades, and anything else she thought she couldn't live without.

While staring at her profile, she turned to look at me with a smile. "What?"

"Nothing. I'm just really happy."

The smile spread even more, lighting up her whole face and those gorgeous green eyes. "So am I, Kyle."

Epilogue

Kyle

I UPSHIFTED, FEELING THE PURR of the engine kicking into gear to swallow up the stretch of highway. If someone would have told me last Christmas I'd be back home the following year, driving my girlfriend to see the Falls, I would've scoffed at the thought. Yet, there I was loving life and loving how excited she was overseeing someplace I took for granted most of my life.

We drove from Manhattan to an adorable inn near the Catskills, spending two romantic nights together before continuing to Canada.

She asked me a million questions along the ride. Making the mistake of explaining how during the holidays there was a spectacular light show illuminating the Falls caused her curiosity to get the best of her.

"How much further? Are we there yet?" I chuckled at the way her legs bounced with excitement, like a child on her way to Disney World.

"Not far." The sun hung low in the sky. I purposely timed the trip so we would get there with just enough daylight left to see their magnificence before nightfall hit.

This side trip was just the first of several surprises I had waiting for her.

Thirty minutes later, I slowed my rented Lexus as we approached the border. The guards asked us our passports, purpose of our visit, and how long we'd be there. Once they were satisfied, we crossed into my homeland and headed to the Falls. "Welcome to Canada, sweetheart."

I pulled into a lot, jumped out of the car, and jogged around to her side. The clean Canadian air caused the exposed skin on my face and neck to tingle. Her anxiety caused her to open her door before I was able to.

My eyes devoured her body as she unfolded herself from the front seat. In jeans that fit like a second skin, Eskimo fur-lined boots that laced up to her knees, and a new ski jacket that cinched around her waist, we almost didn't make it out of the hotel.

I offered her my gloved hand, and she took it with an electric smile. Before walking toward our destination, I pushed her up against the closed door, caging her with my arms. "Vanessa Lee Monroe, this is just the beginning of all the places I want to take you to. From here on out, I want to see the world through your eyes."

"I can't wait, Kyle Steven Cleary."

Leaning in, I kissed her passionately until we needed to come up for air. "Let's go."

We walked past stunning illuminations of wildlife, holiday adornments, and of course a Canadian flag. My first instinct was to start singing the anthem, but I refrained. A chilled mist filled the air as tourists took in the sight of the most powerful waterfall. Vanessa tugged my arm until we made it to the railing. Just like many others who were there, she stared in awe at the beauty before us.

"I've never seen anything like this, Kyle. It's spectacular. Thank you so much for bringing me here."

"You're welcome." I moved to stand behind her, using my body as a shield against the wind—and the fact that I'd use any opportunity to have her body pressed against mine.

"Can we come back in the summer? I want to go on the Maid of the Mist."

Her enthusiasm and the fact she mentioned the future trumped my dislike of that boat tour. "Yes, of course."

She bounced on her toes and chastely kissed my cheek. "Thank you! I can't wait."

I smiled back at her. "Me neither. Tomorrow, we have a helicopter tour where they'll fly us right over them."

"Really? Oh my God, I've never been in a helicopter!"

"That's just the beginning of things we'll do that you've never done, Nessa."

She twisted in my arms. "I love you."

"I'll never get tired of hearing you say that." I kissed her cold lips, anxious to get her into our warm hotel room to love her properly.

As the night wore on, we didn't move. Vanessa refused to budge, stating we had a great viewing spot to enjoy the light show. Colorful streams of light danced on the Falls, like the sky on the Fourth of July. The crowd ooo'd and ahh'd as the colors shifted and played on the water.

Even though there were families with children present, this was still one of the most romantic places. Couples and lovers exchanged glances, embraces, and kisses during the show. I knew I'd never forget this moment, but I wanted to capture it. I took off my glove, reached in my pocket, and grabbed my phone.

"Nessa, turn around." When she did and saw my phone in *selfie* position, her face lit up just like the waterfall behind us. I stood beside her, angled my phone just right, and clicked the button.

A kind woman next to us who was there with her family smiled. "Would you like me to take one of you?"

"That would be great." I handed her my phone, positioned Vanessa in front of me, and wrapped my arms around her waist.

"Smile," she said before clicking the button. Before she handed me my phone, she glanced at the screen. "Are you here on your honeymoon? You make a gorgeous couple."

Before I could offer a reply, Vanessa did. "No, not this time. But maybe one day."

That was not the response that came to my mind or one I thought Vanessa would say, but it was the best. Not wanting to make too much out of it, I thanked the woman for taking our picture and went back to watching the splendor in front of us.

We stayed until we couldn't feel our toes and were almost asleep standing up. I made sure our hotel room had a view of the Falls so she wouldn't miss anything. It was a good thing, too, because just as I suspected, she put on her pajamas, curled up in a chair, and watched the show through the glass.

Her sweet voice was filled with joy. "It's the most beautiful thing I've ever seen."

With my eyes glued to hers, I said, "It sure is."

My family pounced.

No warning, no easing her in… just hugs and kisses and squeezes and exaltations the moment we walked through the door.

Throughout, Vanessa smiled and nodded incessantly. The way her hand gripped mine, I worried this was all too much too soon. But to arrive before my entire extended family would have meant we needed to leave our hotel room at the crack of dawn. Having her warm body wrapped around mine in that big luxurious bed, there was no fucking way we'd be leaving it a minute sooner than we had to.

The chaos in my parents' home went on around us. I leaned in and whispered, "You okay?" I wasn't convinced at the way she nodded with the same plastered smile on her face.

My aunt Betty emerged, holding out two gift boxes stacked on top of each other. "Welcome! Welcome! You must open these immediately. I worked all night getting them ready. You didn't give me much notice, Kyle, but now that I see your beautiful girlfriend I think the colors I chose will perfectly complement her." She thrust the boxes at us, forcing me to grab them in my other arm.

There we stood with about twenty or so relatives circling us, all chattering above my constant pleas of, "Give her space to breathe."

No one was listening. I craned my neck above the circle of humans searching for my mother. Just before I took control of the situation, she appeared out of nowhere, pulled Vanessa free from my grip, and called over her shoulder, "Leave the poor girl alone!" Not entirely trusting of my mother's intentions, I followed directly behind them as my mom led her toward my father's office. "Steven, come with us."

My father nodded and obeyed, and before I knew what happened, the four of us were safe and alone with the door firmly shutting out the rest of my family and their craziness.

"Oh, lord. I'm so sorry about that, Vanessa. I'm Debra. This is my husband Steve, and we are so thrilled to have you here." She pulled my girl into a warm embrace before kissing each of her cheeks. "I wanted to deflect them. I hope they didn't scare the life out of you."

Vanessa offered a warm smile. "No, no. Kyle warned me before we arrived. I think they're sweet."

My father stepped closer and mimicked my mom's hug and kisses. "They're a bunch of nuts. Just say the word and I'll kick them all out," he said, clearly revealing his patience level with my mother's family.

"Steven," she scolded. "They're excited Kyle finally has a girlfriend."

Kill me now.

Vanessa met my humiliated gaze, curling her lips between her teeth. All I could think of was if the guys were here, I'd never survive their ball busting.

Through the door we could hear muffled jabbering, and every so often Vanessa's eyes would widen when one or two intelligible words filtered through the noise.

"Vanessa, darling, they are here just to greet you. Since they didn't behave themselves, as I warned them to, I'll send them all away. The four of us will be spending a nice quiet Christmas Eve together. How does that sound?"

"Perfect," I responded for her.

Vanessa gave me a look before amending, "You don't need to do that. I'm fine if they all stay."

"No, we're not." I ignored the way Vanessa glared at me and demanded, "Mom, get rid of them, please. Or,

I'm taking her back to the hotel."

Knowing that threat would strike a chord, my mom immediately stood and said, "Don't move." She stalked out the door and we heard her say, "Everyone out. Come back tomorrow for Christmas dinner."

My dad's sigh of relief was obvious in the way his body sagged. He looked me in the eye and said, "Thank you."

Vanessa

MEETING KYLE'S ENTIRE FAMILY IN one shot was not only overwhelming, but in a weird way, comforting. Knowing he came from so much love made me love him even more than I had. Marriage, kids, happily ever after were not things I considered for myself. Now with Kyle, I wanted it all. I wanted the chaos, the overwhelming family that got into your face, the love.

It hadn't occurred to me how much I had missed out on being loved during my life. I had it in spades from my friends, but now having a reference of what a loving family looked like forced me to admit so much had been missing. And now having had a fairly large dose of it while in Canada, I decided I wanted more.

Kyle had been awesome in making sure I was comfortable during our stay, as did his parents. His physical traits were very similar to his father's. The same color hair, same smile, even the same crystal blue eyes made it easy to see how well Kyle would age over the years. But his personality was strictly his mother's. Where his father was a quiet, reserved man, his mother was a firecracker.

She and Kyle had the same devious spark within them, the same humor. So many times the two of them had me in stitches with stories they recounted of Kyle's childhood.

When it was just the four of us, we had a lovely time getting to know each other. Mrs. Cleary, or Debra as she insisted I call her, was everything my mother wasn't. I'd never met a woman more kindhearted and giving as she was... well, maybe except for Brae's mother, Ellen.

It hadn't taken long for me to lose the nerves and relax among the clan of Canadians related to my man. Bouncing between a quiet, intimate holiday and a loud family reunion, I was able to get a taste of both worlds and loved each equally.

At Christmas dinner, the smile on Aunt Betty's face when she saw us wearing her sweaters, was adorable. I loved every part of that over the top, gaudy declaration of the holiday memorialized in wool.

When everyone left an hour earlier, Kyle and I retreated to his corner of the house to exchange our gifts for each other in private.

Being an only child, his parents converted two of the guest rooms, as well as the bathroom, into a huge suite for him. It took up the entire right side of their palatial home. Windows framed two sides of his room, affording a magnificent view of the snow-covered forest that surrounded their property.

I smiled when two strong arms circled my waist. He kissed the side of my neck and asked, "Penny for your thoughts?"

"I love it here," I admitted with a sigh. His hold tightened, and through the reflection in the window I could see the joy on his face. I twisted around, bringing us nose to nose. "Thank you. This has been the best Christmas I've ever had." His expression instantly changed at my declaration. He parted his lips to say something, and I pressed my fingers to his mouth to stop him. "Don't look sad. I truly believe every year I spent wishing I could skip over the holidays had to happen for me to appreciate what I have now with you."

"Baby, this is just the beginning. I want to make all your dreams come true, together."

"Well, we're off to a great start. Your country is stunning."

"You only saw a tiny bit of it, but with time you'll see so much more." He kissed me chastely. "Are you ready to exchange gifts?"

I grinned and nodded like a five-year-old. As it was, I needed another suitcase to get all my gifts from his family back to New York, but I'd been anxiously waiting to exchange with Kyle, specifically to give him my surprise.

"I'll go first!" As I dashed out of his hold toward my bag, he moved to sit on the small couch with a chuckle. I pulled out several boxes from my suitcase and carried them over to where he sat. "Okay, this one is last," I said, holding the one I was most excited for in my hands after handing him the others.

First he opened the monogramed flogger I ordered online. While turning it in his hand, he bounced it a few times testing its weight. "Nice one. I love the personalization, nice touch. But, is this for me or you?" he asked, grinning.

"Both. Keep going." One by one he opened and laughed at the little things I picked up that were so Kyle—a ceramic syrup dispenser in the shape of a beaver, a silk bow tie that matched his eye color perfectly, and a

Catwoman figurine sporting the exact costume I had on for Halloween.

"This is going on my desk," he admitted, turning her in his hand to inspect all parts of her body. "She looks just like you."

"That's why I picked it up."

"I love them all, Nessa." He lifted the bow tie and raised a brow. "Best idea you ever had was using my bow tie as a sex toy."

"I agree. Okay, now for the last but not least." I presented the last box to him with a shy smile. "I hope you like it."

I had no idea why I was nervous as he opened the gift. A few seconds later, he lifted the navy square glass bottle from its tissue paper nest and smiled. Embossed across the front in silver was *Mr. Flirt*. He lifted the cap and sniffed. "This is amazing, Nessa. You made it?"

"Well, with Frederick's help… a lot of help, but yes. I explained to him what you reminded me of and we were able to recreate all that in this cologne." Kyle always smelled amazing, but what was in that bottle perfectly captured *my* Kyle in every way

When my focus moved from the bottle to his face, the level of emotion in his eyes stunned me. "I… I'm…" He gingerly placed the bottle on the small table before us and pulled me into his arms. "I am so in love with you," he finished saying once I was nestled on his lap. "Thank you, I love it. So much so, it's going into the new product launch this spring."

"That's not why I did it, you know that." I held his face and stared into his eyes. "I can't begin to thank you for not only helping me love again, but for changing my future in such a positive way. You have no idea how happy you've made me."

He held my gaze for a very long moment. "I do actually." He lifted his chin toward the closet in the corner. "I have about ten or so boxes in there for you to open, and you will soon. But those are all secondary to my main present. First, I want to give you what I'd been dying to."

A contented smile spread over my face. "You already made me my perfect perfume."

"Yes, I did, but this is even better." With me still on his lap, he reached behind himself and pulled out a folded piece of paper from his back pocket. A gold round sticker held it together where the edges met. I gently lifted the seal and unfolded, my heart pounding at seeing the first line neatly typed across the top.

Air Canada

Depart December 26, Toronto > Paris

Flight #AC880

Returning January 7, Paris > New York City

Flight #AC889

Business Class, 2 passengers

It was my turn to be stunned. I couldn't believe I would finally see Paris. A dream I held for so long; as time passed it seemed less and less likely to happen. And here, this man who had already given me the best gift I could have ever wanted just made my dream come true. "We leave tomorrow?" My question came out in a high-pitched tone that failed to hide the level of my excitement.

"Tomorrow. Even though we are heading there on business in a few months to tape the commercial for *Risqué,* I want to show you Paris properly beforehand."

"Wait, you were bringing me to the shoot?"

"Of course. Anyway, back to my gift. Personnel has cleared an extra five days of vacation for you. It's a good thing you know the boss so well."

"But—"

Before I could finish my sentence, he added, "The girls know. Everything has been handled, including your wardrobe." He pointed to the closet and smirked. "I'm ruining the rest of your surprises, but you have all you need for your stay wrapped in those boxes in my closet."

I curled my arms around his neck, squeezing a bit harder than necessary. "Not everything. The most important thing I need is you, Kyle Cleary. I once thought I didn't need a man to have a happily ever after and all I needed was myself. I was so wrong. I love you."

The smile I loved more than any other lit his face, and if possible it made him even more handsome. "I love you, too, Vanessa Monroe. And you're all I need as well…" He kissed me long and hard, pulling away to then say, "… and maple syrup."

The End

Acknowledgments

Taming Mr. Flirt was as fun to write as the first book we collaborated on, Finding Mr. Wrong. Once again, we laughed, cried, and swooned… and we can't wait to do it again for a third time. We hope we don't forget anyone, and if we do, please know it wasn't intentional.

First, we'd like to thank the readers. We all love to read and talk about the books and characters we love, and we're so thankful for your support.

To our beta readers, your feedback, comments, suggestions, and more importantly, your honesty, were incredibly helpful. Thank you from the bottom of our hearts.

Thank you to our very handsome cover model, Dima Gornovskyi, who was a perfect Kyle Cleary, and David Wagner for providing that amazing shot we used for our cover.

Sommer Stein at Perfect Pear Creative Covers, your talents are unsurpassed. You did it again. We didn't think we could love a cover more than Finding Mr. Wrong. But, with Taming Mr. Flirt, you managed to do just that.

To Nina Grinstead and the team at Social Butterfly, PR. Thank you for helping us spread the word and prepare all the amazing readers for Taming Mr. Flirt's release.

To all the bloggers, thank you for all the time you spend supporting authors and reading our stories. You take time out of your personal lives, and we are very thankful.

Nichole Strauss, Insight Editing Services, thank you for helping prepare our book for release.

Julie Deaton, Author Services by Julie Deaton, thank you for proofreading our book and for your awesome comments.

Tami at Integrity Formatting, you're always a pleasure to work with. Thank you for making our words look pretty.

Brower Literary Management, specifically, Kimberly Brower and Jess Dallow, no matter how ridiculous our questions, you ladies are quick to respond and are always efficient. We are honored to be part of the Brower family.

We are also so very happy to be part of the EverAfter family. Seeing our books popping up on bookshelves is a dream come true, and it's because of you at EverAfter. Thank you for all of your support.

To our families. Thank you for putting up with our long nights, takeout dinners and all the craziness that ensued while we wrote Taming Mr. Flirt. Without your love and support, we wouldn't have been able to write about the biggest flirt to grace the romance world.

A & J

xo

About A.M. Madden & Joanne Schwehm

A.M. Madden

A.M. MADDEN is a USA Today bestselling author, as well as 2016 eLit Gold Medalist for Best Romance Ebook, and 2016 Ippy Award Silver Medalist for Best Romance Ebook.

A.M. is a wife, a mother, an avid reader of romance novels, and now an author.

"It's all about the HEA."

A.M. Madden is the author of the popular Back-Up Series, as well as several other contemporary romances. She is also a published author with Loveswept/Random House.

Her debut novel was Back-up, the first in The Back-Up Series. In Back-Up, A.M.'s main character Jack Lair caused readers to swoon. They call themselves #LairLovers, and have been faithful supporters to Jack, as well to the rest of his band, Devil's Lair.

A.M. truly believes that true love knows no bounds. In her books, she aspires to create fun, sexy, realistic romances that will stay with you after the last page has been turned. She strives to create characters that the reader can relate to and feel as if they know personally.

A self-proclaimed hopeless romantic, she loves getting lost in a good book. She also uses every free moment of her time writing, while spending quality time with her three handsome men. A.M. is a Gemini and an Italian Jersey girl, but despite her Zodiac sign, nationality, or home state, she is very easy going. She loves the beach, loves to laugh, and loves the idea of love.

A.M. Madden, Independent Romance Author.

Sign up for A.M. Madden's newsletter at www.ammadden.com to get up to date information on new releases, cover reveals, and exclusive excerpts.

Contact A.M.

Website www.ammadden.com

Facebook www.facebook.com/pages/AM-Madden-Author/584346794950765

Twitter @ammadden1

Instagram @ammadden1

Goodreads
www.goodreads.com/author/show/7203641.A_M_Madden

Email am.madden@aol.com

A.M.'s Mad Reader Group
www.facebook.com/groups/893157480742443/

Joanne Schwehm

JOANNE SCHWEHM is a mother and wife and loves spending time with her family. She's an avid sports watcher and enjoys the occasional round of golf.

Joanne loves to write and read romance. She believes everyone should have romance in their lives and hopes her books bring joy and happiness to readers who enjoy modern day fairy tales and breathless moments.

She is an independent romance author and has written several contemporary romance novels, including The Prescott Series, Ryker, A Heart's Forgiveness, The Critic and The Chance series which she has recently sold the screenplay right to and will be adapted into a movie.

Joanne looks forward to sharing more love stories in her future novels.

Contact Joanne

Website: www.joanneschwehmbooks.com

Facebook: www.facebook.com/joanneschwehm

FB Group Page:

www.facebook.com/groups/joanneschwehmsreaders/

Twitter: www.twitter.com/JSchwehmBooks

Pinterest: www.pinterest.com/nyy2fan/

Instagram: www.instagram.com/jschwehmbooks/

Spotify: www.open.spotify.com/user/1293937868

YouTube:

www.youtube.com/user/JoanneSchwehmBooks

Goodreads Reading Group:

www.goodreads.com/group/show/156533-joanne-schwehm-s-romantic-reading-friends

Newsletter: www.eepurl.com/cgUvSf

To the Reader

Thank you so much for purchasing and reading this ebook. Please support all Indie authors and leave a review at point of purchase as well as your favorite review forum. Indie authors depend on reviews and book recommendations to help potential readers decide to take the time to read their story. We would greatly appreciate it.

xoxo,

A.M. Madden & Joanne Schwehm

Join the MadJo Romance Reader group on Facebook.
www.ow.ly/ZE0W30cR5if

Keep reading for a sneak peek of Finding Mr. Wrong

Finding
MR. WRONG

USA TODAY BESTSELLING AUTHOR
A.M. MADDEN
JOANNE SCHWEHM

CHAPTER 1

Brae

THEY HAD ALL BEGUN TO look alike. I swore I'd seen this man before. It had to be his boring navy suit or the questions he asked. Even the small conference room with its plain white walls and cheesy inspirational quotes looked familiar. My eyes landed on the plant in the corner that had seen better days. The poor thing looked limp and neglected… much like how I felt.

"We'll be in touch." Firm handshake, fake smile, and I was out the door. I'd heard that line more times over the past month than I had in my entire twenty-seven years—sixteen times, to be exact. Living in the city that never slept, you'd think I'd be able to find a job, but no.

I'd been a marketing sales representative for a large cable company for the past five years. My goals were always met, and I'd even won a few sales awards. But now I couldn't sell myself if my life depended on it.

Here's a tip: never date your boss. Stefan Wilson might be one of the hottest men I'd ever met, but because I caught him pounding his secretary, I was now pounding the pavement. He wasn't the love of my life, but we were in a committed relationship. *Asshole.*

Hoofing it to the subway after my last interview, I checked my emails, hoping for a stroke of luck that one of these jobs panned out. The only email sitting unread in my inbox was from an online cable affiliate who was once my client. I could sell the shit out of her network. Shelly and I had become fast friends and out of all my clients, I missed her the most.

Brae,

I know you're going through a lot right now, but I have the perfect thing for you! It's a social experiment sponsored by Flame Relationship Services. You'll spend six weeks on a tropical island with a bachelor of your choosing. The event is next week, and lucky for you, the female contestant had a death in the family, so she can no longer participate. And lucky for me, you're my friend who has the free time to help me out.

What could be so bad? Bachelor of your choosing, six weeks in paradise while being wined and dined, and a cash prize.

Win/win, especially for you.

So, are you in?

Little minor detail, I need a response today.

Chat soon!

Shelly

After a roll of my eyes, I clicked the link and scanned the rules. What caught my attention was the prize. Half a million dollars? Holy shit! As I continued to scan the fine print, my heart raced in my chest. I could do this. Images of me stranded with a stranger flashed through my head.

This had to be the craziest thing I'd ever considered. If I thought too long about it, my good sense would have me tossing my phone in my purse without a second thought, but maybe, just maybe, this was the answer to my prayers. Yes, why not? I had the time. Without further negative thoughts, and with just a few more keystrokes, I replied to Shelly, telling her I wanted in. Her confirmation and instructions came quick in an email, along with the attached contract. I skimmed it, electronically signed, and sent it back a few minutes later. It was a done deal.

I gripped the lapels of my coat with my fists, pulling them together over my chest in an attempt to keep the cold air off my skin. Tonight, I was meeting my girls at José Ponchos for happy hour. All I wanted was to sit my ass down and maybe forget what I just signed up for as a cocktail warmed my insides.

José Ponchos was packed with business people and the typical Friday night bar goers. It was so easy to decipher between those looking to wind down and those wanting to go down. Some women looked refined, while others looked like they were on the prowl, and it was only five-thirty p.m. for God's sake.

Vanessa, Desiree, and Cassie, my best friends, were sitting in a booth off to the side. Cassie waved to me, ensuring I spotted them, and with each step toward their table, my feet screamed at me to take my stilettos off, but they'd need to pipe down for a bit.

"Hi!" I said as I slid into the booth, and they all looked at me as if I had grown two heads. Apparently, my voice was too chipper. "What are we drinking?"

"Margaritas are on the menu for tonight." Vanessa smiled. "I ordered a pitcher for us." She grabbed the glass container and poured some for me.

In one large gulp, I finished half of it. My face screwed up as my eyes squeezed so tight I thought my eyelashes would stick together. Wow, that was tart. I blinked as a small shiver coursed through me and turned my attention back to the girls.

Cassie reached across the table and patted my hand. "No luck with the job hunt?"

"Who knows?" My shoulders slumped from the sheer exhaustion I felt over the process. "You know how it goes. They say they'll call, but I'm sure as soon as I walk out of the office, my résumé lands in the recycle bin."

"Sweetie, you'll find something." Desiree smiled. "It'll just take a bit more time."

I shrugged one shoulder, and said, "We'll see."

Chatter from the other patrons filled the air. It wasn't so loud that we couldn't hear each other, but as the bar filled, the volume increased.

The way Vanessa eyed me had me asking, "What?" I glanced down at my professional outfit, wondering if she thought it was prudish.

"You look weird. Like the cat that just ate the canary. Plus, your hair is a bit disheveled." I brought my hand to the top of my head to smooth down whatever errant strands there were. "Did you just have a quickie in the ladies' room or something? What's that on your face?" My hand flew to my cheek. "Wait, is that… dried spunk?"

"Eeewww," Desiree and Cassie gasped, and then looked at me with curiosity.

"Oh my God," I said with disgust. "It most certainly is not. I've been running around all day in the freezing cold. I'm sure it's dried snot." *I couldn't muster up the energy or desire for a quickie right now,* I thought with a shake of my head. "Crap, I hope this wasn't on my face during the last interview." I grabbed a napkin and wiped my cheek. My hand snatched my iPhone out of my pocket before I took off my coat.

Taking another sip of my drink, I tapped the screen of my phone, bringing it to life. I clicked on the link Shelly had sent me. "Look." I handed the phone to Cassie, and Vanessa, who was sitting next to her, looked at it as well.

"A social dating experiment?" Cassie gawked at me as if I were crazy, while Vanessa's lips grew into a rueful smile.

"Brilliant. This is genius! You have to do this." Vanessa flapped her hands as if she were fanning herself.

Desiree grabbed the phone away from Cassie and studied the site. "Do you realize what this says? You need to stay on a tropical island with a man for six weeks." She continued perusing the screen with wide eyes. "The upside is he can't be a sociopath since they did a short background check."

"He could also be a hot piece of ass!" Vanessa exclaimed. "Plus, what does she have to lose? She'd get money, a vacation, and a man out of the deal. Sounds like the trifecta to me."

I snatched my phone back in defiance. "The money and vacation are fine, but I don't want a man. No way. After what I just went through, the last thing I want or need is another dick with a dick. Plus, I get to pick the guy. There will be three to choose from, so I'll just pick the one who sounds like he can't commit." Stealing Shelly's words, I said with a shrug, "It'll be a win/win."

"You're crazy." Cassie shook her head. "What if they all want to commit?"

"No she isn't, and she could just pick the one who sounds the hottest," Vanessa countered. "Be sure to ask if he has a big cock. You know, just in case. Just because you're stuck with the guy doesn't mean you can't have fun with him. Besides, who would want to go away with someone who has a little pecker?"

"She can't ask anything personal. Did you read all the rules, Brae?" Desiree interjected, her lawyer mode in full effect.

"Most of them. It's fine. I need the money. My savings will only keep the banks off my back for so long, and I've worn out more pairs of shoes hoofing it to interviews. Winning this money could solve my problems. It would be such a weight lifted off me. Plus, six weeks isn't that long."

I chose to ride the Vanessa vibe because Cassie and Desiree were making me second-guess everything. I needed to be one hundred percent confident going into this. Plus, I'd already signed and Shelly gave me the spot. From what I understood many applied, but once the original contestant backed out she didn't have time to find a replacement on such short notice.

Vanessa's eyes cut to the right, and I followed her line of sight to see a man at the bar ogling her. "I'll be back. You're doing the right thing, Brae. I can feel it. We'll be supporting you. Right, girls?" Her eyes flitted between us as she slipped out of the booth. Everyone nodded and Vanessa was off to talk to the handsome stranger.

"When is it?" Cassie asked before sipping her drink.

"Two weeks from tomorrow. That'll give me enough time to go shopping, pay my bills, and come up with my questions for Mr. Wrong."

Desiree laughed. "You're really going to go through with this?"

"Damn straight I am. By the time the six weeks are over, I'll have a killer tan, half a million dollars, and no man." My confidence soared the more I convinced myself this was a great plan.

"What are you going to do if you fall for him?" Cassie cocked a brow. "It could happen."

"It won't happen. I'm swearing off men for a while. Trust me, I know what I'm doing." Just the thought of liking the man I'd be spending time with sent a chill down my spine. No way. I would stick to my plan.

We all looked toward the bar as Vanessa tossed her head back and flipped her hair over her shoulder, laughing at whatever the man she was talking to had said. Yeah, she wasn't leaving anytime soon.

"Well, ladies, I'm exhausted." I grabbed my coat, slid out of the booth, and kissed them both on the cheeks. "I'll talk to you later." I looked at Desiree, who still had a concerned "mom" look on her face. "It'll be great, Des. Just wait and see. Would you like to come over tomorrow and go over the fine print with me?"

"I'll call you and let you know what time I'll be at your place."

I smiled at her, knowing that was what she needed. She was the caretaker, the sensible one of the bunch. "Great, I'll have wine chilling."

With another quick wave to Vanessa, I hailed a cab and made my way home.

♡♡♡

By the time Des showed up, I had already enjoyed three glasses of wine. She was adamant about going over the details of the dating contract, but I just wanted the money and would do almost anything to get it.

"I see you're going to be taking this seriously." Des shook her head and poured herself a glass of Merlot.

"Des, it's a no-brainer. I'm doing this to satisfy your OCD." We sat on my sofa while Des reached for the iPad. Sliding her reading glasses on, she began scanning the screen. "You look super smart in those." A hiccup escaped me, followed by a giggle.

Des rolled her eyes. "Number one." Her tone was serious, so I did my best to sober up and pay attention. "All of your questions must be geared toward romance, relationships, or dating."

"So, I can't ask how many inches he is?" I asked with a snort.

"No, you can't." Des did not look amused.

"Girth?"

"Did Vanessa put you up to this?" she huffed. "Can you please focus?"

I put my hand up in surrender. "Okay, what else."

"You both must stay on the island for a full six weeks or forty-two days. If you hook-up with someone else on the island, or leave for even an hour, and they find out, the experiment is over and no one gets a dime."

"How would they know? Are there cameras?"

Des scrolled through the contract. "No. It says there will be unannounced visits from people affiliated with Ignite Your Spark. You both must be present."

"What if I need to pee and I'm not there?"

"Will it take you an hour to pee?" She raised a brow in a silent scold. "Again, let's concentrate, shall we?"

"Whatever, I'll hold it."

"There will be planned activities for both of you that you must engage in."

"Like what? Chess tournaments? Scrabble? I'd kick ass in Scrabble."

Des took my glass of wine and set it on the table. "I'm cutting you off." She shook her head.

I let out a sigh. "What activities?"

"Romantic dinners, island excursions, couple massages."

"Oooh! I hope my masseuse is hot!" I raised my brows, and she frowned.

"That would be breaking rule number one—lusting after a man other than the one you're with."

"I'll make sure I get the fat old woman."

Her eyes scanned the page, and then she said, "Hmmm. Challenges." When she didn't get a response, she repeated, "Did you hear me? Challenges. You will both have to complete team building challenges."

"I'm a team player." I went to grab for my wine glass, but she slapped my hand away. "What else?"

"Your location won't be disclosed to anyone other than the producers of the show, except for one person of your choosing to be your emergency contact."

"Awww, will you be my person?" I batted my lashes at her.

"Yes, who else would you choose? Vanessa?"

"Yay, you're my lobster!"

"Brae." Her serious tone worried me a bit. "Did you read the last line?"

I looked at my iPad as Desiree moved her fingers over the screen to magnify the text. Then she read out loud, "Couple will be married on the forty-second day. Family and friends will be welcome to attend."

"I'm sorry, what?" This time when I went to grab my

wine, she let me.

"Married, Brae. You need to marry this guy. You were wrong. You don't get to walk away with a killer tan, half a million dollars, and no man. The man is part of the deal."

"How did I miss that? Let me see that again." I snatched the tablet from her hands, and sure as shit, that's what it said. "You're a lawyer, can you handle my divorce?"

"Yeah… in a year. Plus, you need to make four public appearances together promoting your loving union." Desiree's eyes were filled with concern. "Brae, this man is a stranger. It's bad enough you'll be sharing a room, but a life? You may get the money up front, but it says if you aren't married for the full year, you have to give it back. You're depending on this stranger to be your knight in shining armor. Even if it's temporary, do you want your first and, hopefully, only marriage to be with a guy you'd know for a month and a half at that point? One who's so desperate, he turned to a dating service?"

She was right. I jumped to my feet and began to pace, my hands on my hips and gaze penetrating my carpet. It wasn't like I could get a loan. I was unemployed, for God's sake. There was no way my parents could find out about this. At that thought, my stomach rolled. "My mother is going to flip out. She has so much on her mind as it is. If I call her in two months and tell her I'm getting married, she's going to have a stroke! Not to mention my father! Holy shit! What have I gotten myself into?" I cried, throwing my hands out at my sides.

My heart was beating so hard, I was ready for it to burst out of my ribcage, and my skin became clammy as I continued my fevered steps, the anxiety feeling like a living force inside me. Nausea washed over me and I ran to the bathroom, getting there just in time.

"Sweetie, are you okay?" Desiree pulled my hair back and handed me a cool washcloth.

"You'll be there for me, right? Will you handle things for me?" I wiped my mouth and stood. The more I thought about what I signed on for, the more bile churned in the pit of my stomach.

"Of course I will. We all will be. I'm sure even Vanessa will think this is insane, but you signed the contract. It says here if you break it without just cause, you could be sued." I bet the original contestant was happy she had a death in the family. I was beginning to think she lied.

Back in my living room, we assumed our places on the couch. "Like I said before, I'll just pick the man who sounds like he wouldn't be good at having a committed relationship." I nodded, reassuring myself of my words. "When we get to the island, we'll make a pact to separate after we leave. Easy-peasy." At this point, I was convinced my decision was brilliant, until I saw Desiree's face.

She looked up, with sympathy etched in the lines of her forehead. "Sweetie, it says you need to live as husband and wife for a year. Living in separate places is not the norm for married couples."

"Oh. Fuck." *I was screwed.*

CHAPTER 2

Jude

THE SETTING WAS STRAIGHT OUT of one of those horrid awards shows Americans went gaga over. Velvet ropes corralled the hordes of crazed overdressed New York socialites hoping to get in. Two intimidating men whose physiques looked more like refrigerators than humans stood guard at the door. What the hell was happening, and why the fuck was I here?

Kyle.

Dammit. The fucker said it was a work function he needed to attend, and once he made an appearance, we could take off. I'd bet my last dollar this wasn't a work thing at all. Knowing my friend, that chick he was banging was going to be here tonight and he lied to get me here.

I strutted up to the two kitchen appliances with eyes and gave my name. One quirked a brow at my accent. It happened every time. People assumed I was a Swedish model without a brain in my head, and most of the time I let them assume.

I waited, feigning boredom as they scanned their clipboard. Without a word, one of the ogre twins moved the velvet rope, granting me access.

With each person allowed entry, the crowd became more irate, and my passing through was no exception. Here these poor saps were dying to get in, and I wanted no part of this night. At least Luca would be coming as well. Lucky for Kyle, Luca often stopped me from beating the crap out of him.

When the three of us attended Yale University, Kyle's antics would often get us into all sorts of trouble. Most of the time with chicks; once with the disciplinary committee. Each time, it was Luca who convinced me to let him live another day. What happened when a Swede, an Italian, and a Canadian walked into a frat house? Chaos.

Thrust together because we were foreigners, no one could have predicted the friendship that culminated between us. Even though Luca and I spoke impeccable English when we arrived at Yale, we often depended on Kyle to talk our way out of situations—which proved to be a mistake on many occasions.

Once inside, I forced my eyes to focus in the dimly lit room. It was massive, loud, and jammed with people. My phone buzzed in my pocket. When I fished it out, a text from Kyle announced they were sitting at the bar.

The first thing I said when I reached them was, "I want a Belvedere with a twist... on you." He dragged me here. The least he could do was buy me the most expensive drink I could order.

Kyle smirked. "Fine."

He repeated my drink choice, telling the bartender to add it to his tab.

Only after I took a long sip did I speak. "You. Owe. Me. Big." Another smirk meant he knew it. "Seriously, what the fuck are we doing here? And be honest. I don't buy your crap that this has to do with work."

His eyes cut to Luca before landing back on my scowl. "It is work. Just drink your ridiculously expensive vodka and relax. Where else do you have to be?"

He had a point. After a long, stressful week, I needed to relax a bit. I wouldn't admit that out loud, though. It would serve me well to have him thinking he owed me one.

I scanned the scene. Round cocktail tables and club chairs all pointing toward a curtained stage filled the dance floor and my initial thought was Karaoke. I despised Karaoke.

"What's happening here tonight?"

Kyle glanced over his shoulder at the stage. "Some trivia thing."

This didn't look like a trivia crowd. This crowd was here for very specific reasons. The girls were dressed to the nines and the guys may as well have had stylists for the occasion. My untucked white button-down and dark denim jeans would have to suffice.

Photographers lined the perimeter, snapping pictures of the guests, and a camera crew was setting up at the back of the room facing the stage.

The closer I looked, the more I realized the female to male ratio was a bit skewed. "Why are there so many dudes here?"

"Ask him." With a palm up, Luca deflected to Kyle, sporting his typical Italian *what the fuck do I know* tilt of the head.

"You have thirty seconds to start talking," I said without humor, lifting my vodka while my gaze remained steady on Kyle's face.

Just as I opened my mouth to start my countdown, a

spotlight lit a perfect circle against the black velvet curtain stretching across the stage. Applause drowned out the music and a man and woman emerged, smiling wide while waving to the crowd.

The man wore a tuxedo and looked like he could be the host for Wheel of Fortune, and his booming announcer voice supported that theory. His partner was a busty blonde who squeezed herself into a red sequined gown two sizes too small.

"Hello, ladies and gentlemen! I'm Chip, and this here is my lovely wife, Barbi."

Chip? Barbi? More like Dipstick and Busty.

"Welcome to *Ignite Your Spark*, sponsored by Flame Relationship Services. We believe true love sometimes needs more than that initial spark. It's not just about striking the match, it's also about stoking the flames. Via Ignite Your Spark, we bring two people together who are a perfect fit on paper. Once that spark catches, we provide all the necessary tools to keep the embers of romance from flickering out before they can become a blazing fire."

The busty blonde smiled wide at what her co-host had just said. I heard the words, but they weren't registering in my brain. All I kept thinking was, again, *why the fuck are we here?*

"Chip and I founded *Ignite Your Spark* ten years ago, and are proud to say we are responsible for over three hundred marriages to date. After our own romance sparked to life…" While she continued to ramble on about how they met and came to be, I turned back around on my bar stool and drained my Belvedere.

"So, tonight," Busty continued, "we are proud to announce one of our best social experiments of all time. We stand behind our theory that love often needs help to flourish, but what would happen if you didn't see the person you are emotionally connecting with? What if all you have is that emotional connection to work from? Tonight, our female contestant will blindly interview three males selected at random from our twenty finalists. Once her questions have been answered, she will then choose one to escape to paradise with for forty-two days. If they find love, they will be rewarded financially, and by the most divine gift the universe can offer—finding their soulmate and eternal flame."

Dipstick nodded at his wife like a big toothy bobble head. "Our female Spark is currently backstage waiting to meet her Mr. Right. We had an overwhelming response from over ten thousand applicants vying for the opportunity to find their Mrs. Right. We will now announce who the three lucky Sparks are." He pulled out a notecard and grinned at the crowd. "Spark number one. Will Chad Heathrow please come on up?" The spotlight swung to the crowd, searching and landing on a Ken doll wearing a navy blazer and khaki slacks. I had enough nieces to know Ken dolls were dickless. He high-fived his friends before jogging up to the stage.

"When are we leaving?" I whisper-shouted to Luca, and got shushed by the woman beside me.

Kyle leaned closer, and answered, "Just relax. Order another drink, eh?"

With each word out of my friends' mouths, and Kyle adamant that we stay, I came to the conclusion that Kyle must have signed himself up for this ridiculousness. What an idiot. "Did you sign yourself up for this shit?" I asked Kyle. "Does this have to do with that chick you're banging?" He waved a dismissive hand, and I leaned closer, saying, "I'm outta here."

"You can't!" Kyle gripped my arm in panic. "I, um…

you need to be here."

"Why?" The hosts began chatting with the Ken doll, and all the pieces seemed to snap into place. The way Luca and Kyle ignored me, I knew…"What the fuck did you do?" My voice increased in volume as the noise in the room lulled. Glares from surrounding tables did little to deter me. Kyle's eyes grew wide as Luca laughed his ass off. "Are you fucking kidding me? You signed *me* up for this?" I looked to Luca, who was now facing the opposite direction, his shoulder shaking in a way that meant he was still laughing. "Hey," I said with a snap of my fingers, "did you know about this?"

"Maybe," Luca said on a shrug.

"Motherfuckers!"

"Relax, you won't be picked." Kyle leaned closer when more people around us glared in our direction. "Your odds are one in twenty."

"And if I am?"

A chick turned around and pointed a finger at us. "Shhh!"

"Oh, well, then, it'll be fun to watch you squirm for a few minutes. Remember a couple months ago when you hooked me up on that blind date for my birthday? Let's see, what was her name? Randi? Randi with an i." Luca and I both started laughing. "Yeah, real funny. Especially when she excused herself from the table and I ended up using the urinal next to her. I mean, him." Luca bent over, grabbing his stomach. "Assholes."

"You were just jealous your date's dick was bigger than yours," I said on a chuckle.

"Fuck you. Now, I hope you do get picked." He smacked me on the back. "Payback, my brother. And if you get picked, so what? I could be doing you a favor.

You get to be on a tropical island with a hot chick, or at least I've been told she's not a chick with a dick."

"You've seen her?"

"Well, no. But the original female was hot. When she backed out, I'm sure they picked an even hotter one."

"Backed out? What if she's a cougar looking for my blood?"

Luca laughed, and mumbled, "Well, that would be fantastico," while smacking his knee at his own little joke.

"Shut up."

Kyle glanced at him and fought to hide his grin. "We could hope."

"Cocksucker!"

"Relax. She's not a cougar, although that would be awesome. The age bracket is between twenty-five and thirty-five. These are just details. The point is, it would be a nice getaway with a gorgeous stranger for six weeks. Compared to what you did to me, this is a fucking gift. Think of all the sex. How hot is that?" He lifted his beer and winked. "You're welcome."

"I can have sex whenever I want, and I don't have to leave Manhattan." I dragged a hand through my hair to keep it from gripping his neck. "Have you lost your ever-fucking-mind?" I asked, incredulous. "Who the fuck is going to run my company for six weeks? What I did was hilarious. What you did is a felony. You forged my name!"

"Oh please. I perfected your signature years ago. It's your word against mine in a court of law." He pointed to Luca. "He knows nothing, so don't think he's a witness. And as far as your business, you have an international army. The finance world wouldn't even miss you."

The crowd went wild when the Ken doll waved before

taking his seat on stage.

"Okay, we're looking for Spark number two. Will George Kroft please come on up?"

I sighed in relief at the sound of a name other than mine. The same deal with dude number two occurred. He stood on the stage blushing through his introduction. His round face, protruding ears, and neck were all as red as a tomato. The man stood no taller than five-feet, and his beer belly deserved its own introduction.

Luca let out a short, loud laugh. "Oh boy, do I hope you get picked."

Just as he said that, I heard, "Spark number three. Can Jude Soren please join us?"

All three of our jaws dropped as the spotlight searched the crowd for their last victim. Kyle stood and clapped my back, bringing attention to whom they were waiting for. The beam of light swung to where we were sitting, landing on me.

"I guess I lost my bet," Kyle shouted above the crowd. "What are the chances?"

"Yes, Kyle owes me a hundred," Luca bragged.

"You fucking bet on this?" I scrubbed both hands through my hair and was surprised none came out at the roots. "What. If. She. Picks. Me?"

Luca leaned forward and raised his drink. "Just be your charming self, I'm sure she'll want nothing to do with you."

I was going to kill him—them. First him, then the other one. Dismember their bodies piece by piece. I began cursing everyone and everything in my native tongue, the Swedish words flying out like bullets.

"Dude! I have no idea what you're saying."

I leaned in, getting right into his face. "I never signed

anything," I said through gritted teeth.

Kyle snickered, "Oh yes you did. And if you don't get up there, you'll get sued."

"I'll get sued? You mean, *you'll* get sued."

"Potato, potahto." He whipped out a folded packet of papers and thrust them in my hand. "I swear, I combed through it. You're good."

Before I could strangle him, the host brought the crowd's attention straight to me with a wave of his hand. "Jude, come on up!" This chaos unfolded like a slow-motion picture. The spotlight captured the entire chain of events, with me yelling at Kyle and threatening his life.

And all this occurred while the host insisted, "Hello, we're waiting. Do you already have a case of cold feet? The wedding isn't for forty-two days."

"Wedding?" I bared my teeth to Kyle like a Doberman about to attack. "I'm going to fucking kill you."

"There's a prenup clause that states you each take away what you brought in. She can't get your money—unless you want her to, that is."

Did he just say prenup? "I'm not doing this!" I threw my hands up, no longer giving a shit who heard me.

"Too late! Go!" He pushed me forward and I almost passed out as I walked through the crowd, up the stage, and beside the two hosts. I think I answered questions; I couldn't be sure. Every set of eyes focused on me—the men leering and women hooting and hollering like I was a male stripper.

Busty eye-fucked me while placing a red clawed hand on my arm, and said in a breathy voice, "Are you ready to turn your spark into a raging flame?" Channeling a porn star, she added, "Jude."

What the fuck was happening?

I searched the bar to where my asshole friends sat watching. Kyle and Luca were cracking up at my expense. A question forced my focus away from them and I fumbled through my answer. When I looked back, they were gone.

The only thought running through my head was, *once this is over, I am going to jail for murder.*

The two other victims sat in director's chairs beside a large white screen that split the stage in half. A single chair on the other side of the divider waited for its occupant. The three of us wouldn't be able to see her, nor could she see us, but the crowd had an open view of the entire stage.

Busty took my hand in hers, led me to my seat, and snatched the now damp and wilted papers from my grip.

Dipstick asked for the audience's attention as he read through the rules one by one. I listened to bits and pieces, but words like *true love, soulmates, marriage, happily ever after,* and *forty-two days* were the only ones I heard in a long monotonous drawl.

"Okay, Sparks. Here we go. The only responses allowed must answer the question you are asked. At the end, you will each have the chance to ask one question of your own. It cannot pertain to any personal information, physical appearance, occupation, religion, politics, or finances. Please answer all questions honestly, and be sure to be your own charming selves."

A loud guffaw echoed from the crowd, and when I looked up, I saw Luca losing his shit while sitting beside Kyle at one of the round tables centered in front. Kyle kept reprimanding him, which seemed to fuel Luca's hysterics.

Fuckers.

CPSIA information can be obtained
at www.ICGtesting.com
Printed in the USA
LVOW08s0512070817
544088LV00007B/14/P